TREMBLE

Dana Duthie

Matchstick Literary
1-888-306-8885
orders@matchliterary.com

KEY WORDS

The U.S. has finally had enough of North Korean antics. When the regime kidnaps weapons inspectors at a suspected nuclear facility, a team of SEALS and a wing of Air Force fighter bombers go north. It's about time!

PREFACE

Certainly this book is fiction. As with my first book, "Dark Rain," my intention is to portray the lives and missions of America's front line fighter pilots. In this case, they are stationed in the very front of the line, just a little south of North Korea and the nemesis, Kim Jong Un. Many of the characters in my books are patterned after men I actually worked and flew with. Their names may be scrambled a bit, but hopefully I haven't offended anyone who sees themself in the story.

"Tremble" is actually the third adventure in the life of Brad Mitchell, the hero. "Dark Rain" is in fact the fourth and final story. So "Tremble" is a prequel, and perhaps the other two books will be out soon.

My time in the Air Force ended in 1992 when I retired. Therefore some of my story line is a bit dated. Today's fighter aircraft and fighter pilots are much more advanced. However, the setting for "Tremble" dates back to when I was a squadron commander in South Korea, and is up to date as I remembered back then.

Dana Duthie

PROLOGUE

NORTH KOREA, OCTOBER, 1951

Captain Mike Johnston is flying his last mission of the Korean War. He is due to rotate back to the States in two days. He and his wingman just came off a close air support mission and the flak and air defenses around the target area are substantial. Mike sees a Mig 17 turning below them trying to get a firing solution on his wingman. He calls for a defensive break and pulls his F-86 into a hard turn to bring his gun to bare on the communist pilot. Then all hell breaks loose. The Mig had a wingman and Johnston had turned right in front of another enemy fighter. Bullets tore through the right wing and the aft fuselage. The F-86 engine coughed and sputtered and just quit all together.

Captain Johnston knew he was deep into enemy territory. He turned south and tried to maintain some semblance of control. It was a lost cause. He was losing altitude too fast. Finally he had no choice but to bail out. When he did, he was in an awkward position and the ejection strained and twisted his back severely. He was able to free himself from the seat and got a good chute above him. Below he could see nothing but trees with a clearing here and there. He could see movement of troops in one of the clearings, but they didn't look like American GIs. He steered his parachute away from them the best that he could. He also tried to steer away from the explosion and wreckage of his jet. He knew the gooks would look for him there.

Mike Johnston plowed through the branches of a large tree and his chute got hung up, leaving him dangling about 10 feet above the ground. He could hear someone slashing through the jungle below and to his right. He was a sitting (or hanging) duck, so he pulled out his survival knife and started cutting the risers to his chute. When he had all but a couple risers cut he was hanging in an awkward body position, the remaining risers pulling up his right shoulder. One last cut and …. thunk! He hit the ground almost feet first with no time to prepare. He slammed hard onto his back and then rolled into a bush.

The bush was large and leafy. Johnston's back hurt bad but he also knew he had some camouflage here. He rolled into as small a ball as his 6'3" frame could and held his breath waiting to be found. After what seemed like an eternity, he decided he was alone and that he needed to get away from his chute still hanging in the tree above him. He crawled out of the bush and tried to get to his feet. He almost made it and then fell forward. From out of no where two pairs of hands grabbed him and held him up. He suddenly was looking at the faces of three Koreans - two men and a woman. They weren't troops. They looked like farmers.

CHAPTER ONE

KUNSAN AIR BASE, SOUTH KOREA, 1993

"BOOM!" Brad's feet were knocked off the rudder pedals and the whole jet shook like it had just been broadsided. He knew immediately what it was. He had ham fisted the throttle at almost no airspeed and the engine compressor stalled. At a high angle of attack, when the nose is up and the airspeed is very low, there is not enough air entering the engine intake and when one slams the power into full afterburner the influx of fuel simply ignites and creates a stall of the engine. He'd had it happen a few times before, but not quite this violently.

"Knock it off, knock it off!" He squawked on the radio. "One, knock it off!" This was the Air Force standard call to cease whatever training maneuver they were doing and pay attention to finding each other and fixing whatever problem there might be.

"Two, knock it off," "Three, knock it off." His two wingmen acknowledged the command and responded accordingly. Brad could see one of them real well. He was practically filling the windscreen and Brad's Heads Up Display (HUD) gun sight. After all, that's who Brad was in the slow speed "knife fight" with when the engine blew. He expected the other wingman was about a mile off and under his belly, out of sight.

"Lead's got a compressor stall. Trying a re-light." Brad set up an immediate glide at 125 knots and pointed the F-16 toward the coast. They were only about 12 miles off shore and at 28,000 feet. So he knew that if he couldn't get the engine running properly again, he could dead stick it into Kunsan Air Base – 13 miles on the nose.

"Roger Lead, you had a huge fireball out the back end and you're trailing smoke now." It was Juvat Two, the young Lieutenant they were putting through paces on this Two vs. One air combat maneuvering mission. Brad was the "One," simulating a Russian style Mig attacking a flight of two F-16s. Of course, he was in an F-16 too, so it was one of the Russian's most up to date fighters he was pretending to fly. In the mid 1990s the Falcon had no match that anyone knew of when it came to turning radius and dog fighting. The "C models" the Eighth Tactical Fighter Wing flew out of Kunsan were not equipped with the USAF's state of the art radar air to air weaponry, but their heat seeking missile and gun were still better than anything the North Korean's had, and were comparable to most Soviet armament.

Brad was a little concerned now. The engine did not respond to the prescribed procedure to recover, so he prepared to shut it down and try an air start. "Three, I'm going to have to shut down and restart. Get on the horn and call the SOF and you two get on the ground ASAP. I'll come up SOF frequency in a minute." Brad knew that the chances of losing radio contact when the "electric jet" had no power was always a possibility. There were battery backups and backups to the backups, but historically, what could go wrong did when you're talking about systems that don't get much use.

"Three, Roger. Two, I'm at your left eight o'clock, one mile and a little high. Join to fighting wing and go channel seven." Jim "Lucky" Finnegan was taking the flight of two back to base as directed and wanted to make sure the Lieutenant didn't get lost. "Two."

The three Juvats checked in on the Supervisor of Flying (SOF) frequency and Finnegan explained the situation quickly. Brad heard it all, so he knew his radio was working. "Juvat One's up." He radioed so that the SOF could talk directly to him and Finnegan could get out of the middle. "Two and Three, say gas." Brad was concerned about his wingmen's fuel state.

"Two's Bingo minus two."

"Three's Bingo." That meant they were both at or below the minimum recommended fuel state to return to base, with a little left over for Mom and Apple Pie. Since it was a beautiful, sunny day, they did not need weather divert fuel, but it was always prudent to reserve a little gas for times like this.

"Roger, copy Bingos. SOF, recommend Juvat Two and Three land ahead of me in case there's any problem on the runway." Brad expected that he might have to take the departure end cable to get the jet stopped. Brake pressure was minimum at best without a running engine and hydraulic pressure. If he did have to engage the cable, he knew that without an engine he would have to sit there, tying up the runway until somebody towed him away. Kunsan had a cross runway, but they did not use it much, and the winds today were not very conducive to crosswind landings on a short runway.

"Roger, concur Juvats. We have two other inbound flights as well, but you just take care of your problem and get on the ground. I'll take care of them." The SOF was from the other squadron and not impressed that Brad was trying to tell him how to run his operation. The Supervisor of Flying was a very responsible position in the wing. Squadron supervisors and selected instructor pilots manned the post in the tower whenever there was flying going on. The SOF checked the weather and airfield status every morning and made his flying recommendation to the Wing Director of Operations (a Colonel), who in turn almost always concurred. The SOF kept track of all the airborne flights and weather, and was especially useful in times of an airborne emergency. He had the checklists and flight manual right there at his fingertips, and with his experience, it was almost like having an instructor in the aircraft with you. BUT not quite! In a single seat fighter there was only one person responsible, and the pilot needed to be ready for just about anything.

Brad was ready, but he wasn't happy with himself. Because he had let the airspeed get so low in the dog fight maneuvering, he had been too fast to push the throttle into full afterburner. Obviously when the engine stalled and "banged" it banged something loose, and now he had a damaged jet on his hands. He tried the airstart and then tried it again. No luck. He had only airstarted one other F-16 in his career, and that was one that he was performing a maintenance Functional Check Flight (FCF) on. It had just had an engine change and, shore 'nuff, something wasn't put back together correctly. But at least that time it restarted. This time he was in for a very quiet, descending end to his flight.

Falcon pilots practice Simulated Flame Out (SFO) landings all the time, but they always have the luxury to get out of trouble by pushing the throttle up and letting the jet's outstanding thrust climb them away. This time Brad only had one chance to do it right. Otherwise it would be a "nylon letdown" (parachute landing) and one destroyed $16 million jet.

"Kunsan Tower, Juvat One's 4 miles west at 10,000 for an SFO Full Stop." Actually, it wasn't going to be an SFO, just an FO – nothing simulated about it, but Brad was using terminology he was used to. He had switched over to the tower frequency and was setting up for his approach. He planned on hitting "High Key" at or above 7000 feet in a 125 knot glide. High Key is a point usually overtop the runway from which the approach would start as a spiraling descent to land.

"Roger Juvat. Call High Key. Traffic is two F-16s on two mile initial, and another two on straight in, short final. Kunsan is landing runway 35, winds 340 at 15, gust to 20, altimeter two niner niner six." The tower was manned by Air Force non coms, and Brad expected their Chief was at the helm right now. They couldn't afford anything to go wrong either. The two F-16s on initial were his own wingmen, and the two making a formation landing were two of the four the SOF had spoke about. The others were still 20 miles out and would have to wait their turn to land, land on the cross runway, or divert. If the ground crew had their stuff together, it shouldn't take but a couple minutes to pull Brad and his jet out of the cable, if he had to engage it. Again – something that was practiced all the time.

"Two niner niner six, Juvat." Brad acknowledged the altimeter setting. Altimeter settings, altitudes and headings were mandatory acknowledgement items in flying radio vernacular. Brad had completed the checklist and gone over particulars with the SOF. At this point all attempts to restart the engine were abandoned, and all of his attention was vectored toward a safe landing. All too often pilots of aircraft with an engine out spend too much time at too low an altitude trying to restart, and don't pay attention to aircraft control and landing. Result? Crunch!

"Juvat's at High Key." Brad announced as he passed over the runway on a perpendicular heading at 7300 feet. He went into an easy left bank and let the jet descend on airspeed. He didn't want to get too tight and overshoot at too high an altitude, but he did not want to be too wide with nowhere to land either.

"Roger Juvat, Call Base. Traffic's short final full stop." The last of his wingmen were just about to touch down.

Brad Rolled the Viper out parallel the runway, and abeam the touch down point he lowered the landing gear handle, then used the "blow down" procedures to be sure the wheels were down and locked. Passing about 3500 feet he started an easy turn back in toward the runway and announced "Juvat's base, gear down, full stop." Understatement! He certainly wasn't going around on this one.

"Juvat you're cleared to land. Wind is 345 at 18. SOF advises your landing gear look to be down and locked. Maintenance is on site at the departure end."

Brad rolled out at about a half mile with 800 feet to descend. He picked the nose up a bit and settled into an approach speed of 110 knots. With a steady headwind he knew he had the descent made. He touched down as smooth as silk about 1300 feet down the runway, held the nose up as long as he could to "aero brake" and slow down, and then eased the nose down. He was actually able to stop short of the cable and sat and waited for the tow driver to hook him up. They had him off the runway and along for the ride in just under two minutes. The emergency was terminated and Kunsan went back to normal. For now.

The Eighth Tac Fighter Wing "Wolfpack" had been in Korea since the late 70s. They have a colorful history, especially during Vietnam. There the 8th was the wing commanded by Robin Olds, one of our American modern day "Aces." Although his eight victories were not all in Vietnam, he added to WWII and Korean War totals while commanding the Wolfpack in Southeast Asia. General Olds was a character in himself. He worked hard and played harder, and the fighter pilots under his command learned both very well. After Vietnam the wing moved around, passing through Japan and finally settling into Kunsan, flying the F-4 Phantom. The two squadrons that make up the wing now are the 35th TFS Panthers and the 80th TFS Headhunters (sometimes known as "Juvats"). Both have long histories dating back to the South Pacific during WWII, flying the P-38 and other successful fighters. The squadrons transitioned to the F-16 in the early 80s, and have been dominating the training skies over South Korea ever since. Today is October 15, 1993.

Kunsan is not known as a "garden spot" of an assignment. The base and city of Kunsan are situated about halfway down the west coast of South Korea. It is a cold and blustery part of the peninsula in the winter, and the city is not the modern day miracle of Seoul for sure. The other active flying base in Korea is Osan, much nearer Seoul and a more desirable location – if you wanted something to do besides flying and fighting (or at least practice fighting). Many Air Force members assigned to Osan were accompanied by their families and lived in nice housing in and around Seoul. Kunsan was termed a "remote" assignment, and although there were a few wives and husbands around, they were not sponsored and supported by the Air Force, and the tour was one year long. The good news was that commanders generally had the full attention of their people, day and night – whether at work or at play. The bad news was that they would just get someone trained up right and it was time for them to rotate, replaced by a newbie. During peacetime the yearly clock revolved around an Operational Readiness Inspection (ORI) in the late Spring.

The main players in the wing, from wing commander down to squadron commanders, generally came in on their assignments in the early summer, and had most of a year to prepare for their test – the ORI, which was the Wing Commander's report card. As soon as it was over, they would normally depart (sometimes with their tail between their legs) and the new leadership would come in.

The mission of the Eighth was ground attack primary and both strike (nuclear) and air to air secondary. That's a big load to put on a squadron. The pilots main proficiency task was in conventional bombing, with a currency and accuracy requirement that was fairly stringent. They also had to practice and be proficient in the nuclear attack role, and fly a certain number of air to air training sorties each training period as well. To get everything done, a line pilot flew at least 60-70 sorties every six months. That doesn't sound like much (10 sorties a month), and in fact, at Kunsan most pilots logged 80-90 sorties. However, because of the weather in the winter especially, some of those flights were nothing more than boring holes in the sky under instrument conditions. The squadrons used to rotate to Clark Air Base in the Philippines for 4-5 weeks of intense training in the winter. However, when the Philippine government decided to kick the US out, that precious training resource died. Appropriately (in a lot of USAF pilots' minds), a huge volcanic eruption buried Clark Air Base a few years later, and it was all a moot point. To make up for the missed training there were exercises in Australia, Singapore, Guam, Alaska, just about anywhere in the Pacific region. The 8

TFW was always ready and willing to attend. After all – without wives, husbands and kiddies around, what else was there to do?

The main mission of the USAF in South Korea is billed as a deterrent to the North Koreans. Although the capabilities of the North Korean forces were suspect, there was no denying the fact there were millions of armed men just north of the DMZ with their guns looking south. The leadership of North Korea has been fanatical for years. Kim Il Sun and now his son, Kim Jong Un made no bones about it – they will bury the South. They detested and were very vocal about the American presence, and as long as they were squarely in the Soviet camp, they were a definite threat. In fact, now that the Soviet Union was no more, the status of North Korea was even more tentative. There was no longer the strong guidance and control by the Soviets to keep the Kims in check. Although the Chinese claimed to have some influence, and they did have more than anyone else, there was not much confidence that if the North came south, China would or could do anything about it. The scariest thing about the regime north of the DMZ was the perpetual rumor and intelligence sources that they were developing a nuclear capability. They already had missiles that could strike as far as Japan, and perhaps even farther. If they indeed had a nuke that could be delivered by those missiles, the Pacific Rim should **tremble**.

Although U.S. presence in South Korea was supported and solicited by the government in Seoul, it was not so popular with the people – especially the young people and students. Korean university students have exercised their democratic right to riot almost at the drop of a hat. They are always protesting something, and the most popular topic is the presence of U.S. troops. There is good intelligence that the students are supported from North Korea, and that there was a significant communist influence in the universities. But the main issue on the peninsula is reunification. There was never a peace treaty in the Korean War, and the arbitrary line drawn across the peninsula has separated families for decades. There is a strong reunification movement, but Kim Jong Un has stipulated that the Americans have to go first. Although there have been some cultural exchanges (mostly one way – the North doesn't have much to offer), and some families allowed to see each other, it is still very much a divided country. The "haves" live in the South with their modern military and fancy cars and bustling cities, while the "have nots" live in the North starving to death.

Brad Mitchell finished up his debriefing with the maintenance folks. The Chief of Maintenance was there and none too happy that he had an airplane with a trashed engine. Brad was sure he would have some more explaining to do – probably all the way to the Wing Commander. On paper the General Electric 110 engine was supposed to be able to take any throttle movement. The "wide mouth" engine had great thrust – more than its Pratt and Whitney counterpart, and the "wide mouth" referred to a slightly larger intake that should suck up more air when needed by throttle demand. However, everyone knew that at high angles of attack and slow airspeed (parameters not easy to simulate on an engine test stand) the amount of airflow to the engine was minimum at best, and the pilot had to be ginger with the throttle. Brad thought he was "ginger," but obviously the engine maintenance guys, and consequently their colonel, thought otherwise. Brad had experience and the fact was that he was an FCF pilot working for the Chief of Maintenance when in that capacity. He was able to give the experts more information and parameter data than the normal fighter jock would. Hopefully they would find something wrong and exonerate him.

He went to the squadron and unloaded his flight gear, accepting the standard "ham fist" jeers from his men, and one or two congratulations for his flawless flame out landing. After all, since he was the squadron commander, the "youngsters" couldn't hammer him too much. About that time, the Wing Assistant Director of Operations (ADO) caught up to him.

"Brad. Need to see you and all your flight commanders in the main briefing room ASAP." Said Rich "Bones" Harbinger. Brad wondered if this had anything to do with his misadventure, but decided not – surely he didn't need organized harassment. He'd get enough from these guys as it is. He told Finnegan and Lieutenant Smalley that he'd page them later or debrief at the club tonight. Brad walked into the briefing room.

Colonel Ron Heywood, Wing Vice Commander, Colonel John Lorner, the Director of Operation, and Colonel Jim MacIntosh, the Chief of Maintenance Brad had just left, were all sitting up front. The rest of the room was half full of Majors and Lt. Colonels and a few senior Captains from both squadrons. Brad was sure that whatever was up had nothing to do with his flame out.

"Room, Ten Hut!" Commanded "Bones" Harbinger. Everyone popped to attention and Colonel Nels Rushing, Wolfpack Lead, entered the room and walked to the front. "Be seated." He commanded. "Nice landing" he mumbled as he walked past Brad. Brad caught the wink in the Colonel's eye and felt better already about his personal faux pas of the day. Rushing was a straight shooter and a fighter pilot's fighter pilot. He was a bachelor, which was a rarity in USAF command structure, and he was actually on his second tour in three years at the Wolfpack. He was the Director of Operations just two tours ago. His background included a long stint as an Air Force Aggressor pilot, traveling around to various units flying the F-5 and F-16, simulating Soviet tactics and equipment, training other Air Force pilots. That experience and his career that was almost devoid of a staff job (another rarity) left him with a lot of credibility that the troops appreciated. When Rushing flew he led the flight. When he led there was no doubt who was in charge, and there was usually no doubt who was going to win the quarters normally bet on bombing accuracy. Brad had always thought that Rushing was the kind of leader he wanted to be.

"Gentlemen, Ladies" Rushing referred to the female first lieutenant intelligence officer normally assigned to the Pantons (35 TFS) who was in the back of the room and to the first female F-16 pilot, also with the Pantons, who sat with her squadron mates. "There has been a development up north and the wing has been put on advanced alert status. We'll know a little later today just what that means, but we need to get right into some mission planning. Intel?" Rushing sat down and Major Louie Leitao from the Wing Intelligence Division moved to the podium.

CHAPTER TWO

THE PLAN

"Sometime last night it appears the North Koreans raided a barracks near Yongbyon and killed four of 7 international weapons inspectors in their sleep." Leitao referred to a map that had been projected onto a screen in front of the wing hierarchy. Yongbyon was a small dot on the map about 100 miles north of Pyonyang, the North Korean capitol. It looked to be about 50 miles inland from the farthest northeast finger of the Yellow Sea. "Yongbyon has long been suspected as a major weapons production facility with possible nuclear capability. The inspectors killed were two Australians, a German and one from India. The three not killed are two Americans and a Canadian." The room got very quiet. Colonel Rushing stood up and faced the crowd.

"Evidently the North is holding these inspectors hostage, demanding we withdraw our forces from the peninsula." Lobo said in a very solemn tone. "As you might expect, the words I'm getting from higher up are that we will not negotiate with terrorists, and in fact as we speak, a rescue mission is being planned. Louie." The Wing King pointed to Major Leitao and sat down.

"Yes sir. Right now there are two HH-53 choppers on the ground up at Osan. The wing there is on tap to support them as they gin up to go in to pull the hostages out. The only problem is no one knows exactly where they are. As you might know, we don't have many friendly folks on the ground up there. At any rate, the mission is proposed for tonight. The idea is to waste no time and strike early while we may still have an element of surprise." Leitao paused and took a big gulp of air. In his 16 year career he had never done anything more than interpret and brief for simulated missions. This was the big one!

"The mission of the Wolfpack is to destroy Yongbyon as soon as the helicopters are clear and the Americans are on board." There was a buzz in the crowd. Even an "All RIGHT!" from someone in the back, who got less than an approving glare from Wolfpack Lead. The boys were itching for a fight, but Rushing knew this was going to be very difficult at best. A rescue mission over 400 miles of the most hostile territory in the world to pick up three people we can't even locate. No electronic warfare support or even air refueling for that matter. No time to get them here, though an AWACS and a tanker or two might be able to be scrambled from Kadena Air Base on Okinawa.

Brad finally asked, "Sir. How will we know when to even be there if the choppers don't even know where to go? Seems like we could be flying around in orbit over all their air defenses trying to save gas for the attack that may or may not come. Will we have tanker support?"

"Ok guys – here it is." It was Rushing. "This whole thing stinks right now. Conan's got it right" Conan was Brad's tactical callsign. "The Osan boys have got to figure out how to escort helicopters doing 90 knots over Hell's Half Acre to a rugged valley with a facility the size of a small city tucked away in it to find two Americans who for sure won't be standing on the rooftops waving Old Glory, and a Canadian. We're supposed to be up there with the wrath of God ready to rain down on the place as soon as the good guys are clear. All of this depends on a helluva lot more intelligence and planning. We just don't have the intel yet, but we need to get at the planning." Rushing walked to the podium and Leitao stepped aside.

"Cannon, I want you to take the overall lead." Lobo went on. "I want two gorillas of as many jets as Maintenance can give us – one from each squadron. Stagger the takeoffs by an hour. That way the first attack gets there with or just after the rescue and the other will be about an hour later. If the choppers have to loiter, or if the rescue is unsuccessful, abort the first attack and hopefully something will be accomplished by the time the second one arrives. If the first attack is successful, Intel - come up with a viable alternate target for the second wave. All this is just a WAG (Wild Ass Guess) at a plan right now, but it's the best we can come up with. You guys determine the ordinance based on the targets. No B-61s." Everyone laughed. The B-61 is the nuclear bomb the squadrons had in their arsenal for the last ditch effort. Obviously they would not be dropping 24 of them on one target, though it sure would get the job done. Rushing went on, "I want a down and dirty update at 1500 hours. Maybe we'll have more to go on by then. Keep your seats." The Wing Commander and the rest of the colonels left the room.

Cannon Rand was the 35th Squadron Commander. He had been at "The Kun" going on two years. He had been the Operations Officer of the 80th and extended his tour a year when he moved over to take command of the "Pantons." Everyone knew and respected him. He took the podium. "OK. I guess we got our work cut out for us. The Pantons will take the first wave. Conan, will you lead the Juvat attack?" He asked the 80th Commander.

"Roger that." Mitchell answered.

"OK. Well, let's get started. We should configure the same way. We'll need three tanks of gas. It's a long way up there. Plan on jettisoning the wing tanks when empty. Louie, unless the wing weapons guys and you determine otherwise, we'll go with a mixed load of Mark 82s, and CBU. Let us know if we need something different and/or fuse extenders. We need that determination ASAP in order to give maintenance a chance to load up. Conan, let's keep in touch as we plan through the day and get back together at 1430 here to dry run what we're going to tell Lobo at 1500." With that Cannon Rand and the rest of the 35th pilots left the building for their own squadron.

Brad got up. "Juvats, let's go to work. Assume six flights of four. Flight Commanders plan on each leading a flight and pick your flight members. That will leave two other flights. Coach, you lead one and you'll be the deputy gorilla lead. I've got the other. Hammer, you'll be my Number Three. We'll plug in the names of the flight members ASAP. Lucky, take your flight and get on the route planning. Keep us out to sea as long as possible and then hitting the coast low and hot. Louie, give him your best threat guys to advise. Loogie, get someone on the take off data with the heaviest load and the SMS settings." Brad was definitely organized. He had let each flight commander line up their flight of four, appointed Ed "Coach" Howe, his Operations Officer, as the Deputy Lead, and selected the squadron weapons officer to fly in his number three position. That way, if he took a hit on the way in to the target and there wouldn't be time to shuffle flights around, Dale "Hammer" Handle had the experience to take over the lead.

A "Gorilla" was the pet name given to a mass attack flight of as many aircraft as the squadrons could muster. The idea was to put as much firepower on a target in the shortest time possible. The formation flown varied with the altitude, the threat, and the type attack planned. It could be anything from line abreast at high altitude to single ship, radar trail in the weather. The actual attack was always the toughest to plan. The terrain and target arrangement often determined attack headings, but hopefully they would be varied so as not to give what defenses there might be a chance to aim for the next guy coming down the same chute. This attack would be real complicated – at night and in very steep terrain.

It turned out that Yongbyon was a series of long, low buildings – sort of a cross between chicken barns and barracks. There were a few bunkers and several anti-aircraft and missile defense sites. There was one central building that seemed to be the hub of activity. It was more square in shape and had a little more vertical to it. The satellite photos were pretty good and the targeteers were able to pinpoint recommended targets for each flight. The plan for the Juvats was to actually attack from the west. That meant launching off over the Sea of Japan and going "feet dry" just south of the city of Hamhung. It also meant a much longer time over land (about 200 miles), and therefore a longer time at low altitude, and therefore more fuel expended. The 35th attack was to come from the east where they could loiter off shore over the Yellow Sea for longer if necessary. The Juvat attack from the west was hopefully meant as a surprise as well. In addition, the alternate target for the Juvats was a facility near Kusong, a city more south and west, and their attack from the west made it a lot easier to hit.

The lineup for the Juvats was set. Brad Mitchell led with Handle as his Number Three and two young Lieutenants not selected by their own flight commanders on the wings. Boomer Huston led A Flight with "Pigpen" Smalley on his wing, Randy "Shotgun" Johnson as Number Three and Homer "Slam" Schmidt as Number Four. They were carrying CBU – Cluster Bomb Units – and were targeted on one of the two missile defense sites. They would actually be the first ones down the chute on the attack. B Flight was led by "Clit" Clamoris and had the other missile site and a gunnery position as their target. Their attack was nearly simultaneous from a different direction as A Flight's. Jim "Lucky" Finnegan led C Flight with Mark 82, 500 pound bombs on the command center, along with Brad's flight. Ed Howe's flight and Don "Loogie" Walsh's D Flight brought up the rear with Mark 82s on the outer buildings. The timing was critical and the entire attack was to take just a little over two minutes. Each flight had a different egress heading and would recover at Kunsan in individual flights of four. That way, when pulling off target, each wingman knew where to look (in the dark) for his flight members without getting lost – hopefully. There was a SAFE area designated, although in North Korea no area could be called safe. A SAFE area was actually a Selected Area For Evasion, not necessarily "safe," as in secure. It was usually someplace relatively unpopulated that may or may not have an indigenous contact on the ground to help a downed pilot. At the very least, it was a place where rescue forces knew where to look in the event of a bailout. That would be a problem in this case as well. The only rescue forces were those that were starting the whole show by rescuing the hostages. If a pilot went down on this mission, he needed to plan to be there a while – to evade capture as long as possible, and to hopefully last a day or so until a rescue mission could be organized. It was October and North Korea was a cold, sometimes snowy place. Temperatures at night would be in the 20s. Each pilot refreshed himself on the contents of the survival kit in the jet, and added a few more necessities to his pockets.

The word came down about 1300 hours that the time on target (TOT) for the rescue and the Pantons was 0100 hours. That put the Juvats on target at 0200. The squadron commanders sent as many of the pilots to their rooms for some rest as they could. Brad kept a minimum skeleton crew around to finish the planning and used all of the pilots not "lucky" enough to be selected for the mission for the details. He kept Ed Howe and "Popeye" Parsons, one of the assistant Ops Officers at the squadron to guide the planning, hoping to get them some rest after the briefing to the Wing Commander at 1500. It was all coming together nicely. He had touched base with Cannon Rand, and they smoothed out any details that needed coordination. Since it was really two different missions, about the only thing they needed to do was set up a system to communicate with each other on the way in or out.

Maintenance was humping. Colonel MacIntosh himself was out there driving the train. They were able to put together 27 35 TFS jets and 26 for the Juvats. That allowed for a couple of spares, and the squadrons appointed five more pilots to get ready and start as spares. They would fill in where needed. The pilots not tasked were appointed to do all the preflighting and "hot cocking" the jets. Basically that meant they did the walk around and weapons inspections, started the engine, loaded all the navigation and weapons data into the computer, and checked out all the systems. During that process five jets had problems – two from the 35th and 3 from the 80th. That meant that unless they could be fixed in time, the 80th would go with a maximum of 23. MacIntosh jumped on it. He was bound and determined to get at least 48 vipers airborne. By 2000 hours there were 51 ready and cocked

F-16s on the ramp – 27 for the Pantons and 24 for the Juvats. They were still working on two more.

The rest of the base was abuzz as well. It was pretty obvious that something was in the works. All the maintenance and weapons personnel had been recalled to work, the Security Police Squadron was in full riot gear and was deployed all over the base. The Dining Hall had been alerted to prepare lots of good hardy meals, and the Officers Club was working on a pre-flight dinner for the pilots. Only the South Korean hosts were in the dark. There was a ROKAF F-5 squadron on the base and the base was actually a Korean installation. The Americans outnumbered their hosts by far, but the appropriate respect and rapport was maintained. However, Colonel Rushing had no intention of letting his ROKAF counterpart in on the action. There was often no telling who was the good guy in this country.

Brad Mitchell double checked the route information, the maps, the weapons setting card and everything else pertinent to the mission. When he was satisfied they were as accurate and well prepared as possible he pulled copies of everything for the colonels and said to Ed Howe. "Here you go. I think we're as ready as we can be. I'd sure like to have some more certainty about all of this, but I guess the real problem will be with the Pantons. They could sit out there "feet wet" forever not knowing if this thing's gonna go." He handed his Ops Officer the packets for him and the colonels to look over during the briefing. It was about 1415 hours.

"And Coach, as soon as this dog and pony show is over I want you and Popeye to get some sleep. Life Support has set up some cots in my office. It's quiet in there. Do what you can. As of right now, we've scheduled the meal at the club for 2000 and the mass briefing at 2130. I don't want to see your ugly mug until chow time."

"Yes sir. I'll try." Howe said. Brad knew that the chances of sleeping right now were between slim and none. The adrenalin was at fever pitch.

CHAPTER THREE

READY, SET ......

"Room, Tenhut!" Mitchell yelled as the Wing Commander entered the room. Everyone jumped to their feet, eyes front. Most of the pilots were in their quarters in bed, but a few of the planners, intel types, maintainers and others who thought they had a reason to be there were in the room.

"Seats." Lobo directed and moved to his seat at the front.

Cannon Rand was at the podium. "Ladies and Gentlemen, without any specific guidance I've classified this briefing Top Secret. Sir, we have verified that everyone in the room has an appropriate clearance. Whether they have 'Need to Know' I couldn't tell you. Do you have any guidance on that?"

Rushing looked around the room, frowned once or twice and finally said "Yeah, I think we're good to go with this group. However, ladies and gentlemen – what goes in this room stays in this room unless you have clearance from your commanding officer to share the information to get the mission done. In this case, the "commanding officers" with that kind of authority are the four colonels you see sitting up here." He nodded to the Vice

Commander, the Director of Operations, and the Director of Maintenance. "Go ahead Cannon."

"Sir, the packets you have there are the mission packets for the two gorillas. We're planning on two mass briefings – 2030 hours at the 35th for the Panton mission and one here at 2130 for the Juvats. As you can see, the two mission profiles are quite different. The attacks are very similar, and the recoveries are the same – four by four back here. The Pantons will launch out over the Yellow Sea and set up an orbit waiting word from the rescue force that their mission is complete and that they are clear of the area. We'll hit the coast at the end of this little finger of water about 80 miles from the target." He pointed to an isthmus of water that extended northeast and pointed right at Yongbyon. "We'll be at low altitude about 50 miles out to sea and in a staggered wedge trail formation, each four ship separated by 4-5 miles."

"The attack will be a series of offset pops with each four ship down a different axis. The first two flights will have CBU and will be going after the defenses here, here and here." Randall pointed to the specific drop points on the target photo displayed on a big screen. "The rest of us will be targeting the main building and as many of the out buildings as we can, stringing Mark 82s – six a piece. Egress will be to a specific heading – different for each flight of four, to help us find each other in the dark. Recovery will be in fours. Our SAFE area as it were, is this area here, but there are no indigenous contacts that we know of." CBU are Cluster Bomb Units, canisters holding dozens of smaller bomblets that are hell on troops in the open and can do major damage over wide swaths.

Mark 82s are 500 pound bombs, big enough to create small craters and the destruction one might imagine that would cause. Rand went on to describe the specific targets in detail and Leitao gave a brief description of the threats and enemy defenses. Rand then finished up with an update on the maintenance readiness of the jets and announcement about the pre-brief meal and main briefing times.

"OK. Good! I will be at each briefing and I'd like to finish them with a couple minutes to everyone. In the meantime, Jim can you get as many of your folks together in one of the hangars – say at 1800 hours? I'd like a word with them as well." Rushing aimed this last request at the Chief of Maintenance.

"Yes sir. No problem. How about Hangar 701? It has the most free space right now. We'll be there at 1800." MacIntosh acknowledged.

"All right folks. I don't need to tell you the seriousness of the situation. This will be a difficult mission. Cannon – you guys get as much rest as you can. The rest of you dig in and do all you can to make it work. It's going to be a long night, and I suspect this is just the beginning. This is what you signed up for folks, so brush up on your procedures and dig out your chemical gear. Effective at midnight – when the bombs hit the target we will be in Threatcon Alpha." Rushing just directed the wing to go to its highest level of defense. Everyone will be carrying gas masks and chemical suits. "Until then I don't want any more change to our daily routine than is absolutely necessary to get the hard work done. Questions?" Hearing none, "Let's get back to work. Cannon, a word with you, Bones and Conan. Brad, let's go to your office. John, join us please."

Colonel Rushing, Colonel Lorner, the two squadron commanders, and the Assistant DO Bones Harbinger went behind closed doors in Brad Mitchell's office. "Sit down guys." Lobo directed. He remained standing behind Brad's desk.

"I'm not at all comfortable with this whole thing, and I suspect you're not either." Lobo looked around and saw a nod from just about everyone.

"What bothers me so much Boss, is the uncertainty." It was Lorner. "I don't see how this rescue force is going to be able to find these guys and get out of Dodge in any reasonable time. Our guys could sit out there off shore forever and not know who, what or where."

"I don't think that will be a problem." Rushing obviously knew something the rest of them didn't. "What I'm about to tell you stays in this room." The interest level perked up.

"Evidently there is no intent to rescue anyone, unless they just happen to be there and available. As of right now, the mission up at Osan is to drop in a four man Seal team at 2000 hours tonight – soon as it gets dark. They have three hours to get into Yongbyon, find whoever they can and be ready for a pickup by the choppers. No one really expects to find the hostages, and even if they do, four Seals will be no match for the regiment of NK regulars up there. Apparently everyone is expendable – even the Seals. The choppers will make one attempt, wait only as long as they are not taking fire, and get out. They will be escorted by 6 A-10s

(Warthog tank killers), and covered by the Osan F-16s. Then it's your turn." He looked at Rand and Mitchell.

"Cheesh sir. Why even bother?" Rand spoke up. "Seems like a waste of time and probably four good Seals."

"I must agree with you, Cannon. This is purely political and it makes me sick to think we are going to sacrifice at least six Americans and a Canadian just to make a point, or more likely just to get rid of a nuclear weapons plant. Lacking the will to make an unprovoked pre-emptive strike, we apparently are using the kidnapping and a failed rescue mission as provocation. Bottom line is Washington wants Yongbyon erased."

"So I guess that means the Pantons will definitely go in and we'll be put on the alternate target?" Brad asked.

"No. You can forget your alternate target. Orders are to spank 'em twice. You need to have some alternate aim points on Yongbyon though. Assuming the Pantons can hit their asses, you might as well go for something that's not burning yet. Have you guys coordinated actual targets?" Lobo asked.

"Yes sir. We are both pointing for three defense sites and a total of six buildings. That will leave one Triple A site and six other buildings untargeted." Rand responded.

"We'll look at the run in headings and have a short or long backup target, sir." Brad offered. "I wouldn't want to have the guys changing headings. It's going to be crowded enough coming down the chute."

"Agreed. Do what you can, and check six. By the time you get there the whole North Korean Air Force and defense system will be awake." Lobo addressed Mitchell, then Lorner. "John, I want you in the Command Post during the launches. "Bones, you man the SOF truck as Launch Control Officer. I'll be in the tower. I'll see you all at dinner." Rushing and Lorber left and the three Lt. Colonels followed.

Mitchell and Harbinger returned to the main briefing room and Brad directed the squadron intel folks to pull out the target photos. He quickly selected backup aim points for each bomb dropper. The targeteers made copies of the photos and inserted them in the appropriate mission packets for the later briefing. He then joined a wide awake Ed Howe and a snoring Ron Parker in Brad's office. Sleep wouldn't come easily, but he knew he had to try.

The pre-flight meal at the Officers Club was exceptional for the Club. Usually the food wasn't all that good, but since it was pretty much the only show in town, most of the pilots ate there anyway. Some actually shared "hooches," or houses that had kitchens and did their own cooking. The problem was that because it was a "remote" base, what passed for a commissary food store was pretty pathetic. About all one could buy there was frozen dinners and other not so healthy products. Most of the folks gained weight eating their own cooking. Tonight was unusual at the Club in another way too. It was quiet. Most of the guys were lost in their own thoughts about the coming mission. Some conversed with each other about various topics to try and take their minds off the inevitable. Anyway – the steak was good, and hopefully the guys didn't look at it as a "last supper." Colonel Rushing made the rounds of all the tables, basically making small talk, but in effect letting the pilots know he appreciated them and supported them. That meant a lot to the guys.

The mass briefing at the 35th Squadron was also a solemn affair. Cannon Rand gave a time hack that he had coordinated as well with Brad Mitchell Next up was the weatherman, and unfortunately he didn't have great news. The target weather was ok – scattered clouds at about 3000 feet and light to moderate winds. Kunsan weather was "iffy." The fog was sitting just off shore, and if the winds picked up anymore than they were right now, it would roll in and bring the base down to below minimums. The forecast was for light winds, so the best guess was it would hold off, but no weather forecaster in the Air Force would bet his or her month's pay on it. Osan was the real problem. The fog was on them heavy, and if it didn't break up they would be below minimums all night. The minimums used by the Air Force were basically landing minimums. An aircraft could actually take off in lousier weather, but a safety factor was built in to insure that if an emergency occurred on takeoff, the pilot could bring it back around to land. Different types of aircraft had different minimums based on the equipment they had on board. Pilots also had different minimums based on their experience level. Since this was a big exercise, there were plenty of young, inexperienced pilots scheduled to fly from both Osan and the "Kun." For now the mission was still a "Go," but there was a chance that at least the Osan participation would be scrubbed. Without the choppers from Osan there would be no rescue, and not even Colonel Rushing believed the "Higher

Ups" in Washington would insist on a strike without even trying a rescue.

Next up was Louie Leitao and an update on the threats and targets from the intel point of view. Fresh satellite photos were passed around and each pilot refreshed himself on his particular target aim point. Some made drawings on their clipboards which would be strapped to their knees in the cockpit. Since it would be a night attack, and one always tried to keep the cockpit lights down as much as possible to enhance night vision outside, the exercise of a drawing was probably more for rote memory purposes than anything else.

Rand stood up and displayed a lineup card on the overhead screen. It had every flight call sign, pilot name, tail number and parking location. Each pilot had a version of their own, reflecting just their own four ship flight. On it was also all the weapons data and computer input information they would have to check to see if they were loaded correctly by the "hot cockers," squadron mates who had started, run the checks and loaded the computers.

Rand went over start and taxi times, end of runway arming procedures, take off timing and sequence, and formations to be flown to the orbit point. Because it would be dark, formation flying would be a challenge, especially when they would turn off their lights so as not to be visible to the enemy. There was going to be about a three quarter moon, and with the clouds below them, the jet's silhouette would show up fairly well. Still, the recommended formation was a loose route to a wedge, with about 1000 feet between jets. Basically, the wingmen number 2 and 3 would fly about 30-45 degrees back from the leader and spread out about 1000 feet. Number 4 would fly the same position off Number 3 on the opposite side than Two. Each individual flight lead had the option of changing this formation as he wished as long as they did not conflict with another flight in the orbit area.

"In the orbit area we'll stack with the first flight in on the bottom and work our way up with 1000 feet altitude separation." Rand drew it out on the white board. "We'll fly an oval pattern with 10 mile legs oriented basically east-west. I want us spaced out in the pattern so there's always two flights of four at least headed inbound (east) with radars looking for threats. The last thing we need is for some lucky gook in a Mig to wade into this gorilla while we're sitting up there pickin' our noses." Rand went on to direct a staggered entry into the pattern so that the timing would work. "Leaving the orbit and starting your descent is the time to punch off your wing tanks. We don't need them raining down through the orbits below us."

"Flight leads arrange your radars anyway you want to ensure we get full coverage from the deck up to about 30,000." Rand was allowing the flights to determine who in each flight would be responsible for radar coverage at what altitudes. "Remember, your wingmen are going to have a tough enough time flying formation, so don't expect a whole lot of help. We'll use 'Uniform' radio for all threat and mission calls. Stay off it unless it is something everyone needs to hear. Each flight has a different 'Fox Mike' freq, and I expect you to use it for your gibberish. The VHF frequency on your card is the chopper's frequency. I don't want anyone on it except me, and that's only if I have to know where they are. The Juvats will check in on our Uniform when they get up, and after the attack everyone get off that freq and over to the SOF frequency for recovery. Questions on the radios?" Communications in a gaggle like they were planning was always a major issue and can destroy the whole mission.

The F-16s the wing was flying had a UHF (Ultra High Frequency - "Uniform") radio that was normally used for all communications air to ground (tower, radar facility, etc) and an FM frequency usually used for air to air (between flight members). There was the capability to reverse that so that they talked to controlling agencies on "Fox Mike," but the UHF was the only radio that had a working secure voice capability. The Very High Frequency (VHF) radio was not used much and was usually the communication with AWACs, command and control and in this case, helicopters. The trick was remembering which radio you were transmitting on and not garbaging up the wrong frequency. Best of all worlds? – comm out. If there was no talk, no one who wasn't suppose to hear could be eavesdropping.

Rand went on to describe the attack and the egress headings for each flight, and the recovery back to home base. He also briefly touched on the SAFE area. "Face it guys – there is no 'safe' in the SAFE area. There's no one down there to help you. If you can get feet wet, do it. You'll be much better off in a raft in the Yellow

Sea than in the terrain of Kim Jong Un Land. But – if you go down, dig in, stay hidden, come up on the radio on the half hour until or unless told otherwise. Turn your beacons off until you need them. Chances are no rescue mission will be put up until tomorrow night. The emergency locator beacon would squawk a "Beep Beep" once activated by an ejection. Remember, the only rescue forces are the ones in there just ahead of us. They won't have the gas to turn around and pull you out. Questions?" There was a lot of squirming going on. Almost to a one each pilot silently resolved to be sure he kept at least one bullet in his sidearm. No way did they want to be captured in North Korea.

Rand went on to finish up with the mandatory briefing points and housekeeping items, then he turned the podium over to "Lobo" Rushing. The Wing Commander walked slowly to the podium, shook Cannon Rand's hand and mumbled, "Good briefing." Then he turned to face his young charges.

"Men, I don't need to tell you that this will be a night you will always remember. With the exception of Cannon, Brad Mitchell and Ron Parkins over in the 80th none of you has been in combat. I gotta tell you that makes me nervous but not scared. I know how good you are. I've flown with just about every one of you. The training you have received over the months and years has prepared you for tonight. If you're not nervous and scared right now then you're kidding yourself. Is there anyone out there who does not want to fly this mission?" He paused. "Speak up now. I personally will take your place and you can sit in the tower for me." There was a muffled chuckle. Lobo paused some more. "I didn't think so. Ah well – it was a good try." Laughter. "All right then, let's go kick some butt. Do the Wolfpack proud." Rushing and Lorner left with the room standing at attention. They proceeded to the Headhunters' building for a similar briefing.

The flights broke up into different briefing rooms to finish their particular four ship briefings, and got ready to step to the jets.

CHAPTER FOUR

MELANIE

At Osan Air Base a new wrinkle popped up. A fifth person arrived to go into North Korea with the Seals. She was Melanie Lee Han, a 34 year old CIA operative assigned to the U.S. Embassy in Tokyo. Her job in that capacity was "working" a couple of North Korean assets that the CIA was trying to exploit. Melanie was their contact and interpreter. Melanie was the daughter of an American pilot shot down during the Korean War and a Korean mother. Her father was Air Force Captain Mike Johnston. He had been shot down while flying a bombing mission, actually not too far from Yongbyon. He was injured in the bailout and was found by Melanie's mother and Korean family. The captain was in severe pain and couldn't walk from a compression in his spine. The family hid him in their farm house and kept his presence from the North Korean army. Melanie's mother was 22 at the time and was assigned nursemaid duties. One thing led to another and they fell in love. Captain Johnston elected to "disappear" rather than return to the U.S. after the war. In fact, his dog tags were conveniently found near another crash site in 1975 during a U.N.

sponsored search for remains. He was officially declared "Killed in Action" in 1976.

Melanie's mother and American father lived in hiding for almost eight years after the war. They had a room behind a false wall in the family farmhouse, and because of the American's injury, he could not get along very well anyway. Melanie was born in 1953 and she had a brother born a year later. Their father basically was a "house husband." He stayed home and took care of the children, as well as two other children belonging to Melanie's aunt. The women and healthy men folk in the household worked the farm and did outside chores. Mike Johnston took care of the home, only venturing out at night, and even then very cautiously. But the secret was too difficult to keep. Melanie and her brother obviously had foreign blood in them. Melanie was fairer skinned and had the round blue eyes of her father. Her brother looked even more American. He was blond. These unusual traits did not escape the neighbors, and when Melanie went to school, the authorities became very curious.

In 1959 a squad of North Korean "special police" broke into the family home and grabbed and tortured the family looking for information. They shot Melanie's grandfather and uncle and raped her mother and aunt. Melanie was in the back room with her father at the time. Her father heard the commotion and realized immediately what was happening. He shooed Melanie out the back of the house and told her to run, and he burst into the front room with a pitchfork, to try to rescue the rest of the family.

Melanie stopped and watched through a window as her father impaled one officer and then was shot six times. He died instantly. The soldiers killed everyone else in the house except Melanie's towheaded brother. They scooped him up and took him with them as a prize for the night. Melanie stayed hidden until their trucks were out of sight. She was horrified and scared and completely alone in the world – a six year old Korean-American girl in a world where anything American was hateful and a desecration of the homeland. She ran.

The next farm was two miles away. The family there had been very close to the Han family. In fact, they had all been together when the American jet came down. The Liu Hong Chun family had actually helped by delaying the search party while the Han family spirited Mike Johnston away. The word from the Hans was that the pilot had died that night, but Liu never really believed it. So when he saw Melanie peering in their window sobbing and crying, he had mixed emotions about what to do. But they brought her in and she told her story. Liu's wife cleaned Melanie up and fed her rice and porridge. The family discussed their options. If they turned Melanie in they too could be accused of collaboration. Melanie could implicate them just by claiming they helped her. The decision was easy. Liu's teenage son Lee Chun was dispatched to escort Melanie to the nearest seaport and to sneak her on a boat for China. They smeared Melanie's face with dirt and blackened her hair with tar. Her hair was mostly black anyway, but there were some light streaks in it – nothing like her towheaded brother, but an obvious feature not normally seen. Lee's mother packed up a container of rice and some dried meat and kimshee, and they all hugged and pushed the two travelers out the door.

Melanie and Lee made it to the coast in four days. They hid in the heavily forested terrain during the day and traveled at night. Lee found a fishing boat captain who for all the money that Liu Chun had given his son agreed to take Melanie across the Yellow Sea to China. It turns out the captain had other motives and between the two ports of call he and his crew repeatedly abused and raped Melanie. They dumped her off on a pier in a village just over the border from Kusong, North Korea, and sailed away.

Melanie's story from then on was almost as depressing and distressing. She was adopted by a family in China who saw her physical traits as an asset. They traveled with a small circus and Melanie was paraded around as a freak, painted with make up and her hair dyed blond to make her vaguely resemble Shirley Temple, the American child star someone had seen pictures of. When she was twelve, a wealthy Chinese aristocrat from Peking bought Melanie as a slave and took her to the big city to be her blond girl in waiting. There she was spotted by a local pimp who convinced the mistress that Melanie was worth a lot more as a whore for European businessmen, and purchased her services for close to $100 dollars. Melanie was now 14. She was growing into a beautiful girl, tall and with high cheek bones – model like quality. She grew up in a hurry.

After surviving in this life for almost four years, Melanie decided she wanted out. She sweet talked one of her "clients" into taking her back to Iran with him. He was an executive with an Iranian defense firm who had an apartment in Tehran where he worked, and a home two hours away where he lived with his wife and three kids. Melanie was his mistress in Tehran – at least for a while. During that time her sugar daddy educated and refined Melanie, and she learned four new languages. She already knew Korean and Mandarin Chinese. She became fluent in Urdu, Farsi and had a good command of English and Russian.

At 23 Melanie had had enough. One day she walked through the doors of the Swedish embassy in Tehran and the rest is a much more pleasant, if still clandestine story. She was recruited by the CIA as a language specialist and brought to Langley to work in the Mideast Branch. It soon became evident that with all her experience, and her looks, Melanie had a "talent" for manipulating men. She moved rapidly through the training regimen and was out "in the field" in two years. She had been hardened by her experiences and was in excellent physical shape. At 5'8" she was tall for a Korean, and built like a Hollywood movie star. Men were hitting on her constantly, but she never had time. She had one rather torrid affair with a married co-worker. It ended up breaking up his marriage and several hearts, got him fired and Melanie reassigned to the Tokyo office. Through all this time Melanie kept one secret with her – who her father was. Even though the Agency tried to find out more about her background in their personnel screening, she was always able to deflect any questions, claiming her father was a German in Korea who disappeared and left her mother shortly after Melanie and her brother were born.

So when Melanie Lee Han stepped off the Air Force executive jet onto the ramp at Osan all eyes were riveted on her. She was still in the clothes she was wearing for a "contact" she was about to make with one of her assets in Tokyo – dressed to kill in a mini dress and spiked heels. She was not even given time to pack anything – just whisked off to the Air Base at Yokota, Japan where the jet was waiting to fly her to Korea. On the way a two star Air Force general briefed her in on the operation. Melanie's job was to help the Seals find the hostages, or at least translate if necessary. Melanie knew a lot about Yongbyon, although she had never been there – at least not in 28 years. Her latest "asset" was a North Korean nuclear scientist who had defected two years earlier, and through him she had everything but blueprints of the place. She also was the "point man" of a highly clandestine mission into North Korea just 18 months ago.

"Miss Han, I'm General Russ Everts." The officer in a flightsuit met her on the ramp as she walked off the plane. "Welcome to Osan. We've got about two hours to get you outfitted and briefed in on the mission."

"General." Melanie nodded and shook the general's hand with an iron grip. "Glad to meet you. Any place I can get something to eat? I think I had breakfast this morning, but things have moved pretty fast since then." Her English had improved to flawless over the last few years.

Melanie was introduced to her Seal team, MacDonalds bag with Big Mac and Fries in hand. To be sure the Seals were skeptical at best, but they were also men, and the sight of this gorgeous chick in a mini and high heels was more than a couple of them could stand. "Down Tiger." Melanie purred when it was obvious one of them was going to drool all over himself. "We've got work to do. Where can I change into something more appropriate?" Within a few minutes she was clad in a black jump suit and boots. She had a 9 mm Lugar pistol in a shoulder holster and a very large knife in a sheath strapped to her leg. She looked as comfortable in this get up as in her fancy clothes.

Over the next two hours Melanie got a crash course in parachutes and the gear they would have with them. Then they got a briefing on the area and the mission from the Major flight lead of the HH-53s choppers. Melanie made a few inputs on the terrain and Yongbyon, both from memory and from the information she had recently recovered from her assets in Japan. She knew quite a bit about the buildings in the complex and was able to narrow their focus down to two locations as the likely holding areas for any hostages. They went over and over the pickup point, and although everyone was well versed, none of them had a warm, fuzzy feeling. Melanie got the opinion that she and her teammates were expendable. That feeling was reinforced even more when the flight surgeon from the hospital distributed to each of them a pill that she said would make it a quick and painless end. Melanie put hers in a breast pocket of her jumpsuit.

At 1900 hours they stepped up the ramp of an HC-130 Hercules aircraft. Each of them was dressed in all black, had painted their skin black and dark green camouflage, wore a parachute, and carried a weapon of choice. Melanie chose an AK-47 Russian made automatic rifle. She had been well trained through the recent years in how to use it and she was an expert marksman.

Melanie sat down beside Master Chief Ron Woolsey, the leader of the SEAL team. They stayed away from the rest of the team for a few minutes and got reacquainted. Woolsey had been the leader of a three man team Melanie supervised just a year and a half ago. That was the main reason he was selected to lead this team. He'd been in the country before and knew a little about the environment.

CHAPTER FIVE

18 MONTHS EARLIER - OVER THE SEA OF JAPAN

The new C-17 cargo plane climbed out from Yokota Air Base near Tokyo heading west. It was 2330 hours, the weather was cloudy and stormy over their destination and there was very little moon tonight. On board were four of the ten people in the world who knew what tonight's mission was. Even the aircrew only knew they had a very different mission to fly, but nothing about their passengers and their plan. They were soon to find out. In fact, because the big cargo plane was manned with two complete aircrews, it was obvious they would be aloft awhile. The pallet brought on board with modern, hi-tech communications gear served to tweak their curiosity even more.

The mission was the brainchild of Charles Durkee, Director of the Central Intelligence Agency, with the input of Melanie Han, one of the CIA's best agents in Japan. Durkee, the CNO of the Navy Admiral Steven Paradise, and General Johnny Joiner, Chief of Staff of the Air Force, along with their boss Marine General Robert Sanchez, Chairman of the Joint Chiefs of Staff, were in the White House "Situation Room" with the President, Robert Madigan. None of the White House staff or other "strap hangers" were present. Suffice it to say, the classification of this mission was well above Top Secret. Other than the men in the "Sit Room" only the three man SEAL team, Melanie Han, and Technical Sergeant Roberta Hall, all aboard the C-17 were read in on the mission.

The mission was the assassination of Kim Jong Un, Supreme Leader of North Korea. All other attempts to get along with or replace the Kim regime in the country had been unsuccessful and President Madigan felt that the potential that Kim Jong Un would escalate his constant threats and antics would lead to war on the Korean peninsula was too high. All diplomatic efforts and economic sanctions had been exhausted and this plan was deemed as a last resort, but necessary.

The C-17 climbed to its operational ceiling of 42,000 feet, then entered North Korean airspace at the northwest corner of the country over the border with Russia. From there on the flight path mimicked that of an Aeroflot airliner out of Vladivostok across North Korea bound for Seoul, South Korea. Upon crossing the border, the Air Force jet rapidly descended to 31,000 feet and the pilot turned the IFF (Identification Friend or Foe) code to one used by the Russian airline. The thinking was that by "squawking" a Russian airliner code and flying the typical airliner altitude and route, North Korean radar operators with their drastically outdated equipment would believe this new target was a "friendly" airliner.

Approaching Pyongyang the aircrew noticed the stark difference in flying over North Korea as compared to other night flights they'd experienced. The countryside was dark - virtually no lights - until Pyongyang came into view. Because of the clouds and weather, their glimpses of the city were sporadic, but when it was visible, it was lit up with huge bright lights, as if it was in full regalia for some nighttime celebration. As they got near their "drop zone" the pilot signaled the jump master in the rear of the aircraft. The three man SEAL team stood up, checked each other's equipment, moved toward the rear of the cargo compartment, and donned their oxygen masks. To Melanie and Sgt. Hall they looked like some cyborg warriors from a Star Wars movie.

The jump master activated the huge clam shell doors in the rear of the C-17. They swung open and the ramp lowered. A flashing yellow warning light turned to green and the jump master pointed to the dark space behind the aircraft. Quickly, one by one the three Seals jumped out, spreading their arms and legs and looking down in their sky diving position. This is what is termed as a HALO jump (High Altitude, Low Opening). They soared in and out of the clouds, trying desperately to keep each other in sight and as close together as was possible under the circumstances. What seemed like many minutes was only a short time as they broke out of the clouds over the city at about 6000 feet. Master Chief Ron Woolsey had the lead in the jump and he had accurately flown in the blind to put them over the northwest edge of civilization. At 3500 feet his automatic chute deployment activated and he was jerked into a slower descent under a black canopy. He looked up and saw the silhouette of one of his partners, but not both. It turns out that the chute on Mike Stroud, the team's communications expert did not automatically deploy at 3500 feet, so he had to manually activate it passing 2800 feet. That put him below his two partners and separated by about a mile when they landed.

Aboard the C-17 the jump master closed the doors and Melanie and Sgt. Hall went about firing up the communications gear on the pallet. Hall settled into a built in "cockpit," surrounded by computer screens and radios. Melanie nervously paced the cargo deck waiting for their first check in with their SEALS, call sign - "Cheetah." In the meantime, Sgt. Hall checked in with General Joiner back in Washington via High Frequency radio. Meanwhile, the crew in the flight deck continued their route of flight toward the south. As they neared the DMZ (Demilitarized Zone) and border with South Korea, they turned off the IFF and made a hard turn out to sea so as not to actually cross into South Korean airspace. The Republic of Korea (ROK) radar operators were much better equipped and trained and would challenge a flight coming into their airspace without a flight plan, especially in the middle of the night. By the time they turned off the IFF and headed over the water, the radar operators of the north would probably be puzzled but in no position to activate any response. They probably just thought the Russian airliner was responding to directions from South Korean air traffic control. After all, Seoul was only 50 miles south of the DMZ and if the airliner was going to land there it made sense it would maneuver for approach and start a descent soon. The C-17 proceeded out southeast of North Korean airspace and set up an orbit. They rendezvoused with an Air Force KC-10 air refueler and the two big jets set up an orbit, prepared to stay aloft for hours.

Back on the ground in the dark the three SEALS managed to get together. They buried their chutes and excess equipment and struck out for their final objective. They were dressed as North Korean soldiers, and since all of them were of oriental or mid-eastern descent, they looked like many of the millions of local soldiers to any casual observers. Sgt. Stroud was actually a Korean-American and spoke the language fluently. It was 0200 hours. They had 4 1/2 hours of darkness left to move about three miles to the city proper of Pyongyang, and then another 4 miles down back streets and alleys to their eventual destination. But first a check in with "the boss."

"Athena, this is Cheetah, over." Stroud tried over the radio once he got it set up. "Athena, this is Cheetah, come in."

"Cheetah, Athena has you loud and clear. Say status." Melanie answered back.

"Cheetah is intact, good to go. About seven miles out."

"Roger Cheetah. Check in once in place. Use code clicks if necessary." Melanie directed. Use of code clicks simply meant clicking the mic button in Morse code in case the area was too congested for voice transmissions.

"Cheetah copies and out." Stroud answered and packed up the radio into its back pack. They set out for downtown.

This operation was Melanie's show. She set it up and she will be the on scene (or at least in the general area) commander. The go, no-go decisions were hers to make unless she heard something different from Washington. Her airborne command post was set to stay up for at least 24 hours if necessary. The C-17 would top off its fuel tanks periodically on its buddy tanker and the aircrews aboard would rotate shifts every six hours, getting some rest in between in a relatively sound proofed crew cabin behind the cockpit, complete with a full kitchen, showers and even a library of books and a TV with videos. The tanker would be replaced every 4 hours by replacements from Kadena Air Base on Okinawa.

That day was Kim Jong Un's birthday and there was to be a huge parade and military show of force down the main avenue named for Kim's father, Kim Il Song. The younger Kim was slated to be in an observation "box seat" style affair specially built for these kinds of events. The box was about 50 yards long, by ten yards deep, equipped with plush theatre style seats, completely stocked bar and served by dozens of minions. There was a raised stage it the middle where Kim could stand in full view of the proceedings behind bullet proof glass. The parade was to start at 10 AM with Kim and his party in place shortly before.

Cheetah made good time through the suburban area. There were small houses and huts, but without electricity, or at least if they had any, they had the lights off. In fact - it was very early in the morning. When they got to the city they moved quickly but cautiously through the streets until they spotted the first of the soldiers making preparations for the day. At that point the Cheetah team simply marched on through as if they knew what they were doing and where they were going. After all - they did. They arrived at the warehouse building across Kim Il Song Avenue from the reviewing "stand" about 0530, still before sunrise. They made it to what was basically a catwalk around the inside of the warehouse about 30 feet off the floor. The third member of Cheetah was Eric "Shooter" Wilson, a sniper originally from Kentucky (with a mideastern mother), and widely revered the best shot in the SEALS. He took up a position on the catwalk where with the window cracked about six inches, he had a clear view of the stage area behind the bullet proof glass across the street. He also had a long rifle with a big scope.

Master Chief Woolsey went about collecting boxes, trash, piles of aluminum siding, anything laying around in the building that he could use to build a little "nest" behind Shooter, so that he wouldn't be immediately detected from inside the building. Though they had very little intelligence from North Korea, Woolsey suspected that as paranoid as Kim Jong Un is, he would demand all of the surrounding buildings be thoroughly searched. In the meantime, Sgt. Stroud unloaded his radio on Woolsey and traded him for a back pack filled with C-4 explosives, basically rolled into small "tubes" of what looked like clay or caulking. He then went out in search of his next "team."

What intel Melanie was able to gather was that about 2-3 hours ahead of any event that Kim was participating in, a team of "sweepers" congregated around whatever his planned route or location would be and conducted a thorough electronic and physical sweep, looking for explosives or anything else out of the ordinary. Stroud joined the sweepers as they conducted their search of the reviewing area, especially concentrating on the bullet proof glass that would separate Kim from the outside. The last to leave the area, he deftly stuck three "tubes" of explosives, about 4 inches long along the bottom of the glass where they could only be seen by someone on their knees looking up. The tubes were connected by a very thin wire to the middle set where a miniature receiver and detonator was placed along side the tube. Hopefully the search from the hands and knees had just been accomplished. Stroud walked on with the sweepers until the next block, then he beat a quiet retreat away and back to the warehouse. There he took his place next to Shooter and set up the signal device for the detonator, and then the radio to call Mom.

The parade went off right on time. After all, if Kim was there on time, the parade had better start off appropriately or heads would roll - literally. Kim was in his traditional all black suit that looked like pajamas and his entourage - all in uniform, had arrived and were milling around in the lounge behind and beside the "stage." The Cheetah team thought it a bit odd that Kim's designated "wife" was not also there. After all, it was supposedly his birthday and she, or one of the other of his concubines usually accompanied him to public rallies.

The parade started with a fly by of just about everything in the NK Air Force's inventory, followed by tanks, rocket launchers and other heavy machinery. Then came the troops, goose stepping in perfect unison and dress. Cheetah had seen these parades on TV before and they knew when Kim would be most interested and on display. They watched him and after the tanks and heavy artillery he stood perfectly erect and waved almost a salute as a large, black stretch SUV went by, just ahead of the first line of troops. It was time.

In perfect unison with Shooter, Stroud activated a trigger switch that sent a signal to the receiver attached to the C-4 under the bullet proof glass across the street. Shooter had the middle of Kim Jong Un's forehead dead center in his powerful rifle scope and he pulled the trigger one second after the glass shattered. Kim Jong Un went down in a heap with a clean hole in his forehead and the back of his head blown away.

The guards, and all of Kim's surrounding minions reacted to the bomb and rushed the viewing stand. The parade kept going, at least for a while until it was obvious something was wrong. The black SUV was suddenly surrounded by screaming soldiers all pointing toward the stand. The Cheetah team quietly but quickly left their perch, gathered all their toys and beat feet out the back of the warehouse. Two hours later they were back in the woods, this time due north of the city, heading west. When they had time to stop and rest, Stroud got the radio up and working and they called home.

"Athena, this is Cheetah, over."

"Cheetah, this is Athena. Got you loud and clear. What news?" Melanie came back right away, anxious to pass on good news to the President and his team in D.C. The President had left the Situation Room after news that the team had parachuted in safely last night, and then came back in time for the event, White House communication folks were able to tune in to North Korean TV and were watching the parade as the events unfolded.

"Athena, Cheetah is mission accomplished, on the egress now." Stroud relayed.

"Roger Cheetah. Good work. Call when you are ready for extract. Be advised Athena will be off the air now for two days. We'll be back up in 48 house to coordinate your extract." Melanie and her C-17 would return to base now and then launch off again in two days to be up to talk to the SEALS and their recovery team from a US Navy submarine stationed off the coast of North Korea. Melanie then called the President's group in Washington.

North Korean TV focussed on the viewing stand and the bomb destruction for a short period, then it zoomed in on the black SUV in the middle of the parade route, currently surrounded by North Korean troops. After a few minutes, the troops backed off from one side of the vehicle and the back door was opened by one of the guards. Out stepped Kim Jong Un to wild cheers and waves from the troops. A woman got out of the car with him and he waved solemnly, then got back in the car and it quickly moved off toward the Presidential palace. The CIA Director knew immediately what had happened.

"We've been duped Mr. President." Durkee meekly announced. "The man in the review area was obviously one of the many doubles Kim often employs. That was definitely his latest "wife" with him in the car."

"Shit!" The President explained. "So what the hell happened? Did they know we were coming."

"I think that's unlikely sir. If they had, they would have been looking for a sniper. I think this is something else." The Director answered. About that time a phone rang in front of the President. He answered, listened, and passed the phone to Durkee, "One of your folks has an urgent message for you."

The Director took the phone and listened. Then thanked the caller and hung up. To the President he said, "Sir, it appears we may be saved any scrutiny here. Evidently the North Koreans uncovered what they thought would be an assassination attempt on Kim by the Seoul government using explosives."

"Well, I guess that's the good news to deflect the fact that we got the wrong man." Madigan said. "But what do you expect Kim will do about it? I can see the horde swarming over the DMZ looking for blood and revenge."

"That's certainly a possibility sir, but whatever comes we need to stay completely out of it." Durkee said and everyone agreed.

"We can offer our support and protection of South Korea, but we cannot let on we were the instigators here."

"Agreed." The President said as he rose to his feet. "Gentlemen, thanks for nothing. Let's go about our business and see what happens. In the meantime, make sure we get those three SEALS out of there."

The extract went off like clockwork. The Cheetah team made it to the coast in about 36 hours. Two crew members from the attack submarine USS Virginia came ashore in the middle of the night with a Zodiac boat and the five of them disappeared beneath the waves on the Virginia in short order. Melanie didn't pass on the word about the "failure" of the mission. She wanted to get them home first.

Kim made a lot of loud threats, launched a couple of long range rocket tests, and the NK Navy intercepted and destroyed two South Korean Coast Guard cutters. The North claimed they were in North Korean waters. The ROK vehemently denied that and threats were tossed back and forth for a few days. Then things returned to their "normal" state of disarray.

CHAPTER SIX

THAT WAS THEN. THIS IS NOW. NOT SO FAST!

The mission to rescue the hostages and destroy the nuclear facility was scrubbed. At least most of it was. The weather at Osan was the show stopper for the A-10s and F-16s. The choppers could actually have launched, but without escort they would be taking a real risk. So everything was put on a 24 hour slip – same time, same station tomorrow. Everything that is, except Melanie Lee Han and her Seal friends.

The four engine C-130 Hercules took off in visibility that was counted in yards at best. The pilots could see the centerline stripe of the runway in front of them for a few feet, and that was enough to keep the big plane straight. They lifted off and went straight onto their instruments to climb above the fog. If they had lost an engine on takeoff, no big deal. The C-130 can fly on three (or two for that matter) of its big propeller driven engines for hundreds of miles. As it was, everything went fine and soon they were cruising west northwest out over the Yellow Sea, careful to stay out of North Korean airspace. To be even more sure they would be alone, all lights were turned off and strict radio silence was maintained. The Identification Friend or Foe (IFF) system was turned to standby, so even the South Korean air traffic control was kept in the dark. They could see a radar target, but could not interrogate its signal. Since the target was going away from the ROK, no one really cared.

Melanie reflected on her day. She woke up in her apartment in Tokyo early, went for her morning jog in Yoyogi Park, took the bus to her office in the embassy for a morning meeting and update on the daily intelligence traffic, got all duded up for her meeting with one of her contacts, and was on the way to see him when her beeper went off. A quick call to the office and she had the taxi turn around. Within an hour she was in an Air Force staff car on her way to Yokota Air Base. That all seemed like ages ago, and yet it was only about 6 or 7 hours. She figured she would try to sleep a little if she could. The troop seats in the back of a C-130 are not very comfortable, but she needed some rest. This was going to be a long night or more.

The 24 hour delay actually helped the Seals and their new cohort in their mission. They would have more time to locate the hostages, if that was even possible, and hopefully set up some communications with the choppers coming in. One of the men carried the latest in communications technology – a very powerful radio that was about the size of an overnight case. Another Seal had a collapsible antenna that could extend up to fifty feet, and another 100 feet of antenna wire that attached onto that. The new plan was to drop in one valley further to the east of the Yongbyon valley, trek overnight to their "target," and get whatever done they could tomorrow before the mission started to get hot.

About 100 miles out to sea the C-130 pilot put the big plane into a steep dive, still heading west. Passing 3000 feet he jerked it into a hard (for a C-130), steep banked turn, still descending and brought it around to almost due east. They leveled off at basically wave top altitude and kept the engines pushed up to red line. The dive and the turbulence at low altitude kept all the "passengers" awake and anxious. Fortunately the C-130 only has a small port hole in each man way door, so unless one went to look out, they wouldn't see how low they really were. Suffice it to say the salt spray splashing up onto the fuselage was not a good thing for the paint job.

As they approached the coast the co-pilot turned up their Radar Warning Receiver (RWR) to pick up the signal from enemy radars and interceptors that might see them coming. The pilot climbed as necessary as they broke the coast to avoid the trees and rocks, and from then on the attitude varied drastically, hugging the rugged terrain. Ten miles out from the drop zone they went into a moderate climb and let the change in nose attitude slow the craft to jump speed. The jump master open the gaping rear doors under the tail and yelled "Stand in the Door!"

Melanie was the third in line. Her "keepers" insisted on "protecting" her as best they could, keeping her between them as much as possible. Although she wouldn't dare tell them so, she secretly appreciated their concern. She had jumped before, but never at night and not under such dire circumstances. She was glad that the powers that be didn't decide to input the team via a HALO jump as was the method a year and a half ago. In fact, she was probably the reason that option was scrapped. A novice jumping out at a few thousand feet is a lot simpler than a HALO jump which even the seasoned parachutists and sky divers avoid when able. She looked down into the expanse of darkness with very few lights to be seen.

"Ready!" The jump master yelled as the yellow jump light illuminated. Passing 3000 feet altitude the co-pilot punched the green light activator, and about that same time the RWR lit up like a Christmas tree. The defenses around Yongbyon could "see" them on radar and air defense crews were scrambling to their missiles and gun sites.

"Go! Go! Go!" The jump master yelled and one by one the 5 infiltrators stepped off the ramp into the darkness. Immediately the jump master hit the "Close" button on the doors and radioed "All Clear!" to the cockpit. Even before they heard the word the pilot had rolled off onto one wing and was dumping the nose over to get back at low altitude and headed west. The co-pilot punched the chaff button, which expended aluminum balls and strips out into the air that were supposed to cause radars to break lock and transfer to the chaff. It didn't really matter. As soon as they put some rocks in the form of a ridgeline between them and the North Korean defenses they disappeared for all intents and purposes. The pilot was breathing hard though and he left the engines at maximum power until he was 60 miles offshore, still heading west. Both the co-pilot and the jump master were looking back, as much as the lousy rearward visibility of a C-130 would let them, for any Migs sent to investigate.

Sixty miles out in the Yellow Sea the big lumbering C-130 started an easy climbing turn to the south and southwest and headed back to South Korea. Because the fog was still hanging over Osan, they landed at Kunsan and debriefed with the wing intelligence personnel.

Melanie's parachute landing wasn't pretty. She was able to guide into a small clearing so as not to get hung up in the trees. But just as they preached in training and earlier in the night, depth perception in the dark is deceiving at best. She wasn't quite ready for old terra firma when it jumped up and bit her. She sat down hard on her bum and scraped up her chin a bit in the ensuing roll. Within seconds she was out of her chute and harness and was pulling it together to bury. Master Chief Woolsey was at her side before she knew it. "You ok, Ma'am?" Melanie gave a thumbs up and frowned, putting her finger to her lips to indicate "shhh."

She hadn't seen anyone around when she was in the silk, but who knew in a country that hardly had any lights anyway?

The Seals huddled up and took stock of one another. One had slightly strained a knee on landing, but he could move, although with a limp and not too fast. The radioman got hung up in a tree and had to cut his way loose. He had a few scratches, but nothing serious. The serious part though was that some of his parachute was still hung in a tree. They had to take the time to climb up and retrieve it. No chances of discovery could be taken. About an hour later, after they had eaten some rations and drank half their water, they struck out east over the ridge toward Yongbyon.

Back at Kunsan, Brad Mitchell took advantage of the delay for a little diversion. He thought about doing a little bird hunting, but decided with everyone on edge around the base, firing off a few shotgun shells might not be a great idea. He remembered the last time he went.

He had been at the Kun just a few short weeks back in the spring. It was the weekend before Easter and the wing commander had selected a few of the guys to go pheasant hunting with him. Brad was one of the lucky ones, although he never really knew why. No one had hunting guns and rifles with them in Korea, but they each checked out scatter guns from the Security Police. Brad thought that was a bit futile. The guns were wide bore shotguns with a short range – good for a lot of pellet dispersion, but not much accuracy. As it turned out, that's all they needed.

Korean pheasant must be at the bottom of the chain when it comes to intelligence. The guys were hunting around the runway and taxiways. In fact, that was the rationale for the hunt – keep down the aircraft bird strikes by eliminating the threat. Anyway, the birds were so slow and/or dumb you almost had to go up and kick them to get them to fly. It wasn't sporting to shoot them where they sat and looked at you. They were big and beautiful birds though, and in a matter of a couple hours, each of 5 guys had bagged 15-20 birds.

Brad hustled to his hooch with his bag full of pheasant, but had no idea what to do with them. One of his hooch-mates was a big time hunter, but he was on a cross country flight and wouldn't be back until the next day. Brad decided to just stuff the whole bag o' birds in the freezer as they were. There was a wing dining in that night and he had to climb into his mess dress (formal uniform) and get to the club.

Brad was sitting at the bar, nursing a gin and tonic when Captain Karen Ohara (Scarlett), the flight surgeon assigned to the Juvats came up and sat next to him. She introduced herself and they went through the niceties of the day. Karen was waiting for Bobby Fox, a flight commander in the Juvats. Brad knew about them and decided Bobby was a lucky guy. Soon the conversation turned to Brad's activities of the day.

"What did you do with them all?" Karen asked about the pheasant.

"I just left them in the bag and stuck the whole thing in the freezer." Brad replied. "I'm hoping my roommate will know how to clean them. After that, I haven't a clue. Any idea how to cook a pheasant?"

"You did what?!" Karen looked aghast. "You didn't clean them first?"

Brad was a little ashamed. "I'm not sure how. The only bird I've ever cleaned before is a dove. All you do with them is stick your thumb up under their sternum and pop the breast out. I assume there's more to….." Brad didn't have a chance to finish. Karen had him by the wrist and was pulling him out of the bar.

"Come on. Where's your hooch?"

They went to Brad's hooch and Karen stripped off her mess jacket and rolled up her sleeves. Brad did the same. He figured he'd better at least help. Within 45 minutes the good doctor had every bird cleaned, rinsed, wrapped in saran wrap and back in the freezer. She let Brad clean up the mess. He thought that was the least he could do, and they made it back to the club in time to inhale a quick drink before the gong went off to take their seats.

Karen surprised him later on Easter Sunday. He had mentioned to her later in the week after the dining in that he still didn't know what to do with the pheasant. At about 7 A.M. on Easter Sunday he woke to a bunch of banging and clattering going on in his kitchen. He stumbled in wearing just his skivies to find Karen cooking.

"Uh. G'morning." He offered with a yawn.

"Hey! Sorry 'bout the noise." She came back. "You got any more pans? Nice shorts, by the way." Brad thought about covering up, but decided she was a flight surgeon and had seen all there was to see anyway. They decided there were no more pans to be had, so Karen raided the next door hooches for all their kitchenware. She made pheasant enchiladas and the invited the whole squadron. Needless to say, the guys were impressed.

CHAPTER SEVEN

"A" TOWN

"Hey Joe! Ju lub me? I lub ju." The bargirl leaned against Staff Sergeant Mike Syzmanski's arm, rubbing what breasts she had on him to get his attention. Her typical Korean butchering of the English language wasn't as humorous as it was when he first arrived on the ROK. They didn't know too many words anyway, just the ones necessary to hook their prey for the night – or the hour – depending on how quick they were. This one was new. Mike had been in this bar in "A-Town" probably 30 times in his ten months at Kunsan. He knew all the bar girls and whores, even in the biblical sense, and he didn't remember ever seeing or bedding this one. Ahhh! A new challenge.

Sgt. "Syzmo" Syzmanski was an intelligence specialist assigned to the 80th TFS. He had just worked about 14 hours copying route maps for the pilots of the squadron and processing intel data for their mission. When the 24 hour delay hit, his boss told him and everyone else to get some rest. "Rest" to Mike Syzmanski was unloading in A-Town with his buddies and some rot gut Korean beer, followed by a romp in the hay with whichever bar fly he could talk down in price. He had a reputation as a partier and a stud, and the girls swarmed around him. He was a good looking guy and he always seemed to have plenty of money. Besides, he always paid in greenbacks – illegal but much more valuable to the Korean girls.

One of the reasons Mike had hit the bars so much was that he had turned into an alcoholic over the last few years, and he had a chip on his shoulder about the young lieutenants and captains in the wing. Mike Syzmanski had been a cadet at the Air Force Academy. He had taken the glider and flight training offered at the Academy and was slated for pilot training after graduation. Then in his senior year, he got caught supplying beer to a bunch of underage cadets at a party downtown in Colorado Springs. The party was raided and the Commandant, and the]Superintendent made an example out of Mike. At least that's the way he saw it. He was kicked out of school and forced to serve out his commitment as an enlisted man. Since he was a Geography major with a Political Science minor he was assigned to intelligence and trained as a targeteer. He spent a tour at Mountain Home Air Base, Idaho, and was assigned to Kunsan almost a year ago. Two straight assignments with ex-classmates and underclassmen who were now F-16 pilots. His ex-roommate at "The Zoo" was even a captain in the 35th. They hardly spoke. Mike figured these guys all thought they were better than him. Bullshit! The final straw was when one of the so called "underage" cadets at the party showed up at Mountain Home as a First Lieutenant fighter pilot. That's when

Mike hit the bottle. He also used marijuana and had shot up a couple of times as well – being very careful not to get caught. Tonight he was just tired – wanted a few beers and this sweet new piece of Korean tail.

"Sure. Sit down. You want a drink?" Syzmo offered the girl. She was pretty for a Korean, and she seemed to have some Filipino or Thai blood in her. She also had bigger boobs than the average girl – silicone enhanced probably, but Mike didn't care. She sat down and started rubbing his inner thigh. Mike figured this was going to be easy.

About 2300 hours Sergeant Bucky Michaels came in the bar, looking like the cat who'd just eaten the mouse. He was one of Syzmanski's running buddies. "Where ya been, Bucko?" Mike teased. "You missed out on the new blood."

"Syzmo, you wouldn't believe it. I've been in on the debrief of the C-130 guys that just went north." Michaels sort of whispered, but it was loud enough that anyone who understood English could hear. He was convinced though that the only ones within earshot were the bartender and the barfly hanging on Syzmanski's arm, and they didn't know but about ten words of English.

"Oh yeah? Did they get it done?"

"Yeah, they delivered their passengers and I guess they lit up the defenses up there" Michaels was assigned to the Wing Intelligence Division as a briefer/de-briefer and he and Major Leitao had de-briefed the Hercules pilots when they landed. He knew very well that any of this information was Top Secret, but he figured Syzmanski was read in. After all, they were in the same business.

A-Town. Every U.S. military base in the Pacific had an "A-Town," or a "B-Town," or a shanty town of some sort right outside its gates. Actually, this one was about ten miles off base toward the City of Kunsan, but it was typical – small bars with loud juke boxes, dirty bars with rot gut whiskey, beer loaded with formaldehyde, and girls of all ages looking for a quick buck. There was usually a hardwood dance floor where the guys could rub all over the girls and there were plenty of rooms upstairs to get the deed done. Especially at a remote assignment like Kunsan, A-Town got lots of action. The fighter squadrons were especially popular. They would usually invade en mass once a month or so. Each squadron had its favorite series of bars and would make the cycle of four or five in a couple of hours, buy up all the whiskey, dance with all the girls, whatever came next for some. They called it a "Sweep," and it was where each new pilot, or anyone assigned or "adopted" by the squadron was given their nickname, or combat call sign. Sweeps involved a lot of drinking, singing of filthy fighter pilot songs, dancing and mostly just good red blooded macho fun. Some of the guys would partake of the easy sex, but most would finally wander back to base a little after midnight to sleep it off before tomorrow.

The use of combat or tactical callsigns was a time honored tradition, not just in the Air Force, but in all military flying environments. As a matter of fact, even special operators in non-flying units adopted similar nicknames. In the Air Force it was at one time even used to designate mission call signs. For example, a flight of four F-4 phantoms in Vietnam might have the call sign of "Buick," which was the tactical name of the flight lead. He probably drove a big Buick at one time in his career and was always associated with it. The remainder of the flight might be "Hustler," "Pig Pen," and "Geronimo," instead of "Two, Three and Four." That tradition was rather short lived though when in the heat of the battle one day "Geronimo" got very excited when he saw a Mig taxi up behind his element lead, "Pig Pen," and forgot who he was flying with when yelling for a defensive maneuver. Because "Pig Pen" didn't get the word, he was blown out of the sky and he and his back seater spent the rest of the war as guests of the North Vietnamese in the Hanoi Hylton. At least "Geronimo" was able to turn in on the Mig and shove a missile up its tailpipe, so the mission wasn't a total loss. But the powers that be in the Air Force put an immediate end to the use of tactical call signs as the identification of operational missions. From then on, although it might still be "Buick Flight," the call sign of the leader, the members of the flight would be "Buick Lead," or "Buick One," and the others would be "Buick Two, Three and Four." The tradition of nicknames continued and does so even today, although they may be more tempered in "political correctness" nowadays. For example, Larry Clamoris would probably not be "awarded" the name "Clitoris" in today's military.

The callsigns came about in different scenarios for every unit. Like mentioned, the Kunsan squadrons of Juvats and Panton's "awarded" their members with the monickers during a Sweep in A-Town. There was no one rhyme nor reason as to how the names were selected. Sometimes it was by physical appearance. Brad Mitchell was a big guy and since the squadron often sat around and watched the Conan movies, almost cult-like, the old heads selected "Conan" for their new squadron commander. Another was Greg Iliff, who had a big forehead and was prematurely bald. His callsign was "Bulb," like Light Bulb? Others inherited their monicker because of their position in the squadron or wing. Colonel Rushing was the commander of the 8th Tactical Fighter Wing, otherwise known as the "Wolfpack." Hence he became "Lobo," the lone wolf leader. Sometimes the guys and gals were named because of a derivative of their real name. Captain Ohara was the squadron flight surgeon and she was named "Scarlett" after another famous Ohara. Mike Sykes was named "Psycho," Dan White took on the name "Snow." Bob Fore was "Skin," another not so politically correct term. Then there was Bob Huston who inherited his name during a squadron basketball game against another squadron. He was 6'3" but he could jump, and somewhere in the first half of the game he rammed a ball home with a two handed dunk. "Boom" went the cheer from the bench, and from then on and through his career and later he was "Boomer." The call signs usually stuck throughout their Air Force career. Sometimes they inherited new ones, especially if they weren't real fond of the one they got from the Juvats. Boomer though was Boomer throughout his Air Force career and through his follow on career as a defense contractor. He is still Boomer to his friends to this day.

Mike Syzmanski and Bucky Michaels sometimes participated in the squadron Sweeps, in fact that's how Mike got the handle "Syzmo." But mostly the enlisted guys were different. Many of them were hard core partiers. Some were lonely American farm boys who had never had a woman say she loved them before – even one who uses some pretty bad English pronunciation. It didn't matter to them what she said, it was how she showed it that mattered. All too often these rendezvous led to one sided romances and even weddings. The Korean girls knew that a gullible American was their ticket to bigger and better things – the U.S.A. The immigration rosters are loaded with ex-Korean bar girls who were now Mrs. Staff Sergeant – just long enough to get to America. Then it was "Adios sucker, I'm outta here." Certainly some of these romances actually lasted and relationships flourished. But that was the exception.

Not a worry for either Mike Syzmanski or Bucky Michaels. They were old hands at this. Booze and sex, and maybe a little weed were all they wanted, and they were always successful, even though they spent the majority of their pay checks. The way they saw it, what else was there to do? Syzmo's friend, Miss Kim, had a friend – Miss Lee – and the four of them were having a great time. The guys were drinking Korean San Miguel beer – strong stuff, and the girls were drinking watered down Shirley Temples disguised as Mai Tais.

Finally Mike had had enough "foreplay" and was ready to get down to it. "Ok, Miss Kim – how much for tonight?" He propositioned. The girl giggled and jabbered on with her friend a minute. Then finally, "Mikey, I like ju velly much. Thutty dollah, ok?" A bargain, and Mike thought he must have really made an impression. The going rate was normally $40.

"Ok," He said. "I'll be right back. Gotta go pee." Syzmo went off to the little boys' room – a large closet with a trough against one wall, and a sink that didn't work on the other. Bucky came along to relieve himself too.

Back at the bar Miss Kim deftly pulled out a small pill box from her pocket and dropped a tiny tablet in each of the guy's beers. "Ok, ladies – where to?" Mike said as he returned to the bar.

"Finish beer, Joe. Then we go next door." Kim pushed the beer bottles toward the Americans who obliged as any macho American would. Gotta show these wenches we can hold our liquor. They each drained their beers and then threw the bottles against a wall that was bricked over and had a fireplace painted over it. This was the Hot Lips Bar, one of the bars on the "tour" of the Juvats, and the bottle breaking exercise was tradition. Far be it from Mike and Bucko to be different. They went out into the street and arm in arm with their ladies of the night and stumbled around the corner toward paradise (for the night).

It was Two AM when the phone rang in the Wing Commander's hooch. Lobo was finally asleep. He'd been on the horn talking with Pacific Air Forces Headquarters and his counterpart at Osan, discussing the plan and contingencies. He managed to get PACAF to send up an AWACs command and control airplane from Kadena

Air Base, Okinawa for tomorrow's mission. He finally got to sleep a little after midnight.

"Rushing." He mumbled into the hotline to the Command Post.

"Sir, this Major Hansen. We've got a couple dead GIs down in A-Town." It was the Chief of Security Police, being patched through from the scene. Rushing sat up straight.

"What? Who are they? What happened?"

"Sir, they still have their IDs, and one of them's in uniform. That's Sergeant James Buckley Michaels. The other one is Staff Sergeant Michael Syzmanski. They both have had their throats slashed and it looks like they were beat up pretty good. The Command Post is tracking down their positions in the Wing." Hansen described the scene.

"I know who they are. Michaels is in Wing Intel. I just saw him at a debrief a few hours ago. Syzmanzki is in the 80th Squadron. Damn!" Rushing exclaimed. "Jeff – cordon off the area and do a real good search. Wolfden – get the mortuary folks down there ASAP, and have Major Leitao and Lieutenant Colonel Mitchell meet me in the Command Post in ten minutes." Jeff Hansen sensed this wasn't an ordinary murder, not that he'd ever been involved in an ORDINARY murder. He acknowledged his instructions and signed off. "Wolfden" was the call sign of the Command Post and they got busy doing their job as well. Rushing got dressed.

"God damnit guys, what were these two doing down in A-Town tonight of all nights? Didn't you guys give them enough work to tire them out?" Rushing was none too happy with the two supervisors.

"Sir, I told Syzmo to get some rest just like everyone else. I thought he was. Unfortunately he does his own thing and he's a bit of a partier." Brad Mitchell tried to defend himself. The truth was he didn't keep that tight a reign on his enlisted folks. He assumed they did their own thing when they weren't at work, and since fraternization between officer and enlisted was frowned upon, he didn't worry about their private lives. Besides, he knew Syzmanski's background, and had decided to leave the kid alone to his own attitude.

"Unfortunately I have to say the same about Sergeant Michaels, sir." Leitao echoed. "After the C-130 debriefing I just assume he went to the barracks to turn in. Do you think there is a connection here?" The major was thinking like an intelligence officer now, assuming everything is secret, or ought to be, and if it's not, it's probably compromised. Most hadn't even thought that there might be a security problem involved. Rushing had thought about it, and he also thought the coincidence of these two men who knew way too much turning up with their throats cut behind a Korean bar was just too much.

"Let's hope not, but I think we'd better assume so. What did they know?" Lobo asked. "Obviously Michaels knew way too much. He was in on the debriefing of the Seal insertion mission. How about Syzmanski?" He looked at Mitchell.

"He copied all the routes of the ingress of the squadron's attack, sir. No doubt he'll have the whole route memorized. Other than that I don't know how much he was in on." Brad was not so sure there was a compromise. "Are we sure this wasn't just another robbery gone wrong, sir?" There was usually a robbery a weekend in A-Town. Sometimes Korean thugs, but just as often another American GI taking advantage of an inebriated big spender. They didn't usually lead to murder, but it was not unheard of. A maintenance airman and a bar girl were found shot to death just a couple months ago. Turns out that was a disgruntled Korean boy friend, and the Korean police took care of him.

"Could be, but they both had their wallets on them. You'd think a thief would have cleaned them out." Rushing responded. To be safe, he got on the phone to the Command Post, "Wolfden – get me PACAF on the phone." then to Mitchell, "Conan, first thing in the morning get to work changing the Juvat ingress route. Maybe you can start from the west and just swing around to the south and still hit 'em from the east, but just get there a different way. Brief me up on your plan at 1400 hours. We'll assume that neither of these guys knew the Panton route, but find out all you can about who they talked to and 'shared information with' yesterday. If it appears the Pantons were compromised as well we'll change their plan as best we can too." There really wasn't much they could do with the plan for the 35th squadron. They had to orbit until they were ready to attack, and the only safe place to orbit was where they had planned.

Major Jeff Hansen had his cops fan out and door to door search just about all of A-Town, looking for anything that smacked of a fight or a robbery. They found an empty shed with a couple of chairs and some fresh blood on the floor. There was not much else there, but it was probably the scene of the crime. They also ascertained from interviewing bartenders and other "patrons" that the two were last seen in the Hot Lips Bar, where they busted their beer bottles and left with two unknown bar girls. Just on a whim, one of the civilian Office of Special Investigations (OSI) agents swept up and bagged all the broken glass in front of the fake fireplace in the Hot Lips. In the meantime the bodies were "bagged" and transported to the Base Hospital for autopsies. Hansen was able to coerce (with some well greased palms) his Korean counterparts and they let the Americans take full jurisdiction. If there had been a Korean death or a Korean involved in any way, it would have been a different story. But as far as anyone knew, this was either two guys who slit each other's throats (not very likely, but…), or two Americans done in by another American.

Nels Rushing briefed the PACAF Vice Commander who was rousted from bed and none too happy about the news. They also connected with the Wing Commander in Osan and the CINCPAC Deputy Director for Operations, who had been dispatched to Osan to command the whole operation. Since there were Navy Seals involved, as well as a CIA agent, this was a "joint" exercise, and the Commander in Chief of Pacific Command (a four star admiral) would be in charge. He in turn, sent his Air Force two star DO, General Steve Woodward, to be the on scene (or at least as close as generals and admirals get to the scene) commander.

"Gentlemen, the CINC has had several conversations with the SECDEF and the President on this issue, and I can assure you we will not turn back now." General Woodward spoke. "If we've been compromised, we'll just have to live with it. Work around it the best you can. I will confirm all this with the CINC, but unless you hear otherwise, press on with the mission. Let me know if you can confirm any compromise." Vice PACOM agreed and all expressed their understanding. It was obvious to Nels Rushing that nothing was going to stop Washington from beating the shit out of Yongbyon, North Korea, and it didn't matter that there might be a lot of losses. It pissed him off, and he couldn't hang up without saying so.

"Sirs, with all due respect, I want to go on record as objecting to this whole mission." Lobo hung himself out to dry. "You have already sent in five good Americans to what is almost certain capture or death. You are dreaming if you think the Seals will find anyone alive but a bunch of North Korean gooks who will be glad to do the same to them as they probably have to the three inspectors. And you expect us to fly an extremely complicated mission in the dark in an all out attack on an enemy that probably knows when and how we're coming. These folks deserve better." There was a long, pregnant silence on the phone. Rushing hoped at least the Wing Commander at Osan felt the same way, but he wasn't surprised his counterpart didn't say anything. Chances were that Colonel Watson of Osan was soon to come out on the brigadier general list, and he wasn't about to do or say anything to jeopardize that.

"Nels, for the record I agree with you." It was Vice PACOM. "I've voiced the same concerns, as has the boss." He referred to his four star commander. "We were told the same thing I'm telling you now. You've been heard. Now, shut up and sit down."

"Yes sir." Rushing responded and they all hung up.

CHAPTER EIGHT

ESPIONAGE

Miss Kim, Miss Lee, and their male cohort were on a train to Seoul. They had to get to their contact point quickly with the information they had squeezed out of the two American airmen in A-Town. The mickey that Miss Kim dropped in the two romeos' beers was potent. Syzmanski had barely made it out the door of the Hot Lips Bar when he about went unconscious. Kim was able to hold him up and guide him around the corner, down the alley and to a small building all set up for their deed.

The man was an expert in torture. He beat up both the Americans pretty badly, but he was adept enough to keep them awake. It only took him a half hour with each of the airmen to ascertain what they knew — and they knew a lot. After beating them up sufficiently and gathering all the intel they needed, he slit the throat of each of the Americans and put them out of their misery.

The train was an an express and it rolled into Seoul's main station within 90 minutes of leaving Kunsan. They took a taxi and hightailed it to a "safe house" used by the North Koreans. It was well equipped with the latest in computer and communications gear. Miss Lee was the comm expert of the three and she soon had their boss in Pyongyang on the other end. They were able to pass on the information about the American SEAL team and its infiltration into the country, as well as the exact route of flight and timing of the 80th fighter squadron pending attack. They even had names of most of the pilots and the fact that the SEAL team had a CIA agent - a woman of Korean descent onboard with them.

When they were done Kim, Lee and their butcher friend left and melted into the crowd of Seoul.

CHAPTER NINE

BACKGROUND AND THE PHILIPPINES

Brad Mitchell had a fairly restful day. He actually managed to get some sleep and slept in until 0800. He fixed himself some eggs and sausage in his hooch, and even managed a short workout at the base gym before noon. Due to crew duty limitations they were not supposed to show up at the squadron until 1600 hours, so he had time to run a few errands. The biggest errand at a remote base is a check of the mailroom. Since Brad wasn't married and didn't have a steady girl back home, he never really got much mail. However, his Mom managed to send a "care package" about once a month of chocolate chip cookies. Today was the day.

Brad was the son of a WWII B-25 pilot who went back to school after the war and then went to work for the State Department. Growing up, Brad spent time all over the world. Whenever they were in the States it was in the Northern Virginia area, in between two years on the island of Saipan, three years in Indonesia, and three years in Tokyo. Brad started high school at the American School in Japan, but graduated from Fairfax High in Fairfax, Virginia. He had always wanted to be a pilot, and since the Vietnam War was in full swing when he graduated from Fairfax, he tried for the Air Force Academy. He didn't quite make the grade, so he opted for the next best thing – the Virginia Military Institute and Air Force ROTC. Another major factor was that VMI was an "in-state" college for the Mitchells, and the tuition was affordable.

Mitchell excelled at VMI. His grades weren't all that fantastic. In fact, he changed majors half way through his freshman year – from Civil Engineering to Economics – to avoid having to take calculus over again. But Brad did well at the military training. He was a Lieutenant in the Corps of Cadets his senior year and did well in the flight indoctrination program, wetting his appetite for pilot training. VMI being the kind of place it was, Brad didn't experience the "college life" his high school buddies did. Parties were few and far between and girls had to be imported for dances. Brad had a few dates, but he never really got serious about anyone until his senior year. Then he was re-introduced to the daughter of a friend of the family and fell head over heels in love with the sweet young freshman from Bridgewater College, about 60 miles up the valley from VMI. Cassie Hightower was a beautiful girl – captain of the cheerleaders in high school – very charming and "debutantish." But Cassie had traveled all over the world too and she'd had enough of that kind of life. Brad surprised her right after he graduated with an engagement ring and it was a long, tough summer for both of them. When it was all said and done, and Brad had his GTO packed up for pilot training at Moody AFB, Georgia, Cassie dropped the bomb. She wouldn't marry him.

Brad was devastated, but he didn't have time to do anything about it. He had to leave. His pride was hammered as well, and the parting was not very cordial. Although by the time he got to Georgia he had calmed down and decided he needed to keep trying, Cassie had decided a clean break was the only way. He never saw her again, but he heard through his parents that she married a long time high school beau and settled down in North Carolina. From then on Brad kept his romantic interludes to one night stands. That was easy at Moody. Valdosta State College had a good selection of college girls "cruising" to meet and marry an Air Force pilot. Fortunately there were enough that were just out for a good time as well. Brad stuck to the latter, but mostly he studied and worked hard to graduate near the top of his class.

By 1969 the Vietnam conflict was winding down and all of a sudden the Air Force found itself with an abundance of pilots. During the war, pilot training assignments were based on class standing and historically the best pilots in the class would opt for a fighter assignment to get to the war and "fly and fight" as they were trained. Towards the end though, the fighter assignments dried up. The next best thing at the time was an assignment back into pilot training as an instructor. Instructors were still getting fighters as follow on assignments. So Brad took a slot as a T-37 instructor pilot at Laughlin AFB in Del Rio, Texas.

Again Brad did well. Not being married, he volunteered for all the extra flying and cross country flights he could get. That increased his total hours significantly and soon put him in position to upgrade to a Wing Standardization Evaluation (check pilot) slot. There he flew mostly with other IPs, giving them check rides, and flew with students only when he wanted to. That helped his outlook immensely. A lot of instructors burned out early, flying with ham-fisted students who were always trying to kill them. Not really – but sometimes it seemed that way.

Del Rio was also where Brad discovered his second love – sailing. The huge Lake Amistad on the Rio Grande was perfect for sailing with lots of wind, and Brad got in with a couple of squadron buddies and bought a 23 foot Ranger sloop, rigged to the hilt for racing. He was very competitive, and anytime there were two sailboats within sight of each other it was a race. The other guy might not think so, but Brad did. He certainly enjoyed his time off on the water. Brad enjoyed his job too, and when it came time for reassignment he was one of the few who was picked to go on to another flying slot. The gluttony of pilots had continued and many were shuffled off into staff and non-flying jobs to bide their time until another cockpit came open. Brad was lucky and he was assigned as a Forward Air Controller (FAC) in the OV-10, flying out of Thailand into Cambodia.

The FAC business was winding down with the war and he only saw the last couple of months of combat. After a year he was up for assignment again and finally he got his fighter – an F-4 Phantom to Hahn AB, Germany.

F-4 training was 9 months long and it was at Homestead AFB, Florida – just south of Miami. Quite a difference from Del Rio and Alamagordo, New Mexico, where Brad went through a six week fighter lead-in course. The F-4 training was 6 months of work "crammed" into nine, so there was plenty of time to enjoy the beach, the water, sailing, the keys, the bikinis. Again, though Brad may have been "distracted" now and then by the gorgeous south Florida women, he was so excited about finally getting his fighter assignment that he kept his nose to the grind and graduated as "Top Gun" in his class.

Hahn Air Base was another thing altogether. Hahn historically has the worst weather of any US Air Force Base in the world. That's saying something, considering the Air Force has bases in Iceland, Alaska, all over the world in some wild and woolly weather. The problem at Hahn was fog – or more accurately, low clouds. Hahn was about 600 feet higher in elevation than most of the rest of Germany, so that when everyone else had a 600 foot ceiling (certainly flyable weather), Hahn was socked in. It stayed that way most of the winter and off and on in the summer. To get in their flying time the squadrons usually deployed to Spain, or northern Italy, or Turkey. Again Brad volunteered to go anytime and built up even more cockpit time. Once again his star rose to the top and he became an instructor and was eventually selected for a Stan Eval position. When it came time for reassignment, Brad was selected to transition to the new F-16 Falcon, and he was assigned to the new wing of Vipers at Shaw AFB, South Carolina.

Brad started off as the Chief of the Stan Eval division at Shaw and after a year he was named as the commander of the wing Gunsmoke Team. Gunsmoke was an Air Force wide gunnery competition held at Nellis AFB, Nevada. Each fighter wing in the Air Force sent a team of four jets to compete on the bombing range. Mitchell was tasked with picking the pilots and the jets to fly, given command of not only the pilots but the maintenance folks as well. They practiced for several months and became very good. Brad was not one of the primary fliers, but he was in charge of the whole operation. The competition went well for the Shaw wing, and they came in 4th overall. One of the pilots, a lieutenant from the 19th squadron was the top gun in two events.

After Gunsmoke was over, Brad was named as the Operations Officer of the 19th squadron. He had been promoted a year early to Lieutenant Colonel and was on the list for squadron commander. Unfortunately, although he was an outstanding Ops Officer and got excellent ratings, he had managed to piss off the Wing Commander with his over zealous ways. It soon became obvious that Brad was not going to get a command in the States, so the Wing Director of Operations pulled some strings and Brad was assigned to the 8th Tac Fighter Wing at Kunsan. Within a month, he was named the Squadron Commander of the 80th TFS Headhunters.

Flying was obviously Brad's life. He had never dated one girl more than once or twice ever since Cassie. Although there were plenty who wanted to rope him and tie him down, he never let himself get into that position. He kept busy flying, working out and playing squadron sports. Brad was a big guy – about 6'4" and 215. He had played basketball in high school and for two years at VMI, and he was pretty good at other team sports as well. His downfall was golf. He just didn't have the temperament for it, and he couldn't stand not doing something well. Just for grins though today, after checking the mail and downing a half dozen of Mom's cookies, he went to the driving range and checked out a couple buckets of balls. What the hell – there's time to waste and what better way to take out any frustrations than on a little white ball. After a half a dozen slices and hooks and one or two decent drives he forgot all about any frustrations. It made him think about the last time he'd played golf. It was at Clark Air Base, in the Philippines. Thinking of that brought him back to the fact that he didn't pay enough attention to the enlisted folks in squadron. He kept thinking that if he'd gotten closer to his folks in stripes that maybe he could have headed off at least the circumstances that Syzmo had gotten himself into. After all, it wasn't like he hadn't been exposed to the trouble young enlisted could get into - especially off base and especially in the Philippines.

The Juvats had a young airman in the squadron admin section when Brad took command who had a very promising future. He was a lousy clerk and didn't do well taking orders, especially from the female first lieutenant Executive Officer or his female technical sergeant NCO In Charge. No, Mike Clark was not a military man, but he was a helluva golfer. He had grown up in Pinehurst, North Carolina where his dad was one of the club pros in that golf mecca. Clark was a scratch golfer and had just earned his tour card when he got in a little trouble with the law. Brad wasn't briefed in on the specifics when he took over the reigns of the Juvats, and Clark didn't talk about it much. Whatever it was led to his earning another card, that of the black sheep of the golfing community and of his family. He simply put it all on a back burner for now and enlisted in the Air Force. His reputation proceeded him however, and he was drafted onto the Air Force golf team where he went on several boondoggle trips to various tournaments, winning his share of fame and glory. No money, but fame and glory. He had been on one of those trips just before the squadron deployed to Clark Air Base for a six week training stint.

When they got to Clark Brad noticed that Clark was on the golf course nearly every day and asked Mike's boss if the boy was holding his own in the office. She allowed as how Clark came in early every morning and then came back from golf mid-afternoon and stayed late tidying up the paperwork. She had no complaints, so Brad decided he didn't either. He even played with and was severely humbled by the young airman a couple of times. Clark Air Base had a very nice golf course carved out of the

Philippine jungle, complete with filipino caddies. But the treasure for golfers in the islands was Baguio. It was up in the "mountains" of Luzon, about 4000 feet in elevation. The U.S. Army/Air Force kept a recreation center there that became very popular during the Vietnam era. It was still open now, but in reality was a waste of Pentagon dollars. There were only a few Americans that rotated in and out for R&R, and mostly the facility was used by the Filipino elite and the occasional Asian golf enthusiast.

Mike Clark had been to Baguio to play golf a few times and he approach Mitchell with a proposition. Take a couple days off with him and some of the other golfers in the squadron and he would give Brad a lesson or two. Brad knew about Baguio and figured this was too good to pass up, so Brad plus 6 other Juvat pilots and Mike Clark launched off on a Sunday to Baguio, played three rounds - two on Monday and one Tuesday morning and were back on base Tuesday evening.

Baguio was a unique course for sure. Being in the mountains, which were basically karst with drastic peaks and canyons, it was a hoot to play. There was one par three where the Tee box was 2000' above the green, which was in reality only a pitching wedge shot. It was all about the wind. If you made the right swing, the ball might land on the green. If not, it would be off in no man's land. The green sat on the top of its own smaller peak and the golfer got to it on a swinging rope walkway, the kind you see in Indiana Jones movies.

The most interesting hole though was a 130 yard par four. It was just the opposite - the Tee box was down in the valley beneath a towering hill that was terraced - about 8-10 terraces, each one 8-10 feet wide. The idea was to take your loftiest club and hit the ball as high and hard as you could. It would fly up and plunk on one of the terraces. Then you took a rope tow ride (where you hang on to a rope that is motorized) to abeam your particular terrace, get off and go hit your ball again - same way with a blind shot onto the green (hopefully). The whole two day jaunt was a lot of fun and frustration, but Brad did pick up a few pointers.

When that deployment was over, the squadron deployed back to Korea. Brad led the Juvats home and the maintenance and admin folks took off later in the day in a C-141. One of the Assistant Operations Officers was left to squire the group aboard. When they landed at Kunsan Brad was met at his jet by Colonel John Lorner, the wing Director of Operations. "Welcome home, Conan."

Brad was pleased to see his boss, but wondering why the personal welcome. "Thank you sir. What's up? I don't THINK we broke any rules getting here." He asked.

"No, nothing like that, though I'd say it wouldn't be the first time." Lorner replied with a smile. "But you do have a problem. It appears your young admin airman Clark didn't show up for the flight out on the C-141. I told them to press on anyway and we'll see what we can do with the Clark Security Police to round him up. You got it from here."

"Ok. Thanks sir. I'll see what I can find out. I know he was pretty steady with one of the bar girls down there. Hopefully the cops can find him."

Brad went directly to the squadron and got on the horn with the Clark AB Security Police Chief. They basically listed Mike Clark as AWOL (Absent WithOut Leave), and the cops sent out a scouting party. Unfortunately they run into this issue quite a lot. Especially the young airmen in the visiting squadrons often are smitten with what they call "love" with some of the nice looking Filipino girls. In most cases the young men have never even been "in love" before, many are virgins and never had any girl tell them how much she loved them (albeit with a distinct accent). As it turned out, that's exactly what happened with Airman Mike Clark. The SPs found him in one of the ratty off base hotels, shacked up with a pretty little Filipino chick. the cops threw handcuffs on Clark and hauled him back to base, and put him on the next Klong (C-130 that makes the rounds of all the bases in the Pacific arena on a periodic basis) to Korea. The Security Police Chief called Brad at the squadron the next day.

"Sir, we caught your wayward Romeo downtown and he's on his way back to you." The Major said. "But you've got a bit of a problem here."

Brad was more than curious. "Oh boy! I can't wait. What's up?"

"Well it seems young Clark went and got himself hitched to this sweet young thing down here, and he was bound and determined to bring her on the airplane with him." The Major explained. "Certainly we didn't allow that, but it also happens that this girl's father is one of the big muckity mucks in our little off base shanty town. He's anxious to see his little girl treated right - you know, with respect and all that."

"Wow." Brad said. "Ok. I guess I'll deal with it. You've been through this before Major, any suggestions?"

"Unfortunately sir, you're right. We've been through it before. The biggest problem is the bulk of the Filipinos are Catholic, so an annulment or a quick divorce is not an option." The major responded. "Sometimes these relationships work out. It takes a while, but the embassy in Manila has issued visas and the happy young duo goes home to the land of the Big BX (Base Exchange - otherwise known as a shopping mall) as a happily married couple. Nine times out of ten however, as soon as the girl hits the States, she does so running, serves the trusting and smitten young American with divorce papers and it's 'Sayonara sucker'."

"Ok. Thanks Major and thanks for the input. I'll keep you advised as to what we do with him." Brad said.

Mitchell had young Clark in on the carpet just as soon as he was deposited on Korean soil. "Ok. Mike. I got the story from the SPs down south. What have you got to say for yourself, and be advised you will be bumped down to Airman Basic for going AWOL? Anything further depends on what you tell me."

"Yes sir. I'm sorry sir." He whined. "We really are in love. She is a great girl and I want to take leave and go back down there to apply for a visa for her. I miss her terribly."

"Mike, you gotta be shittin' me. You know how these girls are. She only sees you as her ticket to the States. She's probably down there now, back in the bar, zeroing in on another unsuspecting mark." Brad said, but it didn't go over too well - especially the last part.

`"No sir." He yelled. "She wouldn't do that. I'm serious sir. If you won't give me leave then I'll just go there when I leave here. My tour's up in two months anyway."

Brad thought about that a minute. Maybe that's the best way to handle this. At least then it wouldn't be his problem anymore. But he couldn't just let the whole thing slide either. "Ok, smart guy. Here it is. You are busted down to Airman Basic. You will forfeit two month's pay, and you'll spend those two months in the Brig. When that's over, your tour here will be up and what you do from here is your business. I can only hope that you take those two months to reflect on this whole matter, and get over it. Go back to the states, stick to what you do best, get out of the Air Force, and go play golf. Forget this girl. Now get outta here!"

Mike jumped up, saluted, and said nothing. Brad could tell he was seething, but he was smart enough to say nothing. Mitchell had one of the Kunsan SPs in his outer office, and he came in and escorted young Arnie Palmer off to the hoosegow.

Two months later Clark got out of the Brig and left the "Kun" for his next assignment to Randolph AFB in San Antonio. It seemed the Air Training Command three star was an avid golfer and he wanted Mike Clark on the ATC golf team. Clark did take leave on the way home to go to the Philippines and gather up his bride. As it turned out however, she was nowhere to be found. Her coworkers mentioned she had found a new boy friend, a sailor who was stationed at the U.S. Navy Base at Subic Bay. Clark tried to find her in Subic and he even visited her father to enlist his help in finding the daughter. The old man slammed the door in Mike's face as soon as he recognized him.

Airman Clark made one smart move on his way out of the Philippines. He stopped by the base Staff Judge Advocate Office to ask about his legal marital status. Since there was no record anywhere to be found of an actual wedding, the JAG basically surmised that he wasn't married. However, they also advised that Clark never return to the Philippines. He might find things a bit sticky.

Case closed. Now back to today.

CHAPTER TEN

GO!

The weather did indeed cooperate the next day. A cold front blew in from the northwest and blew the fog out. It was a clear night in both Kunsan and Osan, as well as in the target area. The Choppers with their A-10 escorts and F-16 cover took off on time and headed northwest to set up their ingress.

At Kunsan the 35th TFS launch went fairly smoothly. The extra day had given the maintenance folks more time and they managed to patch together one more jet. There were two aborts on start that were spared out and a total of 26 jets launched. They took off in 30 second intervals, loaded with three external tanks of fuel, either Mk-82 500 pound bombs or CBU and two heat seeking AIM-9L missiles each. They also had an armed gun, but the pilots hoped they wouldn't have to use it. After the gorilla lumbered northwest for about 50 miles, and it was determined that the external tanks were feeding properly on every jet, the two spares returned to base. They had to fly around a while to burn down enough gas to achieve landing weight, but they managed to get on the ground and out of the way before the Juvat launch.

The pre-mission dinner at the Club was identical to last night's except it was spaghetti instead of steak. The Club didn't have too many good selections. The briefings were a little shorter than the night before – at least for the 35th. The Juvats had a whole new route of flight due to the possible compromise. The non-tasked pilots and targeteers had worked all day on new route maps. The word was of course out about Syzmanski. Not too many folks were overly upset. "Syzmo" was a bit of a shit anyway, but no one needed to be wasted the way he and Michaels were. There wasn't too much talk about a compromise of the mission and everyone went about their business with only one objective – to kick the crap out of Yongbyon.

Brad's mass briefing was a lot like Rand's the night before, only even more precise and organized. He had every threat that was known on the Korean peninsula highlighted on a map. Beside it, he had pictures of the missile or gun or aircraft, and a depiction of what it would look like when it lit up the RWR gear. Each one was thoroughly discussed. The departure formations and stacking procedures in the holding pattern were described in detail as well. No one could afford to get disoriented up there in the middle of a gaggle of 24 jets, all with their lights off. Finally, the attack itself was covered thoroughly. Their ingress would be more of an arcing affair as they were to break the coast from the west, swing around to the south of the target and finally attack from the east. In reality, with the staggered patterns they had planned, they would be attacking from every direction, but the final ingress was from the south and east. The plan was for each four ship (Boomer Huston's A Flight going first) to pop up and roll in at a 20 degree dive angle two by two, with each wingman spread out about 1000 feet on the inside of the roll in, sliding to the outside to drop on target. The next four ship would continue the arc and pop from a different heading, and so on.

The SAFE area was briefed one more time as well, and it was reiterated that any pilot would basically be on his own if he went down in North Korea anywhere – at least for 24 hours. Brad made a mental note to check that his personal weapon – a 45 automatic was loaded and ready. He had no intention of being captured alive.

Finally, Lobo once again addressed his troops. "I don't know what to tell you men about Sergeant's Syzmanski and Michaels." Rushing started. "It seems too coincidental, given who these two were and what they knew, that their deaths were some random murder and robbery. Washington has decided that this mission will go on anyway. All I can say is that you need to really check six tonight. Keep your heads on swivels, and remember – the mission is a failure if you don't make it back. This is not a nuclear war when all stops are pulled. If you don't like what you see, don't stick your nose in it. The bar is open on me at 0400 hours when you guys return. Good luck!"

Brad's four ship briefing was short and to the point. He reviewed the formations he wanted them to fly and specific communications procedures. Finnegan and Russell were good sticks, but Brad wasn't sure about this new kid Fickling. He was a Lieutenant with good hands and was very aggressive – maybe too aggressive. The term often given to lieutenants with their hair on fire was "all balls, dick and no forehead." Brad wanted to be sure that "Freckles" at least reversed the order tonight.

They stepped to their jets at midnight. Each pilot was decked out in his anti-G suit, parachute harness, deflated water wings with their pull ring actuators, survival vest, helmet, and all the mission planning gear. And each of them had their own personal survival gear tucked away in pockets or strapped to their bodies. Brad Mitchell had a 45 automatic pistol in a holster on his hip, extra rounds in the pocket of his survival vest, and an 8 inch "Bowie" knife strapped to his left calf, under his flight suit. The standard survival kit that fits in the seat cushion of the ejection seat contained other gear – matches, signal mirror, two cans of potable water – and attached to it was a one man raft that hung beneath the seat after ejection.

Brad pre-flighted the Viper carefully – especially the munitions. They didn't get to fly with the real thing very often, so he was careful to follow the weapons checklist. There was only so much he could do before engine start. The final pins and flags were pulled by the maintenance personnel either right after start or at the end of the runway before takeoff. He had to trust that they did it right. The crew chief strapped him in and wished him luck, feeling proud that "his" jet was going to war, and hoping this jock brought it back in one piece.

Engine start and checks were uneventful for Brad. In fact, he was thankful that apparently all four members of his flight were up and ready on time. He heard some chatter on the radio that indicated that a couple of Juvats were having problems, and they were spared out as soon as it was obvious they couldn't make it on time. Brad ran through the Stores Management System (SMS) settings one more time, to be sure the hot-cock pilot had loaded everything correctly. Good thing too – he noted that his jet was loaded for Mark 82 bombs, when he was carrying the cluster bombs. He made the change on the computer and gave his flight a "heads up" on the radio to check for the same thing. The crew chief uncovered the missiles and pulled the pins. He checked it out and got the familiar "growl" it gives out when it sees a heat source. The heat source Brad used was the jet taxiing in front of him. Good thing his Master Arm switch was in "Simulate" and not "ARM," he thought, although the missile is not SUPPOSED to fire with weight on the wheels….. no sense finding out.

They lost two more jets at the end of runway checks and the Juvats took the runway with only 23 total. Hopefully they would not lose any to maintenance after takeoff. At five minutes after one a.m. Brad released his breaks and stroked the afterburner. His F-16 rolled about 3000 feet and then lifted off into the dark like a bright candle behind a dark silhouette. Each succeeding Viper followed suit with 30 second spacing. At about 375 knots they came out of afterburner and then from the ground you could see nothing. From each cockpit the rejoin was accomplished mostly on radar while each wingman joined on his appropriate leader. While coming aboard each one did an airborne weapons check, testing all air to air modes of the radar and the Heads Up Display (HUD) and the missiles. When he had his wingmen in formation each leader dropped back on one of them and checked out his system as well. The Juvats were off to war.

CHAPTER ELEVEN

BEHIND THE LINES

Melanie and her Seal team had been on the move all night. The countryside was very quiet. They avoided two small farming villages and had climbed to a strategic position overlooking the complex of Yongbyon. There was enough light to tell that not much was going on here either. They could make out most of the buildings, a couple of guard towers and shacks, but not much movement. They dug in and covered up for some sleep as the sun came up. It was cold and a fire would have been nice to take the chill off, but they couldn't take the chance. The Seals were well trained in using their body heat to warm each other, but they weren't prepared (except in their dreams) to snuggle up to a beautiful woman – even if she was decked out in war paint and fatigues. Melanie decided that Master Chief Woolsey would be the most harmless and she backed up to him and pulled as much heat off his body buttocks to buttocks as she could.

At about 1030 hours things started picking up. Yongbyon had come to life shortly after sunrise as far as the worker bees and daily routine was concerned. But all of a sudden there was something up. Truckloads of soldiers rolled up and fanned out in all directions looking toward the hillside in the Seals' direction. They were too far away to hear any of the frantic orders being issued, but Woolsey decided it didn't look good. The soldiers started climbing the rocks, carefully poking and prodding like they were looking for something – or someone. Silently the Seals fell back over the ridge and quickly moved to the south.

"Do you think they're onto us?" It was Radioman Wilcox. He asked the Chief. "Sure looks like they're looking for somebody."

"I don't know, but if they know we're out here we ain't got a snow ball's chance in Hell in finding the good guys." Woolsey whispered and Melanie knew he was right. If the North Koreans had word that they were in the area they would have their hostages buttoned up and well guarded. The team kept moving as fast as they could to try and circle the valley and take a peek from the other side. The soldiers only seemed to be interested in what might be on the western ridgeline. It was like they had intelligence pinpointing intruders.

After almost 3 hours of running, crawling, stumbling and climbing, the team was positioned near the southeast corner of the complex. They had crossed a small stream and road that ran out of the complex and down the valley, and were up the ridge about 80 yards – still well concealed in the deep underbrush. They could make out soldiers every once in a while on the opposite ridge as they crossed clearings or rocks. There must have been 500 men out there. Woolsey had Wilcox set up the radio.

"See if you can raise Headquarters on the HF. We need to let them know there might be a compromise." The HF was the High Frequency radio one that if anything would work in this terrain, it would. Chances were it would be the only mode of contact until the jets or the choppers were within line of sight.

Melanie had been searching the ridge lines with her binoculars. She could see two of the air defense sites and they too seemed to be in an agitated state of readiness. She could see men running back and forth, and the antennas swinging up and around. At one site she saw AAA pieces rotating up, down, left, right – as if they were working out the cobwebs and getting set for some action. "These guys are gearing up for an attack." She whispered to Woolsey. "We've gotta get through on the radio and warn the Air Force."

The Seals worked quickly and had powered up the radio in a couple of minutes. But, no luck. They couldn't raise anyone anywhere. If there had been an AWACs aircraft up they probably would have been able to talk to them, but without all the normal support, the effort to maintain secrecy was a definite detriment this time. Especially since it appeared the secret was out.

"Chief, look over there." It was Specialist Parker Davis. He had been scouring the Yongbyon complex with his glasses. "It looks like there is something they really value in that one building." He pointed to a small building beside the main road through the center of the complex, but offset a bit from the long, low factory type structures. Everyone shifted their eyes that way. The building was a small concrete bunker with high windows with bars on them. There was what looked to be only one entrance and it was well guarded. At least four armed sentries stood out front. There was a jeep and a dark sedan parked out front.

"Looks like some officers or other big wigs just went inside." Davis said. "Two of them were in civilian clothes and one of them looked like a white guy. At least he was taller and fairer skinned than the gooks. The other one was the boss though. They all saluted him and held the door and practically treated him like a king. He was in a dark suit , but not a uniform."

"Probably the local Communist party chief. They tend to be in charge." Melanie whispered. "The other guy could have been a Russian scientist. They still have some here, though the Russians deny it. How long ago?"

"Just a few minutes." Davis responded. Just then the men in front of the bunker stirred and a group emerged from the building into the clearing in front. Melanie could make out four more soldiers – two of them in NK officer uniforms. One of them looked like a general officer. Then came the civilians Davis had referred to, and then another soldier escorting what was obviously a hostage. He was in pajama like clothes, no shoes and had a black hood over his head. His hands were cuffed behind his back. He was not in very good shape either. The soldier had to keep propping him up.

"Davis, zoom your scope in on that prisoner's feet and hands." Melanie demanded. "Compare them to everyone else's." She shinnied her way over to Davis' position. He had an extremely powerful telescope-like set of binoculars that were much more revealing than her pocket size glasses.

"Yes ma'am. Looks like he's a white guy. His feet are all bloody though." Davis passed the scope to Melanie.

"What are you thinking, ma'am?" Woolsey asked. "Think he's one of our hostages?"

"I don't know, but I can't imagine they'd have two or more places to keep them if they're on site at all, and he certainly is getting a lot of high level attention. Only thing that bothers me though is that if they know somebody is out here, why would they parade this guy out in front of us?" Melanie got her answer.

The soldier propped his prisoner up against the building and stepped aside. The boss man civilian took a rifle from a nearby soldier and fired it into the sky. They all then looked around at the hills and the Seal team ducked even further into the brush.

"Shit!" Swore Melanie, and as she watched the man with the gun placed the barrel next to the hooded man's head and ripped off at least six shots in succession, almost blowing the prisoner's head off. Blood splattered on the building and the body slumped in a heap. Again the head man down below and all his puppets looked up into the hills as if to say, "Did you see that? This is what we've done to your spies?"

The men conferred for a few minutes with the civilian in charge very animatedly. He swung his arms around as if pointing to the hills and wagged his finger as if giving strict orders. The general saluted and bowed several times during all of that. Soon the two civilians climbed into the sedan and sped off into the center of the facility. The general took his turn giving orders and barking and got into the jeep to follow his master. Two soldiers went back into the building and the other four resumed their positions guarding the door.

"There's obviously more prisoners in there or this has all been a big show designed to lure us in." Melanie said. "What do you think, Chief? Can we get to that building?"

Woolsey took a long look at the building and surrounding area, as well as what he could see of the terrain between them and the target. There was a tall chain link and barbed wire fence around the entire complex, and guard towers about every hundred meters or so. They also knew that one of the air defense sites would be just down hill from them on a straight line between them and the objective. Woolsey pulled out his map.

After a few minutes of study the Chief spoke. "It would be a lot easier at night, but we could get right up next to the fence right about here without any problem." He pointed to an area about 80 yards from the objective. "That's about split between these two guard towers and looks to be in a blind spot for both of them. We can get through that fence in a heartbeat, but then negotiating our way in the open to the building would be a trick. We'll need a diversion. Franks, what do you think? Can you take out those sentries?" The Chief was talking to the quiet one of the team, Tommy Franks. Franks was the marksman and he carried a rifle that Melanie had only seen once before, in a C-17 high above their present area 18 months ago. It had a long barrel and a huge silencer, and a scope almost as big as the one Davis was carrying. Franks had been surveying the situation using his rifle scope instead of binoculars. "If I can get a little farther up yonder Chief, I think I can smoke both guard towers and probably two of them critters at the door." Tommy was from Arkansas and although he had a voice that was almost always a whisper, it was very distinctively - - - – Arkansas

Woolsey thought for a little bit, then, "How important is this, ma'am? We can get there and we can probably get in the door. That's about all I can guarantee you. No tellin' how many are in there, and getting them out could be ugly. I'd give it about a 30 percent chance. If we could wait until dark, maybe 50 percent." The Chief put the onus square on Melanie.

Melanie thought for a bit, and then, "Sunset's about 1930 hours, and we're at least two hours from the pick up point from right here – probably another hour back to here getting around that SAM site." She pointed spots on the map. "That gives us about 90 minutes of slop time. Ok, but let's get down there closer in case 'Comrade' comes back and decides to blow another one away for show."

Activity seemed to have calmed down on the opposite ridge line. The Seals had done a good job of covering their tracks and any evidence they had been there. About half of the soldiers had returned to their trucks and were just lolling around smoking and joking with one another. The rest were still up in the hills. Davis had found three small groups that had apparently set up sites to sit and wait. They suspected there were more like that under the brush and hidden from even Davis' powerful "eyes." After about an hour the general in the jeep drove up to the troops at their trucks. They quickly looked a lot more official and busy. The general was animated once again and Melanie wished she could be a fly on the side of the nearest building. He was giving orders to a couple of junior officers who were as rigid at attention as frozen mummies – except they kept bowing and obviously agreeing with everything, including how stupid and incompetent they were. The general finished his tirade and the soldiers were ordered quickly to their trucks. They loaded up and headed toward the south end of the complex – right below Melanie and the Seals.

Everyone held their breath as some of the troops off loaded just outside the south gate to the complex. Other trucks went on down the road. Davis could see two more of them stop and off load at about 200 yard intervals. If the troops came west the team was doomed. They were not very far up the ridge line, and there was a clearing of sorts just behind them. Fortunately the horde fanned out and moved east. They were expanding their search but still expecting any perpetrators to be coming from the west.

"Damn!" Melanie mumbled under her breath. Woolsey looked at her, understanding her concern. If the soldiers stayed in that general area they effectively blocked any route to the pick up point that could be negotiated in less than a day. Just about a mile down the road to the south the terrain got extremely harsh, basically impassable with a rock wall almost 400 feet high that formed a steep canyon for close to three miles. If the team couldn't cross over to the west within that first mile they would have to move much further south before they could come across the canyon, and then back up to the north to the choppers in waiting.

"Can we move the pick up point?" Wilcox asked in a whisper.

"We can't even talk to anyone, and we won't be able to until the choppers are practically on us." Woolsey scolded his junior mate. Then he turned to Melanie, "Tell you what, ma'am. With all this activity going on right now we might be better off doing our thing while at least a bunch of these gooks are looking elsewhere."

"Yeah – I was just thinking that. They basically have a few diversions going already. Let's do it!" Melanie "advised." She was not in charge, but obviously the Chief had come to value her input as important to the operation. Woolsey nodded and then with a few hand signals directed the team up the ridge line to the north.

It took almost two hours for the team to circle the air defense site and work their way down to a point abeam the fence and their objective on the other side. It was pushing 1600 hours. Franks climbed a sturdy tree and put himself in position where he could see both guard towers. "I can take the guard towers Chief, but I'll have to go back up the hill a ways to see the critters at the door." He relayed via walkie talkie headphone.

Woolsey didn't even hesitate. "How many guards in the towers?"

"Just one."

"Smoke 'em now and then come on back down. Davis, belly up to that fence and be sure it's not hot. If not, cut it."

There were two "thumps" from Franks' rifle, about a minute apart. Melanie could see one of the guard towers with her glasses and while she was looking the guard's head exploded like a pumpkin. She swallowed hard. Davis took just over a minute to negotiate the half cleared brush to the fence. "It's cold, he whispered in Woolsey's earpiece."

Melanie turned her glasses to the fence and watched as Davis whipped out a pair of bolt cutters. Working swiftly and methodically he cut an opening, leaving two strands barely intact at the two upper corners. It would be big enough for a person to go through in a crouch – once the two corners were completely severed. Davis was back in a flash.

"Ok, Tommy – get up the hill and get in position to take out the gooks on the front door. We're going through the fence and to this side of that first building. That will put us about 30 seconds away on a dead run. When you see my signal, take out as many as you can. We're gonna try for the wall on this side of the building – right next to where they blew away that poor bastard. Then we'll regroup and go through the door. Ma'am, you stay right here. Keep an eye on that bunch on the other side. See if you can pick us a way through them." Woolsey was thorough, precise, and very obvious that he did not want Melanie in on the action.

"Oh no, Chief. I need to go with you. I speak the language and you might need me to negotiate." Melanie protested.

"All due respect ma'am, but this is all the negotiation we need." The Chief held up his automatic weapon. "The people who count all should speak English. If they don't, they're dead. We need someone out here and you're it." There was no further discussion and Franks disappeared into the brush. Woolsey, Wilcox and Davis checked all their weapons and lightened their loads significantly. Woolsey carried only his rifle, handgun and knife. Wilcox and Davis had the same, but Wilcox also carried a double belt of grenades and a small box marked "Danger! Explosives!" He dumped the radio and they each took off their packs. When they were all ready and Franks had called in to say he was in position, Woolsey looked at Melanie, nodded once and waved his men off toward the fence. Melanie wanted to protest one more time, but she knew it was hopeless.

Melanie watched as the three Seals quickly removed the fence piece and went through. Davis stopped and leaned it back up against the fence after they were through, making it almost look intact. They sprinted to the side of the first long, low building. It was dark and did not appear to be inhabited. Melanie saw Woolsey's arm go up with a clinched fist. He pumped it twice. She assumed this was Tommy's signal to unleash his big gun. She could not see the sentries or the building herself, so she just had to assume all hell was breaking loose in the doorway of the jailhouse. The Seals rounded the front of the building they were hiding behind and disappeared. Everything was very quiet – for about 45 seconds.

There were several gunshots from the direction of the bunker, and at least two muffled explosions like the sounds of grenades going off indoors. Then suddenly all hell broke loose from up the hill to Melanie's south. Obviously the air defense site had a good view of the Seals and their objective. Several machine guns were blazing away. Melanie assumed they were directed toward her team. She wondered if Franks could help.

"Kaboom!" There was a huge explosion from the direction of the objective. Melanie figured Davis had used whatever was in that little box. She wondered if anyone survived the blast. The machine gunners were still blazing away, so Melanie figured they must have targets to shoot at. She couldn't stand it anymore – she moved out.

Melanie quickly moved down to the fence a little south of the escape hole. She crept along the fence until she could see down the corridor between buildings toward the bunker. What she saw made her cringe. Her team and one or two other men were pinned down in a cross fire – between the machine gunners from just above her and a squad of soldiers back toward the center of the complex, just across from the smoking hole of what used to be the bunker. They didn't have a chance. It was obvious from the terrain and trees that Franks could do nothing about the machine gunners, but it was also obvious that he was doing what he could about the soldiers to the rear. Their numbers were dwindling and without anyone from the pinned down Seals even firing a shot. Trouble was, there were truckloads of more soldiers pulling up as reinforcements. Melanie knew she had to do something.

Melanie estimated it was 40 yards from her position at the fence to the edge of the clearing around the air defense site. No telling how far inside the clearing the gooks with the guns were. She wished she had a few of Davis' grenades. She climbed quickly through the underbrush and got to the tree line in about two minutes. It was easy to pinpoint the gunners – follow the noise. There were two of them – one on a permanent barrier about 30 yards inside a fence, which was itself 5 yards in from the tree line. The other was on top of an armored personnel carrier manning a vehicle mounted gun. Both were wailing away at the good guys. Melanie opened up with the AK-47. Big mistake!

The gunners immediately ducked and were most likely surprised, but they did not wait long to react. The APC cranked up and started down the hill in Melanie's direction. The gunner on the ground picked himself up, swung his barrel in her direction and started hosing the forest. Melanie's rifle was no match for the buzz saws her adversaries were wielding. She realized right away that she was dead if she stayed where she was. She tumbled back down the hill and ran as quickly as she could to get out of range. The two gunners just kept mowing down trees and soon there were hardly any standing in the 40 yard area between them and the fence.

Melanie had provided the diversion Woolsey and his men needed. He realized the fire from the hillside was at least diverted and there was no time to waste anyway. The soldiers to their rear were multiplying like rabbits, and it didn't matter that Tommy

Franks was doing his best to keep down the population. It was time to run for it. "Go! Go! Go!" He shouted to his men and their charges. Woolsey stepped out in the path and opened up with his weapon, sweeping side to side, not necessarily aiming at anything in particular – just trying to keep some heads down.

Wilcox led the way with one of the hostages – the one who could walk – or run. They were both shoeless and barely dressed, but at least this one could move. Davis had the cripple. The man's right foot was an ugly mess, just dangling there. It had obviously been broken and smashed and was extremely painful. The man was probably close to 60, not in very good shape, and he screamed in pain every time his foot even touched the ground. Davis was practically carrying him and they could not move very quickly. That was their demise.

Woolsey back pedaled keeping the fire up the best he could, but the speed that the three of them could keep up was their undoing. The soldiers to the rear were reinforced with APCs and just plain numbers. A burst of fire from the rear and all three stragglers went down in a heap. Melanie saw it all and felt helpless. She did what she could with her rifle, but at this point she figured she needed to concentrate on Wilcox and the lead hostage. Even then though, she felt like not much more than a cheerleader.

Chief Woolsey was hit twice in the right shoulder, and must have taken several hits to his bullet proof vest – enough to knock him down. He looked over and saw that Davis had taken one in the back of the head. At least he went quickly. The hostage too was wounded and was a whimpering mess. Woolsey kept firing, using his left arm, but he was no match. He took two more hits and was basically helpless. As the soldiers advanced he looked over at the hostage. The man looked at him with pleading eyes, bleeding from the mouth and a wound in his neck. Woolsey did not hesitate. He pulled out his handgun and placed it next to the man's temple and fired. He was so weak he could not even hold the weapon in its recoil. He rolled over and looked straight up into the eyes of two North Korean soldiers, their rifles to their shoulders, barrels in his face.

Chief Ronald Woolsey took a deep breath, gathered as much saliva and blood as he could in his mouth and spit just as hard as his severely crippled body would spit. The end came quickly.

Wilcox and the other hostage had almost made it to the fence when the gunners in the air defense site decided they had blown down enough trees and refocused on their targets in the complex. They opened up on the two runners and it was like shooting ducks in a pond. The hostage took the first hit in the thigh and lurched forward into the fence. Wilcox took two hits in the legs and crumpled about ten yards shy of the fence. He gathered his weapon and sat in a spread leg position and started firing in the direction of the shooters. "Go! Go!" He yelled to the hostage.

Melanie couldn't stand it – she threw herself out into the open and grabbed the man by the arm and dragged him back toward the brush. The last thing she remembered was a group of soldiers approaching from the fence line. They must have come down from the air defense site, or circled around from inside. Then she heard a familiar "Thump! Thump! Thump!" from the brush in front of her. Tommy Franks had come off his perch and was picking off soldiers like grapes off a vine. Before she disappeared into the woods Melanie looked back and saw Parker Davis literally ripped apart by machine gun and automatic weapons fire from both sides.

"Let's go, ma'am." It was Franks. He bent his 6'4" frame down and hoisted the hostage over his soldier like a sack of potatoes and lit off up the ridge line to the north. Melanie decided there was no choice. There was nothing they could do back there, except die. She followed, but not before hoisting the radio Wilcox had left over her shoulder and strapped it on her back.

They moved quickly considering their new loads. Franks was a big man. His hostage was no small kid either, but Franks had him over his shoulder and was able to motivate pretty well. Melanie felt the weight of the radio, but she refused to let it slow her down. They moved up the ridge line and to the north, basically trying to get away from any known gook position. Melanie knew that all the activity would bring out the reinforcements and probably most of the soldiers looking elsewhere for them. They HAD to get as far clear of the complex as possible. But if they were to have a chance of a pick up, they couldn't go too far in the direction they were moving. The pickup point was west and north and they were moving east and north. After almost an hour Franks finally stopped for a rest. He dumped his sack of hostage rather roughly on the ground, but there was not a peep from the man. Melanie checked him over quickly. He was dead. Apparently he had taken a round square in the back, probably while they were disengaging from the enemy, and he also probably took one that would have severely wounded Franks. The big man broke down and cried.

"Aw shit, ma'am. A'm sorry. Ah blew it." Franks scolded himself.

"Tommy – you gave this guy a fighting chance." Melanie tried to console him. "You saw what they did to his partner back there just to show us who was in charge. There was no way he was going to make it out without you. We just got unlucky and he took a stray bullet." She went through the man's pockets, but found nothing. He did have a Saint Christopher medal on a chain around his neck. Melanie was surprised. The North Koreans were about as godless a people as there was. Either they didn't know what it was, or they really did have a heart somewhere amongst them. Melanie gently disconnected it and shoved it in a pocket. "Let's hide the body." She whispered to Franks.

They didn't take time to bury the hostage. They covered him with brush and dirt as best they could in a hole next to a tree. Franks paused and looked long at hard at the man, as if he was offering his own prayer. He reached out and touched the man's skin with his big hand, then stood up and nodded at Melanie. Franks took the radio to lighten Melanie's load and they lit out into the woods. They moved quickly as long as it was light. But when the sun went down their progress slowed significantly. By that time they had also crossed the valley to the north of Yongbyon and were on the western ridge line. Melanie was afraid there would still be some bad guys out here looking for them, so they needed to be much quieter and slower.

By 2300 hours Melanie figured they were about as close to the pickup point as they could reasonably expect to be. Franks had a GPS receiver and it showed they were within a half mile. Melanie had Franks set up the radio.

"Cobra, this is Dingaling. Cobra, this is Dingaling. Come in Cobra." Melanie whispered over the microphone on the VHF radio. Cobra was the call sign of the helicopters. Dingaling was the "handle" she had been assigned by the mission commander. She didn't appreciate it much then, but at this point all she wanted to do was talk to someone. Nothing. The choppers were probably still out to sea and out of range. She had Franks switch to the HF radio.

"This is Dingaling in the blind. This is Dingaling calling anyone, over." She made this blind call several times, trying to reach anyone who might have been assigned the frequency to monitor during the mission. It could have been the command post at Osan, anyone with a High Frequency radio and reason to be on the air. After almost five minutes of trying she got results.

"Dingaling, this is Sentry 41. We read you about five by. Go ahead." Sentry was an AWACS aircraft, though Melanie did not know that and certainly did not expect that kind of support. Evidently they heard her at about half strength.

"Roger, Sentry 41. I'm not aware of your call sign. Dingaling is on the ground, looking for a ride." Melanie gave away more than she probably should have, but she wanted this contact to authenticate itself quickly so she could tell them what she knew.

"Copy Dingaling. Sentry is a late player command and control platform. We are 300 miles south and about due west of Kunsan. Standby for authentication." Melanie waited while the AWACS controller went through whatever communications he had to in order to get the data on "Dingaling." Everyone on the mission had updated their Search and Rescue information before they launched. In Melanie's case it was all new, since she was not normally involved in these kinds of operations. However, she had been through similar routines with the Agency, and in fact, she used some of her same personal information.

After a few minuets, "Dingaling, this is Sentry 41. Confirm your first automobile." This was her first test question. Melanie immediately answered.

"Beamer." Referring to a used BMW she had in Germany.

"Roger, Dingaling. Confirm who's on first." Sentry's second question. There were four, but normally only two or three correct answers were enough to confirm the real McCoy.

"Will Clark." Melanie shot back, remembering how she always enjoyed watching Clark swing at a ball when he played first for the Giants. He had the prettiest swing in baseball.

"Roger, Dingaling. What's your status?" Sentry was satisfied.

"Compromised! That's our status. Somehow the Koreans knew we were out here. They are ready for anything – both us and an attack from the air." Melanie tried to be as unemotional as she could, but she remembered Woolsey and the rest of the team, and the hostages. "All but one of the Seals is dead. The other is with me. We got two hostages out but they were both killed in the escape. The enemy killed a third one in front of us. We are near the pickup point, but I recommend aborting the mission."

"Roger, Dingaling. Sentry copies. Sit tight. We'll get back to you."

"Can only wait ten more minutes." Melanie responded. "We need to be on VHF to talk to the choppers." She could not use the radio on more than one frequency at a time, and she knew that if the choppers were coming she'd have to be talking to them soon.

"Copy that, Dingaling. Standby."

They waited for what seemed like an eternity. Then Franks sat straight up. He'd been resting and Melanie thought he was grabbing some much needed sleep. "Ma'am." He said, and pointed up towards the western sky. Melanie listened. Soon she heard the faint "Whop, Whop, Whop" of a helicopter, slowly getting louder. She quickly switched the radio over to the VHF frequency, and even before she could pick up the microphone her headset went off. "Tiger Team, Tiger Team, this is Cobra over." Either the choppers did not have the word that the Tiger Team was dead, or just didn't know "Dingaling's" call sign.

"Cobra, this is Tiger. We are down to just two of us and no baggage, over. Did you have contact with Sentry 41?" There was a long pause and the approaching noise from the choppers' engines seemed to stagnate. Melanie could only guess that they were about two ridgelines to the west. "Cobra, do you copy, over?" No answer.

After what seemed like an eternity Franks jumped up. "Ma'am. They're leaving. What the.." Sure enough the chopper noise started to fade. The helicopters were either moving back to the west or going lower, decreasing the sound to anyone listening.

"Cobra, this is Tiger. We hear your engines. What status, over?" Melanie sounded as calm as she could considering they were being left in the unfriendly forest with a bunch of real unfriendly bears.

"Roger Tiger, this is Cobra. Sorry to be the bearer of bad news but our mission has been cancelled for tonight. We expect to be back for you in 24 hours. Meantime, keep your heads down. The rest of the mission is still on." Apparently Melanie's message to Sentry had reached the powers that be, and the powers decided there was not much reason to risk the rescue mission just yet. She felt a cold chill up her spine, as if someone had just written her epitaph. She wondered what good it does to risk the attack when the North Koreans obviously knew they were coming. Just to punish them? Melanie decided the politicians had inserted themselves into the fray and military advice to the contrary, all hell was about to break loose. Melanie broke the news to Franks and they dug in to watch – or at least listen to – the fireworks. Melanie shivered a bit, a **tremble**.

CHAPTER TWELVE

"PICKLE, PICKLE, PICKLE"

The 35 TFS mission had gone fairly smoothly so far. They did lose two jets to a maintenance problem. The number three jet in the third four ship had developed an electrical problem and a generator warning light. In keeping with standard Air Force philosophy to never send a crippled fighter home alone, Rand directed the Number Four in the same flight to escort his element leader back to Osan (the nearest recovery base). So they were down to 22 for the attack. They had set up the orbit out to sea as briefed and had seen nothing on the radar or RWR gear to give them any concern.

The A-10s were escorting the choppers by flying a figure eight pattern over and to the side. At the designated "push off time" the helicopters pressed in toward the coast and hugged the nape of the earth. The A-10s moved back and out to one side so as not to highlight the choppers if anyone was looking. Although A-10s could fly low to the ground, they did not practice it much at night. These pilots were not equipped with night vision goggles or infrared systems, so they had to rely on their own un-enhanced eyeballs. Therefore, in order to keep track of one another and the choppers as well, they limited themselves to about 500 feet above the ground. That provided the first activity of the night.

Just as the choppers crossed the coast the radars of every North Korean air defense site for miles around lit up and targeted the A-10s. They obviously saw the fighters but not the choppers who were flying on night vision goggles and not more than 50 feet above the ground. The A-10 drivers went into a defensive mode, expending chaff and flares and diving into defensive turns to avoid any potential attack. Chaff is bundles of aluminum that when expended into the air was supposed to cause unsophisticated radars to break lock. It worked sometimes. The flares were not needed just then and did nothing more than confirm the position of the target for the gunners. Flares were intended to pull the guidance of an incoming heat seeking missile onto the flare. However, if there was no incoming missile all the flare did was light up the sky just behind the jet. The cockpit settings the pilots had set up were based on an expectation that they would surprise the sleeping giant and not be detected until they were well inland and around the target area. At that point they figured they would need everything working for them if detected. The defensive turn was used to put the threat on a beam detection vector. Radars were designed to detect and track aircraft with a closing velocity, or even one going away. But if the target is on a beam maneuver, maintaining its distance and neither closing in or departing, the radars had difficulty tracking. The only problem with that maneuver right now was that the helicopters were pressing on and the A-10s were basically going the wrong way.

They had no choice. One AAA gunnery site opened up and others fired for effect, lighting up the sky with tracers and making it very obvious that the cat was out of the bag. The A-10 flight lead called for an abort to their mission. There was no sense wading into a gunfight when you were clearly outnumbered. They moved out to sea and set up an orbit to wait for the choppers and escort them home to Osan. Cannon Rand agreed with the decision and quickly got up on the radio to the AWACS that was supposed to be in the area.

"Sentry 41, this is Panther One. How do you read?"

"Panther, this is Sentry, we read you loud and clear sir." The controller came right back.

"Roger Sentry, looks like someone set the table with an extra plate for dinner. These guys definitely know we're coming. The A-10s took fire approaching the coast and have broken off their mission. Cobra is still inbound." Rand relayed what he figured the folks in charge needed to know. Although he was a typical fighter pilot, itching for some action, he wasn't sure he wanted to lead his squadron into this hornet's nest. They had discussed the possibility of a compromise when they had heard of the death of the two intel types in "A" Town, but they still expected that surprise would be on their side.

"Roger, Panther. Stand by." Sentry was obviously working two or three radios at once, probably talking to the Osan Command Post and General Woodward.

"Sentry and Panther, this is Cobra. We have contact with Tiger Team." It was one of the chopper pilots. The helicopters were close to their rendezvous point. "We're about four minutes out from the pickup point."

"Roger, Cobra. Standby. Sentry's talking to 'Big Eye.'" Big Eye was the call sign of the Osan CP. After a minute,... "Cobra, this is Sentry 41. Abort your mission. I say again, Cobra – abort, abort. Relay to Tiger that we will attempt a pickup tomorrow night at the same time. Acknowledge."

"Roger, Senrty. Cobra copies. Authenticate 'Alpha Omega.'" Cobra was using the code authentication system that changed every day. It was a series of letters and numbers. To authenticate the challenging party reads off any two letters in succession, and the authenticating party reads back the next letter or number in succession on the card of the day. It was quick and reliable.

"Roger, Cobra. Sentry authenticates 'Yankee.'" The AWACS controller had expected this challenge and was ready with his response. After all, any gook with a good accent could come up on a radio and cancel an attack. This way the choppers knew that their night was officially over. All they had to do now was get out of Dodge.

"Cobra copies. Egressing west." The helos were leaving but with heavy hearts on board. The men in these choppers were trained and lived to rescue those who needed them. To leave two on the ground was not sitting well.

Cannon Rand heard all of this on his VHF radio while the rest of his gaggle may or may not have been listening. Chances are they turned down their VHF volume so as not to be distracted. Their mission was to be basically "comm. out" but using the FM and the UHF as necessary. "Sentry, Panther. Any words for us?" He asked the AWACS if their part of the mission was cancelled too, expecting it would be.

"Roger, Panther. You are a GO. Repeat, your mission is still a GO, over."

Rand was confused, but decided the decision wasn't his to question at this point. But the communication was. "Roger, Sentry. Understand GO. Authenticate 'Lima Two.'" He challenged the order.

"Roger, Panther. Sentry authenticates 'Mike.'" AWACS shot back. It was a good message.

"Copy that. Panther pushes in three minutes." Rand switched to FM radio and informed his gorilla of the situation. "Green 'em up." He ordered, and each pilot called up his Stores Management System and confirmed that they were armed up and ready to fight.

Exactly on time the Pantons pushed off from their orbit point and dove for the water. Rand had directed that they keep it as low as they could safely stand since the bad guys knew they were out there. Each flight of four jettisoned their empty wing tanks as they left the orbit. As they approached the coast there appeared several fresh air to air targets on the radar. The North Korean Air Force had been ordered aloft, even though they had no fighters with the capability of doing anything against a low level night attack. The NKAF did have Russian Mig-23s and Mig-21s, but neither had much of a night clout. In fact it was known that the NKAF never trained at night. Rand figured these pilots were probably scared to death. Nevertheless, they were a threat to watch. The Mig-21s could only be vectored from Ground Control Intercept (GCI) radars, and the Mig-23s were not much better. They did have a 1960s version radar missile, but the onboard radar on the jet was not good against ground clutter behind a low level target. The GCI controllers could only guide their intercepts on what they saw themselves. With the Falcons coming in at low level and the terrain of North Korea, target acquisition would be spotty at best. Regardless, the RWR gear of every Panton lit up as they approached the coast. Radars on the coast could see them coming, but that's about all. The route and "feet dry" point selected avoided flying over or within range of any of the missiles that might be launched, and they blew over the top of any gunners so quickly all they could manage was barrage fire – a wall of AAA fire hoping for a "golden BB" to get lucky. It was a WWII tactic, and effective if your target is flying at WWII speeds. But with an F-16 doing 500 knots, no gunner had a chance.

The flights crossed the coast and hugged the terrain as best they could. Wingmen generally had to fly above their leaders to look down and see both the jet and the ground at once, thereby keeping from colliding with the rocks and trees themselves. Consequently every once in a while an enemy radar would "paint" a target and a wingman's RWR would light up.

"Two's paint, 10 o'clock."

"Four's the same."

These kind of calls were numerous and almost to the point of garbaging up the radio too much. Rand decided though it was good info to have. At least then they knew where to look for any shooters. "Paint" meant that someone or something was highlighting that particular jet with a radar of some sort. They were approaching their pop up points. Everything below Panton Lead was very dark with only a light or two on the hillsides. Above however, there was plenty to look at. There were at least five air to air targets in the vicinity of the Yongbyon area. They were not threatening because they only had a general idea where to look for the intruders. Rand was beginning to wonder if the NK fighters might be a collision hazard in the attack. He made sure everyone else saw what he saw, and as he approached the pop point flicked his throttle toggle switch back to the air to ground mode.

Rand pulled his jet into a 25 degree climb and pushed the power all the way up, not stroking the afterburner though. No sense lighting up the sky too much. Besides, he didn't want to go that fast. He was pushing 500 knots now. His heads up display (HUD) showed a target fall line that pointed down and to the left toward the target as computed from the inertial navigation system. He punched off two hits of chaff and took a quick look at the RWR gear. It lit up like a Christmas tree, some of it from the direction of his target. That checked, because his target was a missile site and his plan was to spread a rain of cluster bombs right down their throat. Sure enough, as he rolled over the top at about 3000 above the ground and centered the "death dot" in his HUD, he could see through it to the target area, offset just a bit to the right. A quick correction to center up the bomb fall line, a glance at his wingman tucked in to about a loose route formation, and he mashed the weapons release button and the microphone button at the same time.

"Panther One, Pickle, Pickle, Pickle." That was the signal to the wingman to release his bombs at the same time. If he had been too preoccupied with flying formation and could not manage his own simultaneous attack, he could just release off Rand's call. As long as their jets were closely aligned in the dive his bombs should fall right in line with Rand's.

The attacks went well. Two missiles did fire and some of the AAA put up a barrage, but they were silenced early on by the attackers with CBU. One element lead aborted his attack and took out a Mig 23 that was in his field of view in the pop. He jettisoned his bombs in his dive back down to egress. Several wingmen got lost from their leaders on the way out, but they all followed their prescribed egress heading and got back together on the climb out, "feet wet."

It was all over in less than two minutes. The number three attacker in the last flight was the designated BDA (bomb damage assessment) reporter. All he could really do was take a quick look in the pop and down the chute while he was delivering his own ordinance. Two air defense sites were completely destroyed. Another three were still relatively intact. One attacking flight missed the mark altogether and blew down a bunch of trees. Six of the long structures on Yongbyon were destroyed or on fire. The central bunker had been hit, and was completely out of commission. There was no telling how many casualties there were.

CHAPTER THIRTEEN

"CONAN'S HIT!"

Juvat Lead was listening in on all the conversations on the radio. He knew about the aborted rescue and the Pantons' orders to proceed. He really expected their own mission to be aborted, especially after receiving word from Cannon Rand that the Panthers had done significant damage. It really made no sense to continue the attack, but what did he know? He was only a military man. What possible expertise could he lend to decisions like that?

"Sentry 41, Juvats are up and approaching orbit. Any words for us?" Brad thought it was at least worth a try.

"Roger, Juvat. Your mission is a GO. No changes." The Controller could sense the frustration in these pilots' voices as if asking if this was really a necessary mission. He authenticated with Sentry and the Headhunters readied their cockpits for war.

Brad double checked everything. His SMS was set up to ripple the canisters, spreading the bomblets over about a 300 foot area. The Master Arm switch was in "ARM." Switching forward to air to air mode his missiles growled the familiar "ready" growl that an AIM-9L gives off. The growl gets a lot louder when it detects a heat source. His radar was in a slight look-up mode and in 40 mile sweep. That meant he would be looking from the ground up to about 12,000 feet and out to 40 miles ahead. Realistically a fighter size target would not show up until around thirty miles, and maybe not at all if it was down low, obscured by the terrain. He turned his RWR volume up so that when it went off he couldn't ignore it. That was a problem with the equipment. It would indicate friendly radars as well, and in peacetime flying the pilot got used to ignoring the noise. Not tonight. Brad re-checked that his chaff and flare switch was properly set and programmed. He had decided on chaff only – three bundles with each hit of the dispenser button, and no flares until he needed them.

"Juvats push on time." Brad passed to the gaggle. Boomer Huston's flight was the first to leave orbit because they were the first on target. Based on the time hack they all got in the mass briefing, Boomer had adjusted his last orbit to be at the eastern end and the "push point" right on time. He did not acknowledge the radio call. This was to be a comm out mission, and no news was good news.

Brad's four ship jettisoned their tanks, then pushed over and used the dive to accelerate. Brad leveled off at about 500 feet above the water. He figured that was low enough. The gook radar could see them coming anyway, unless they were right down at wave top, and he didn't want to risk that at night. His wingmen would have a hard enough time keeping him in sight – no sense making the water another major hazard. He could make out "Freckles'" jet out on the right side about 1500 feet out, a little high and 30 degrees back. "Hammer" Handle and "John Boy" Russell would be out on the left side and farther back. Brad couldn't see them, but he was confident "Hammer" would have them in position.

"Two's got hits on the nose 30 miles, and 20 left, twenty two." It was Freckles alerting the flight he had air to air targets over the coast. Mitchell had seen the one on the nose and now picked up the other. It was impossible to tell at this distance whether the targets represented one aircraft each, or a formation of more than one. Brad figured it would only be one. Since the North Koreans never trained at night, they would be scared to death of the dark anyway, and wouldn't be flying around in formation. They did not normally fly much formation anyway. Their tactics were very regimented and highly controlled by GCI. If there were more than one in the same flight they were usually in trail – one following the other on an identical track, as directed from below.

"One's hits there." Mitchell let his wingman know he saw the threat as well. He figured the bad guys probably would get word they were coming and maybe even a vector for an intercept, but he doubted they would be able to pick the flight up on their onboard radars – assuming they were Floggers (Mig – 23s). If they were the Fishbeds (Mig – 21), they would just be shooting in the dark, unless the GCI controller was real lucky.

"Three's paint, on the nose." Hammer was picking up a radar threat on his RWR gear. That meant the controller at least had him on the scope. Brad could only imagine what must be going through the gook controller's mind right now. If he had one hit he probably had a dozen or more hits on his radar. There was a gorilla approaching from the west and it would be a daunting target. One thing a good controller would not want to do was vector a fighter in on the lead target, turning him right in front of the flight behind. That was a good way to lose one of your interceptors quickly. Of course, that was assuming the controller was good, or more importantly, that the interceptors weren't considered dispensable. Brad decided they'd better assume the worst. He turned the flight 20 degrees away from the nearest threat.

As they approached the coast their RWR screen lit up like a Christmas tree. Radars all along the coast lit them up. They were ready for this and at five miles from the coast Brad went into a pre-brief hard turn to port, putting the coast on the wingtip, and the radars on a beam look. "Juvat's beaming now, chaff, chaff." He alerted Hammer to look out for the turn, and the whole flight to punch the chaff button. It worked. Half way through his turn the RWR went blank. They stayed on that vector for about 30 seconds and then turned hard back toward the coast. Although as expected, the radars picked them back up again, it was too late to order any shots or intercepts. Freckles did have one of the interceptors on his radar though and a perfect head on shot with an AIM – 9L.

"Two's locked on, good growl." He wanted permission to shoot.

"Cleared to shoot." Brad didn't hesitate, and neither did the Lieutenant. The sky to Brad's right lit up and the missile flew straight and true. Just as the flight broke the coast a Mig fighter of some sort blew up about a mile ahead of them and 1000 feet high. If the Mig was an immediate threat, or if their mission was to kill Migs there would have been no requirement for Freckles to ask permission to shoot. He was a disciplined wingman though, and although who knew how much of a threat this guy really would have been, he decided to ask before being the first Juvat Mig killer of the "war." Brad was glad to oblige. What the Hell – the only good Mig is a dead Mig.

They jinked through a couple of barrages of AAA fire and screamed up the first valley into the mountains of North Korea. Mitchell could see that Freckles had climbed a little more to be able to avoid the ridge lines while still keeping his leader in sight. Brad went back to navigating and watching for air threats. The rest of the gaggle got through the coastal defenses ok as well. In fact, one other Juvat became one fifth of an Ace by shooting down another Mig that was just in the wrong place at the wrong time. Once the Falcons were at low level over the rugged terrain there was very little the North Korean radars could see, much less do anything about.

The Headhunter attack was different from the Pantons in that although they approached from the west, they basically circled around south of Yongbyon and then attacked from the east, staggering the final run headings so that the last flight was almost on a north to south run in. That probably helped them by surprising the defenses at and above Yongbyon. As it turned out, the attackers needed all the help they could get. The Koreans were even more prepared this time. After all, the intelligence they got from their contact in "A Town" included the Headhunter expected time on target.

"Three has multiple hits above the target area." Hammer was showing a whole bunch of Migs in the air. The NKAF must have launched everything they had, and somehow they knew when to be there.

"One hits there. Watch them for anyone running on us." Mitchell then switched to the UHF radio. "Juvats, heads up. Multiple targets above the target." He wanted the rest of the gorilla to know what he saw.

"Juvats, this is Sentry 41. We're showing 12 -14 targets in the area. Looks like they've set up east to west orbits, staggered from 2000 up to 15,000 feet." It was the AWACS. They had moved another hour up the coast and from their vantage point out to sea could see the whole arena. The AWACS radar was much stronger and could differentiate targets.

Brad replied for the whole gorilla. "Roger that Sentry, Juvats have multiple tally Hos and one No Joy." That was basically a joke, saying they had plenty to look at, but had no clue about what they couldn't see.

Eight miles from the target area Mitchell came hard right 30 degrees to set up his offset for the attack. Although he couldn't see Hammer and Russell, he was confident they turned with him and in fact slid to the outside, or south of the run in. They would pop with about a ten second delay. That would put Hammer and Russell on a slightly more westerly heading for their bomb drop. Brad took one last look at the air targets and apparently they had no clue what was happening a little to their south.

"Juvat One's up." Mitchell keyed the flight radio and started his pop, pulled the nose of the jet up to a 30 degree climb, pushed the power to full military (no afterburner), pumped two hits on the chaff button, flipped the flares on for the next time, and switched to air to ground on his mode switch. He took a quick glance to see that Freckles was right where he should have been – off the right wing and about 500 feet out. Looking back down he saw the blasts of Boomer Huston's flight full of CBU on a radar sight.

Brad looked left and down for the target. There were still fires burning from the Panton attack. That was good, because evidently the gooks had turned off everything else to try and blacken the target. Either that or the previous attack had knocked out the power. He could pick out his target area – the air defense site on the western ridge. They picked him out too, because the RWR gear screamed in his ear. He hit the chaff button one more time, but this time, because he had switched on the flares, he dispensed two flares as well. BIG MISTAKE!

Brad rolled out with the bomb fall line splitting the center of the air defense clearing. The "death dot," or pipper was tracking up nicely. The target opened fire. He could see muzzle flashes, and about the time he mashed the pickle button there were air bursts all around. As soon as he was sure the bombs had released he jinked right, then left and dove for the dirt. He hoped Fresckles was still there.

Hammer's attack was about the same, only a few seconds later. On the egress though, Russell's RWR lit up with a threat from six o'clock – an air threat. One of the Floggers had obviously got lucky and had locked him up for a shot.

"Four's breaking left. Raw at six." His voice was up a couple of octaves. He went into a hard, 6 – 7 G turn to the left, pumping out chaff and flares and pulling the power back to idle. This would at least decrease the heat source for a heat seeking missile, and hopefully the flares would decoy it. After about 90 degrees of turn he brought the power back up and split his attention between the attacker and the onrushing rocks from below. The flares worked and the missile blew up a few hundred feet behind him. The Mig overshot the turn and seemed not to want to dive down with his target. He shot out in front of Russell's jet. The Lietuenant was back in full afterburner now, but he was also getting in the way of the egress of the rest of the Juvats pulling off target. It got very crowded.

Mitchell heard the plight of his wingman and saw the sky full of targets and made a quick decision. Since he and Freckles had dispensed their bombs and still had 3 missiles between them and a hot gun, he figured they could help out the rest of the gorilla by trying to tie up the air threats. This was not a briefed option, and in fact turned out to be a real bad idea.

"Two, let's pitch back right and climb. Go air to air." Brad commanded to his wingman. Freckles understood and started salivating. After all, he had one Mig tonight. Maybe he could get one more and be that much closer to "Ace" status.

"Two."

The rest of the gorilla's attack was a gaggle of airplanes and missiles, but miraculously there were no midairs. Five individual attacks were aborted and bombs jettisoned in defensive maneuvers, but the rest found their targets, or at least close enough to do some damage. Two Migs were shot down by Falcons in the pop up maneuver. The Korean pilots seemed clueless as to where their targets would be and found themselves as sitting ducks to the attackers climbing out from the dark below. A few got off a shot or two, but they were mainly shooting in the dark (so to speak).

Mitchell and Freckles had their jets in full afterburner and Brad took a quick look at the gas gage. Since they had jettisoned their wing tanks out to sea, all they had was the centerline external tank and internal fuel. The "Bingo" fuel for the mission was 8000 pounds. That was the minimum required to egress from the target area at low level and climb out on the pre-briefed route back to Kunsan, landing with 1500 pounds. Brad knew though that they could cut the route short, and if need be they could land at Osan, which was further north and closer. He had right at 8800 pounds. "Two, say fuel." He queried his wingman.

"Two's eight point two." Freckles relayed he had 8200 pounds. It made sense that a wingman would have less gas than the leader, mainly because he had to jockey the power back and forth to fly in formation, whereas the leader generally kept a steady setting.

Brad flipped the radar to a better air to air search mode – one that looked closer but in a narrower field – specifically for threats that were close in and above. The problem with the mode though was that it would automatically lock on to the first target it sees. His radar locked immediately onto one of the last Juvat jets rolling in for the attack. Fortunately he broke the lock and searched around for others. It was almost impossible in the heat of the moment to differentiate good guys and bad guys. Brad did not want to shoot down a buddy, nor did he wish to alert a buddy with a RWR gear screaming because of his radar lock.

"Two, too many good guys. Break lock and only look 5000 feet and above. We'll keep it down here low and out of the way." He flipped over to UHF radio. "Sentry, this is Juvat One, off target and to the northeast. Swinging to air to air. Any threats we can take care of?" Brad asked the AWACS for help.

"Roger, Juvat. There's one at your three o'clock, four miles, 3000 feet, trying to close on the last aircraft. Another at 4000, a mile behind the first. Several more higher, and no immediate threat." The controller was good.

"Copy. Coming right." Brad brought the jet into a moderate turn, keeping his speed up and flipped to a close in search mode. He had pulled it out of afterburner, both to conserve fuel and so as not to highlight himself so much to whatever threats there were – both in the air and remaining on the ground.

"Two' locked on the nose three miles, left to right." Mitchell had the lock as well, but Freckles managed to get a call in edgewise.

"Roger, I've got him. Check for the other one." Brad was closing fast on a beam intercept on the Mig who was trying to run down the last flight of Falcons. Back to UHF. "Juvats running west off target, heads up for bogey at six trying to close." He wanted to warn the F-16 that was the obvious target of this defender. He wasn't sure how far the Falcons were out in front because his radar was locked on the Mig and in that mode the radar would not display other hits. He would be at a firing solution in seconds.

"Juvat Three Three's got Raw at six and Raw at four, breaking left." It was the last flight of Juvats.

"Shiiit!" Mitchell swore and immediately broke the radar lock. His "target" had gone into a defensive turn to the right and dove for the dirt. It might be Juvat Three Three. Brad was confused and had his head on a swivel.

"Juvat One, Bogey six o'clock and closing. One mile." It was Sentry 41. Mitchell had locked onto the wrong target and managed to sandwich himself between the trailing F-16 and the attacking Mig. Great!

"Juvat's breaking right." He punched the chaff/flare button and rolled the power back to idle. He cranked his head hard over his right shoulder – not an easy task at 7 Gs. What he saw was ugly! The Mig was a Fishbed (Mig 21), and he had cranked it into a hard turn as well. He was on a collision course, as if he was trying to ram the F-16. "Gawd!" Brad thought. He unloaded the turn, rolled left, stroked full afterburner and pulled straight up, trying to get out of the plane of attack, a different vector than his adversary. Too late!

Freckles had pulled off the first attack as ordered by his leader and climbed and rolled back to the left to find who he thought would be the trail Mig. He heard the chatter on the radio, and turned a full 360 degrees without seeing anything. When he rolled back heading west what he saw was awesome. He thought his leader had just blown away the bad guy, because there was a huge explosion in front of him, down low and about two miles. He checked his gas.

"Two's Bingo minus five." He radioed that he had 7500 pounds of fuel. No response.

"Juvat One, Two. Say status?" Nothing. What the heck? Where was his leader? He headed west toward the coast and swept his radar out to 20 miles, figuring he'd pick up Mitchell somewhere ahead of him. They had a pre-briefed egress plan in case they were separated, so he wasn't concerned. But he wondered why no radio contact. Then came the dreaded sound.

"Beep. Beep. Beep. Beep." It was the sound of a parachute locater beacon. Either someone had bailed out of a jet, or their beacon had malfunctioned and was going off over the "Guard" emergency frequency.

"Juvat One, Sentry 41, come in." It was AWACS. He had the big picture and they also heard the beacon. He no longer had Brad Mitchell's jet on the screen. He had also lost the target that was closing on Mitchell's jet. "Juvat, Sentry. Come in Juvat."

"Juvat One, this is One One, come in. Say status." Ed Howe joined the communications search.

"Juvat One, this Three, over." Hammer tried his luck.

"Three, this is Two. I'm off target and outbound. No contact with Lead." Freckles decided he'd better let everyone know it looked like he was Tail End Charlie tonight, with no clue where his leader was.

"Roger Two, say fuel." Hammer took over the concerned leader role.

"Two's 7000." Freckles replied.

"Copy. Start a zoom climb as soon as you're ten miles out to sea and cut the corner on the egress route. Three and Four will set up at 15,000 feet 20 miles out. Break. Break. Juvat One One, this is Juvat Three. No contact with Juvat One. We have Two in tow and will wait for him in orbit. We have a beacon on Guard" Hammer had a cold shiver running down his spine. A **tremble**.

"Roger, Juvat Three. Copy the beacon. Break Break. Sentry, what do you have on Juvat One?" Howe was hoping for the best.

"Juvat One One, Sentry 41. We had two targets, one was Juvat One and one was a bogey closing fast from his 4 o'clock. Targets merged. No contact now. Just the beacon." The controller confirmed the worst fears.

"Juvat One One, Juvat Two. Sir, I saw a fireball. I thought it was Juvat One's bogey. Could have been …." The Lieutenant couldn't finish the sentence.

"Roger. All Juvats, this is Coach. Juvat One One and One Three are going into a max orbit. Everyone else head for the house. Three, say gas." Howe was setting up an orbit to try to talk to his lost pilot once he was on the ground, if that's what happened …. And if the pilot was even alive. **Tremble**.

"Three's got eight point four." Eighty four hundred pounds.

"Roger. Sentry, alert Big Eye. See if they can mount a SAR mission. We will orbit up here and about 20 miles out for as long as we can. We'll plan on recovering at Osan. Three, new Bingo 5000." Howe set the minimum fuel for the two of them to allow for a landing at Osan without much to spare.

"Three."

"Sentry copies." The controller got busy. The rest of the Juvats headed south to Kunsan, heavy hearts in hand, and wondering if this had all been worth it. Freckles joined up with his remaining flight members as well. But by then Hammer decided they had taken enough chances tonight and he took the three ship into Osan to be sure there was enough fuel.

CHAPTER FOURTEEN

DARKNESS

Brad couldn't believe it. He had pulled out of the extended flight path of the oncoming jet, but the Mig changed its vector as well. The silver jet's pilot pulled its nose out in front and just kept on coming, belly first. Mitchell didn't have time to do anything. Instinctively he rolled away so as not to hit cockpit to metal. The two jets collided belly to belly with the Mig slicing through the F-16 fuselage just behind the cockpit. The Mig driver never had a chance. His cockpit buried into the engine bay of the Falcon. Brad felt the impact and for a few seconds thought he still had an airplane under him. Then all the warning lights lit up and there was a huge explosion just behind the cockpit. He looked back left and realized there was no wing there. He was tumbling. He looked down at the altimeter and saw he was about 800 feet over the ground.

Fumbling around for the ejection handle, Brad realized he was basically floating in the seat straps. This was not good. He was not in a good position, but he had no choice. He pulled the ejection handle. He felt a sharp pain as the seat shot out of the cockpit. He was slammed back into it as the straps tightened up and within seconds he was hanging from a dark parachute canopy, looking down on a huge fireball and explosion on the hillside to his south. From the glow of the fire he could tell he was low and over hilly terrain with lots of trees. His back and neck hurt, but he pulled on the right risers to steer away from the fireball as best he could. He tried to remember the training he'd had many years ago. How do you prepare for parachute landing in the dark, in the mountains, in the trees, when you're scared shitless?

Crunch! It didn't matter. He slammed into the canopy of a large tree and then into the hillside below it. The chute tangled up in the trees and his impact was slowed a little. He rolled a few feet and then the straps hung him up. He was half lying, half leaning on a hill that was fairly severe in slope. His back hurt like Hell. He reached up and released one side of the chute and spun around so that at least he could get both feet on the ground. He released the other side and fell like a sack of potatoes, rolled another ten feet or so and slammed up against the next tree. It was very dark. He lost consciousness.

Melanie Han and Tommy Franks saw the whole thing. The fireworks from the attack had been interesting, but they were too far away to see what the results were. They saw lots of air bursts from AAA guns, a few missiles, a couple of explosions over the target area, and they heard the jets as they egressed out to the west. Then, toward the end there was this huge explosion just above them and to the north. They couldn't tell exactly what had happened, but in the glow of the explosion they saw a parachute come down less than a half mile from their position. Melanie decided this was not good. Whether it was a good guy or a bad guy pilot, the North Koreans would be all over the place searching for him. She was about to order that they get the Hell out of there when Franks perked up.

It was the radio. A U.S. locator beacon was going off over the Guard emergency channel. He quickly turned the volume down so as not to give away their position, then said, "Ma'am, that's one of ours." Franks pointed to the chute, or at least where it had been. The pilot had no doubt landed by now.

"Ok. Let's see if we can get to him, but be careful. Half the local troops are probably thinking the same thing. Can we keep the radio on while we move?" Melanie asked.

"Yes ma'am. But I can't switch radios or channels with it on my back. We'll have to keep it on one setting. I'll keep the headset on and turn down the volume. I'd bet those critters are scrambling around like chickens with their heads cut off after that attack. You really think they'll be out this far?" Franks had been impressed by the firepower displayed by the Falcon attack.

"I don't know, but let's assume the worst. Keep the radio on that UHF frequency so we can hear the beacon. I think that's the emergency freq the Air Force uses. Maybe somebody will be looking for our flyboy." Melanie gathered up her gear and the two of them lit out toward where they figured the pilot had come down. The beacon came and went sporadically – more prevalent when they were at or near the crest of hills, fainter down in the nooks and crannies. Franks wished he had a homing device so he could zoom in on it.

Conan was wrapped around the tree in an uncomfortable position. He basically was lying on the ground with his back to the tree and bent around it backwards in an awkward angle. The impact of the tree and the pain in his back and shoulders was what did him in. He lost consciousness for a minute or two. When he woke up he thought he was having a real bad dream. Everything was dark and there were ropes and lines everywhere. He reached down to check. His pistol was still there. So was his pain. He noticed though that his flight jacket must have been ripped off in the ejection, and he also had a big tear in the right leg of his flightsuit. It was cold. He was hurt. He was thirsty.

He remembered the survival kit in the seat pack. Pulling his way to his feet he groped around for the parachute lines and pulled his way up to the first tree. Finally he remembered he had a small flashlight in his left sleeve pocket. Should he use it? Was he alone? He waited, still as he could, but the chattering of his teeth from the cold and knocking of his knees from the fear would have given him away to anyone around. After a while he decided it was worth a try.

With the flashlight in his mouth Brad worked fast, using both hands. He found the seat pack, got the survival kit and immediately drank one of the cans of water. He stuffed the other one and the rest of the kit in his pockets. Then he remembered the Emergency Locator Beacon (ELT). He found it and assumed it had been working. He turned it off and turned the hand held radio on, switching to "Guard" frequency. He wondered, should he dare talk? He stood as still as he could and listened.

There! What was that? Brad panicked. He heard, or thought he heard something in the bushes. He froze. He waited. There it was again. It was a snap of a twig, probably dozens of yards away, but any noise out there meant something or someone moving.

"Conan, Conan. This is Juvat One One on Guard. Do you read?" It was Ed Howe from his orbit. He had detected that the beacon was off and figured that his downed wingman might be up on the radio.

Shiiit! Mitchell thought. He grabbed the radio and turned it off quickly. Damn. If any one was out there they sure as Hell heard that. "Gotta get outta here." He thought to himself. He stuffed the radio in a pants leg pocket, grabbed at the rest of the gear and stumbled down the hill, away from the noise he had heard.

Tommy Franks heard the call from Juvat Lead. He stopped and whispered to Melanie. "Ma'am. The pilots are trying to get their guy on the radio and the beacon has stopped." Should we call them? He started to take off the radio pack.

"Yeah, I guess. But what do we …… Shhh! What the…." She stopped in mid sentence and they both raised their weapons to point at an oncoming silhouette crashing through the woods.

Whatever it was it was only 10 – 20 yards away and heading down the hill they were climbing. The intruder came within 5 yards of Franks and then stumbled and fell face forward down into the ravine. He fell with a sickening thud, and then was still. Franks lowered his rifle. Melanie leaned forward and squinted into the dark. "What was that?"

"Not sure, Ma'am." Franks was not very reassuring. "You stay here. I'll go check." He slowly climbed down to the still figure on the ground, prodded it with his rifle barrel, and then shined his light on the man.

"It's the pilot, Ma'am. I think he's ok, but he's pretty scratched up." Melanie came down the hill to join them. She shined her light down into Brad's face just as he opened his eyes. Brad recoiled at the sight of a light in his eyes and reached for his sidearm.

"Whoa there, Feller." Franks whispered as he held firm to Brad's arm. "We're the good guys."

Brad wasn't sure of that. When Melanie shined her light up on themselves what he saw was an oriental looking man or woman – he couldn't tell which, dressed in black fatigues and with black paint smeared all over the face. He looked over at Tommy though, and was a little more relieved. He figured there weren't too many 6'4" blond guys in the North Korean army. He knew there were two Seal team members on the ground someplace, so these must be them. "Who are you guys?" He asked.

"We're what's left of the hostage rescue team." Melanie's female voice surprised Brad. They weren't briefed the agent with the Tiger Team was a woman. "We've been watching the fireworks and staying put we guess until tomorrow night. By the way, your buddies are trying to reach you on the radio. Are you ok? You don't look very comfortable."

"I think I wrenched my back during the ejection. It hurts like Hell. Did you see a gook pilot? The Son of a Bitch rammed me. Did he get out?" Brad pulled the radio out from his pants leg and turned it on to Guard channel. "Are we safe using the radio around here? I heard a noise in the woods back where I came down. That's what I was running from."

"Gawd Damn, Sir. You sure gotta bunch of questions." Franks helped Brad sit up. "We haven't seen anybody, but they're probably out here lookin."

"We only saw one big explosion, and one parachute." Melanie offered. "We can probably use the radio a little, if we have to. But my guess is the army will be out looking for you if they know you went down. Otherwise they're probably pretty confused and busy putting out fires back at Yongbyon." She wiped the blood from a scratch off of Brad's face. He looked into her eyes and they stared at each other for what seemed like an eternity – at least to Franks.

"Ahem. 'Scuse me sir. You wanna use this radio." He broke up the little mutual adoration society.

"I'll use this one." Brad said. He turned the volume up and heard the tail end of one of Howe's transmissions. "...... we're going to have to RTB for gas. Sentry 41, keep trying."

"Juvats and Sentry, this is Juvat One - Conan on Guard, over." Brad broadcast to the world that he was alive.

"Conan, Coach. Thank God. You ok?" Howe shot back.

"Roger. Let's go Channel Alpha." Brad directed they get off the universal rescue frequency and onto one of the dedicated alternate frequencies so that not everyone with a UHF radio would hear. They acknowledged and Brad switched his radio to the "A" position.

"Conan's up." He checked in.

"Coach is up." Howe acknowledged.

"Sentry 41's here." The AWACS controller chimed in. "Coach, understand you are leaving orbit, sir. No traffic between you and Osan. We'll keep a lookout for you sir, but my front end says we have to get on the ground too." The AWACS pilot had stayed aloft as long as he could and had turned the big jet toward Osan as well.

"We're Bingo minus a bit and we need to get on the ground." Howe relayed. "Everyone else made it out ok. The rest of your flight went into Osan. Juvat One, Understand you are ok?"

"I've got a bit of a back problem, but I'm with the Tiger Team. There are three of us. Understand there's a pick up planned for tomorrow?" Brad wanted to get out of this Hell hole.

"I don't know what the plan is. Do you Sentry?" Howe didn't want to step on anyone's thunder when he had no clue what the plan was.

"Roger, Sirs. The orders to Cobra were to abort the mission tonight and return same time tomorrow. I don't have any update from there. I'll see what I can find out." The controller knew that what he told these three folks on the ground had to be correct.

"Juvat One, suggest you go off frequency and check back in 30 minutes. We'll still be aloft then and I should have orders for you."

"Juvat copies. Back in 30 using the callsign Conan." Brad decided to revert to his personal tactical callsign because the whole flight had been Juvats and he figured that's what they would return as tomorrow. "Conan" made the distinction better.

"Hang in there sir, we'll be back manana." Howe tried to reassure his downed warrior.

"Roger." Brad wasn't reassured. He looked at Melanie and Franks. They had heard it all. It was pushing 0400 and it was cold. Brad suddenly realized he had no jacket. He shivered. They decided they would just stay put at least until they heard from the AWACS. They huddled up and tried to warm one another as best they could. Franks passed around some jerky he had in his pockets, and they all drank some water.

AWACS came back up 30 minutes later and confirmed. They were to be at the pick up point tomorrow night at 0100 hours. Melanie had suggested they change the pick up point due to activity in the area. Moving it further west would make more sense.

"Sentry copies. We'll pass that on. Suggest you come back on the radio starting at 0900 hours every 30 minutes on the 30. We'll try to get someone airborne for guidance." Brad agreed and signed off for the night, saving the battery in the radio. They tried to sleep.

CHAPTER FIFTEEN

HIDE AND SEEK

Franks had been awake for some time. He didn't need much sleep and did most of his best work in the dark anyway. Besides, he was convinced they were not alone in the forest. He prodded Melanie and Brad with a stick. "Shhh!" He whispered, and pointed in the direction of the top of the ridge.

Melanie sat up quickly, but Brad was a bit slower. His back was stiff and sore. He winced in pain. He heard the noise too, however. It sounded like several people – men. They were talking and shouting and thrashing through the woods, heading toward the trio.

"We better get outta here." Franks suggested. They gathered up their gear and slowly made their way down the ravine they were in, away from the oncoming invaders. Franks stayed behind for just a minute or two to tidy up and make the place look like no one had been there. They had moved on about a quarter of a mile when Melanie stopped dead in her tracks.

Just ahead was a clearing of sorts. It was a semi plowed field – maybe a quarter of an acre. There was a small tin roofed shack and a smaller out house-like building with a pen attached. In front of the house they could see a large tree and dangling from it was a corpse – or at least a body – hanging from a branch, tied up by the feet. Brad started to step out into the clearing when Melanie grabbed him by the shoulder. She shook her head, "No," and whispered, "Trap?" They waited a while and soon from the side of the clearing towards the ridge they had been evading, six uniformed North Korean soldiers stepped out into the open. They saw the man swinging from the tree and laughed and joked. One of them poked at the body with his rifle butt. Another went into the hut and came out dragging the body of a naked woman by the hair. He was laughing and seemed to be daring another to do something. Brad could hear Melanie gasp under her breath. She could obviously understand what was being said.

They watched as one of the soldiers un-strapped his belt and dropped his trousers, grabbed the limp body of the woman by the buttocks from behind and proceeded to rape her. The rest of the soldiers stood around him cheering him on. When he was finished he just dumped the body in a heap and stepped aside. Two more of the men had their way with what must have been a corpse. She never moved, screamed, reacted in any way. Neither did the body hanging from the tree. When they were finished the men sat down, as if they were waiting for orders, or their next move. One of them talked on a radio briefly and Melanie could hear that there were more soldiers coming.

"We need to move on. There are more of them. Evidently there is a larger village nearby and the inhabitants have all been killed – just like here." Franks pulled out his map. He and Melanie pondered for a while and then decided where they must be, based on the terrain and the proximity to a village. They figured they were about five miles from tonight's pick up point, but in the wrong direction. There were bad guys that way.

Brad looked at his watch. "We need to be able to get on the radio in a little less than an hour. AWACS will be looking for us."

"Let's see if we can get around this clearing and on the other side. At least that won't be between these guys and anyone coming from that village." Melanie pointed to a dot on the map.

They crawled very slowly and quietly for at least 50 yards before they dared try to walk or run. Franks again came last and covered their tracks. Trouble was it was foggy and starting to drizzle. Tracks in the mud would be harder to hide. After about 40 minutes they dug in under a tree. They had climbed to within about 20 yards of the top of a ridge, hopefully high enough that the radio wouldn't be blocked by the terrain.

At 0900 hours Mitchell turned on his radio to Channel A. "Sentry, this is Conan, over. Sentry, this is Conan." He waited.

"Conan, this is Sentry 61, standby to authenticate." It was a new controller, a female, and probably a new AWACS. There were two regularly stationed at Kadena Air Base on Okinawa, and it's not likely they had anything more important to do right now. The crew from last night would still be in crew rest at Osan. Either this was a new crew in their airplane or a new airplane. Brad reviewed his authentication questions in his mind.

"Conan's ready."

"Roger, Conan. What was your first dog's name?"

"Marni. Repeat, Marni." Marni had been a collie he had when he was a kid.

"Copy, Marni. What's your mother's maiden name?" The controller came back quickly.

"Carter. Repeat, Carter." Brad responded.

"Roger, Conan. Sentry has a good copy. Sir, is Tiger Team still with you?" She wanted to be sure she had everyone accounted for.

"Roger that. There's three of us, and this place is crawling with bad guy regulars." Brad sounded a little tight.

"Copy that. The mission tonight is still on. Will you be able to get to the pick up point?" Brad looked at Melanie. She shook her head and stuck her hand out for the radio. Brad hesitated, but decided it was better for her to talk directly than for him to be the messenger. There would be less talking that way, and Franks was getting nervous about how close the gooks might be.

"Sentry, this Tiger Team. I do not advise the same pick up point. Don't think we can get there and it's too close to last night's fireworks." Melanie said woman to woman.

"Copy that, Tiger. Stand by. I'll check with Big Eye." The controller had to contact Osan and the command structure if there was any change to the plan.

"We can't stand by. We need to get off the radio and beat feet." Melanie was sounding impatient. "How long do we have to be able to talk to you?"

"We've got about two hours loiter time. Suggest you come back up in thirty minutes."

"Too soon. We need to be on the move for a while. We'll come back up in one hour – 1000 hours. In the meantime, I suggest a pick up point west of the target area about three ridge lines. We have a map, so just have Cobra give us some coordinates. We'll see if we can make it." Melanie signed off.

"Sentry copies." The trio picked up their gear and moved on. The rain was coming down harder now. Along with being cold and making the going sloppy and slow, the rain on the forest canopy made it difficult to hear anyone else out there. They had to be very careful and stick to the thickest part of the woods and the worst terrain. After an hour they had probably only moved a mile. The only good thing about the weather was that they hoped it would keep the North Korean army under wraps somewhere warm and dry. They all trembled. Brad remembered his survival training back in the early 70s.

CHAPTER SIXTEEN

SURVIVAL TRAINING

Just before the end of the war in Southeast Asia, Brad was assigned as a Forward Air Controller flying the OV-10 out of Nakhon Phanom, Thailand into Cambodia. Since it was a combat assignment he had to go through survival training first.

The first segment was water survival based out of Homestead AFB, just south of Miami. It was pretty much a boondoggle, four days of sunshine in Florida. They did go over the use of the survival kits that were equipped in most aircraft, learned how to inflate and crawl into the small one man life rafts, as well as the large 12 man rafts. They practiced fishing with just a line and a hook - no rod and reel. In fact, Brad remembered one of the guys in his raft hooked a small thresher shark and things got a little exciting until the instructor took the line and tossed it overboard.

The most fun part of the few days was actual para-sailing behind a power boat. This was back before that became such a tourist attraction, and the parachute they used was the same one they would be hanging under if they ever had to jump out of their aircraft. It wasn't very maneuverable and in fact, as soon as they got up about 100 feet the instructor released the tow rope and the "student" floated down under the chute. The idea was to learn to release the chute as soon as your feet hit the water to avoid being dragged along by the wind. There was also an exercise where the student was placed under the chute floating on the water and the goal was to get out from under it by laying on your back and grabbing a handful of nylon at a time over your head and pulling it toward your feet until you were free.

After water survival Brad went upstate to Hurlburt AFB in the panhandle of Florida for FAC and OV-10 training. That was where he met Pete Trask, soon to be his roommate in Thailand and best friend forever. They had a great time at Hurlburt, sailing, hitting the beaches, and oh, by the way, working a little bit.

After Hurlburt they were sent to basic survival training at Fairchild AFB in eastern Washington. This one wasn't much fun. It was two weeks long and covered everything from basic boy scout functions to prisoner of war training. The highlight (or lowlight) was the several day stay in a mock POW camp, complete with interrogation sessions, isolation, starvation, and attempts to escape. The Air Force instructors were good. They had done their homework and tailored the interrogations to the particular "prisoner." ramming home personal information designed to make the prisoner angry and humbled. Brad and Pete actually did escape one night with a couple other "inmates" and evaded for a couple days through the countryside until they came upon a gas station with a convenience store. They managed to collect a few quarters amongst them and went into the store and bought Snickers bars. They thought they were in heaven sitting outside enjoying some real food when AF cops rolled up in a jeep and "arrested" them, throwing them back in the camp. It seems the convenience store owner was used to "escapees" coming by and for every one he turned in to the base cops, he was rewarded with time on the base firing range to practice his shooting to zero in his hunting rifles.

Brad and Pete went together to Thailand, stopping by Clark Air Base in the Philippines for jungle survivor training. This one was four days of academics learning what you could and couldn't eat that grows in the jungle, and which snakes it was best to avoid. Then they were taken by helicopter out into the jungle and dumped off to hide and survive for two days and nights, and to navigate with a compass to a pick up point. All the while there were natives in the jungle hunting them. Again for a price. If you were discovered you had to give the native a chit you were given at the beginning. The Filipinos could trade in the chits for money.

Brad and Pete navigated to the pick up point quickly and fairly easily, then they searched around for a hiding place. Brad thought he was the "cat's pajamas." He found a tall climbable tree with lots of foliage. He climbed up about 50 feet and nestled into a fairly comfortable position and covered himself with leaves and branches. He settled in for a nap and was astounded at how quiet everything was. He wasn't there thirty minutes when he felt a tap tap on his shoulder. He about jumped out of his skin and then turned to see the toothless grin of a Filipino native perched right there beside him with his hand out, looking for Brad's chit. As it turned out, every one of the "inmates" were found within two hours of their original deployment, so they basically made a camp at the pick up point with the help of their "hosts" and camped out eating bugs and critters for the two days.

Fast forward!

CHAPTER SEVENTEEN

DIPLOMACY

The President of the United States had been in his Situation Room at the White House as the mission unfolded. The events leading up to the attack on Yongbyon were complicated and potentially a threat to the entire free world. However, as in many of the Administration's exploits, the U.S. did not have strong backing of its allies when it came to doing anything about a rogue regime like North Korea.

The North had long been suspected of having a program well underway to develop nuclear weapons, as well as chemical and biological. They also were defying even the Chinese by shipping long and medium range rockets to the Mideast. Several of those shipments had been intercepted and that caused tensions to increase even more. In the meantime, talks toward reunification of the Korean peninsula were at a stutter step at best. Just when the South believes some progress has been made, Kim Jong Un pulls the plug on whatever cultural or family exchange may be planned. Every time he blames the U.S. and its military forces in the South.

The American – South Korean relationship was becoming strained as well. The recently inaugurated ROK government was much less military oriented than its predecessors. The massive student demonstrations that rocked Seoul almost weekly were taking their toll on the politicians. The students wanted the U.S. out and a more liberal government in Seoul. None of them were around during the Korean War and they didn't understand the reason for American troops on Korean soil. Most recently, a series of rapes of Korean women by an American Security Policeman from the base at Osan became the cause for more demonstrations and even violence. Although the SP was in custody and going through court martial proceedings, the Koreans wanted jurisdiction. To emphasize their point, a band of Korean students beat and severely injured an American teenager who just happened to be in the wrong place at the wrong time one night in Seoul.

Cooler heads had finally prevailed in Seoul, and the emphasis had finally returned to containing the North Korean weapons program and curtailing the production of weapons grade plutonium. With some unprecedented pressure from the Chinese and the Russians the North had agreed to a visit by a U.N. inspection team to Yongbyon. However, there were not supposed to be any Americans on the team. That stipulation was lost somewhere in the bowels of the U.N. building, and never got to the inspection agency or the Chief Inspector. When the team showed up with two Americans onboard the North Korean's raised a stink and delayed their trip into Yongbyon almost two weeks. They spent an uncomfortable two weeks in a flea bag hotel in Pyongyang, supposedly because the hotel they had been booked into was full.

Another fate of timing came from the U.S. Navy. Just as the inspection team arrived in Yongbyon a Navy frigate intercepted a North Korean freighter in the Persian Gulf. It took two shots across the bow for the skipper to finally heave to, and in the meantime the crew could be seen attempting to hoist large boxes and barrels to the deck, probably to throw them overboard. When the American seamen boarded the freighter, the North Korean captain and first mate both committed suicide in the locked bridge after trying to set the ship on fire. The Navy put out the fire and opened the cargo compartments to find several tons of weapons grade plutonium and almost a dozen fuselages of medium to long range rockets. Unfortunately the whole episode was leaked to the press and the headlines all over the world put the North Korean government on the defensive once again. When they took the inspection team hostage and killed four of them, they blamed the whole thing on the U.S. Navy and American imperialism.

President Robert Madigan had flown back from his ranch in Idaho and been in constant briefings and conferences with his top security advisors and world leaders. What to do about a rogue nation killing or holding hostage several citizens of at least five nations was not a slam dunk. The Australian government was out for blood. The Canadians had been highly concerned as well, but at least as far as they knew, their citizen was alive - initially. The German government and the Indians were much less keen on a military or clandestine response. The Indian government especially was practically willing to overlook the whole thing as an accident, even though one of the murdered inspectors was theirs. The feeling in White House circles was that India too was participating in illegal shipments of its nuclear arsenal and did not want to rock the boat. The Germans were the most perplexing. They wanted diplomacy above all else. It didn't matter that they had a dead body in some North Korean jail. They refused to go along with a hard line response.

To say the least, the rescue mission and attack was a sensitive issue. The South Korean government was vehemently against any action that would involve their forces or even give the perception that they supported it. The Japanese and Chinese as well were not in favor of military action. The Germans, Indians, French, anyone else the President conferred with, wanted U.N. official action, not unilateral or even the small combined action of a few countries. However, the Madigan Administration was not prepared to stand by and let the U.N. waffle about what to do when there were American citizens in peril. The decision to mount the rescue mission without the major supporting force it deserved was a compromise at best. Against the advice of the Chief of Staff of the Air Force and CNO of the Navy, the Chairman of the Joint Chiefs and the Secretary of Defense caved in to the diplomats, and supported what they considered a token response, hoping against hope that no one would be lost.

All that hope came crashing down when word came that there were no live hostages, only two Tiger Team members left (one of them a woman), and a downed American pilot. The Canadian government was especially peeved, convinced that it was their hostage who was executed in front of the bunker when the North Koreans became aware of the U.S. plans. Their press and the Mideastern press had a field day with what they called American "cowboy" ways. The French went so far as to propose a U.N. resolution condemning the U.S. action. The South Korean government officially protested the use of forces from their bases to attack the North, and their students went wild in the streets. Only the Australians and the British were supportive of what the U.S. had attempted, but they were not much help against the wrath of the world.

There was constant communication between Pacific Air Forces and U.S. Pacific Command Headquarters in Hawaii, General Woodward in Osan, and Washington. When it became obvious that the environment on the ground west of Yongbyon was almost as hot as the tempers of the so called American allies, the Secretary of Defense requested an emergency meeting of the President and his security advisory team. Everyone was there. It was 9 PM Washington time.

"Ladies and gentlemen, the President." White House Chief of Staff David McGee announced his boss.

"Take your seats please. Ok Russ, where are we?" The President addressed the Secretary of Defense Russell Matson before he even reached his chair.

"Sir, the AWACS on scene talked to the three survivors just before they had to land for fuel. They told them to be back up on the radio at 9 AM this morning their time." The SecDef explained.

"Right. Missy, other than my phone ringing off the hook with every world leader wanting my head on a stick, how's the temperature out there?" The Secretary of State, Melissa Anderson was next.

"Mr. President, it's ugly. We've got people demonstrating in the streets in at least a dozen countries. There are threats against several of our embassies. There was a bomb set off a couple hours ago near our embassy in Germany. We don't know if it's related or not, but there were three German citizens killed and Chancellor Schmidt is blaming it on us." The SecState replied.

"Yeah, I know. He was one of my later calls. Screw the Germans, Godamnit! If they had any balls they would have been in there with us retaliating for their dead inspector." Madigan was furious, and obviously a little tired. He, like the rest in the room, had very little sleep over the last 48 hours.

"I understand sir. You should also know that the students have taken over two universities in Seoul. They are burning furniture, have several professors hostage, and are demanding an immediate withdrawal of our troops from bases in Korea. The Ambassador has restricted all Americans to quarters and many have moved onto the bases we still have control of. The Seoul government is currently locked down in an all night Parliamentary session. I'm not sure what that means, but as you know, we do not have a majority of support in their Parliament right now." Madam Secretary painted a bleak picture.

"Yeah, well screw the Koreans too. We should have let them go to Hell back in 1950 when they begged for our help. Chuck, what do we know about our three nomads?" The President looked to his CIA Director for some good intelligence.

"Mr. President, satellite coverage is slim right now with the weather. We can tell that there are literally hundreds of soldiers on the ground near the downed F-16 and all up and down the ridge line to the west of Yongbyon. The good thing about all this, if there is a good thing, is that our agent Melanie Han is one of the three. She knows the territory and obviously the language. She's also a tough cookie." Director Charles Durkee offered.

"I don't want a personal reference here. I want to know what we're up against trying to get these folks out." The President glared at his top "spook."

"Up to 200,000 troops armed with fairly sophisticated Soviet weaponry and a scared shitless local populous. My estimation, as hard as it is to say, given I have one of my own on the ground, is the odds are too great against us." Durkee grabbed for a drink of water. He suddenly went very dry.

"General?" The Commander in Chief looked at the Chairman of his Joint Chiefs.

"Sir, I don't recommend sending the choppers back in there unescorted, or even without a substantial pre-strike to soften up the LZ. They are too vulnerable. However, a coordinated attack clearing the way in and out, with AWACS, air refueling, electronic defense suppression, and at least the same size force we used last night might do the trick." General Felix Marquez was a Marine four star, and the first Marine to hold the top spot in almost 20 years. He was also the first Mexican American in the job. In addition, he was a very smart and solid tactician.

"Mr. President, I must protest. We cannot go back in there with our guns blazing again." It was the Secretary of State. "I'm not sure we can patch up the damage we've done already."

"With all due respect, Madam Secretary, would you have us just leave those three American citizens to the wolves? These people have served us well. We just can't leave them there." General Marquez personified and now verbalized that at least the Marines NEVER leave a man (or woman) behind.

The White House Chief of Staff was the next to speak up, and he probably wished in a second that he hadn't. "As tough as it is to say General, isn't that the risk these people take when they put on the uniform, and especially when they volunteer for a mission like this? We have to expect some losses."

The Chief of Staff of the Air Force, General Johnny Joiner came unglued. "With all due respect sir, Bull shit! These people don't sign up for our military so that they can be thrown to the wolves. They expect and deserve support and a fighting chance.

I also don't remember issuing any 'volunteer only' orders for this mission." Joiner was a graduate of the Virginia Military Institute. He had been briefed on Mitchell and his background, and knew that his downed pilot was a fellow Keydet. That wasn't the source of his anger however. He was known as a concerned leader dedicated to the people as well as the mission. He was an experienced fighter pilot with two tours in Vietnam, and he was used to the politics of war. Used to it, but disgusted with it. He was about to fall on his sword for this one.

The SecDef shot Joiner a glance of disdain. General Marquez broke in quickly to try and diffuse the obvious tension in the room. "Mr. President, if we let these three folks go we will have a much larger morale problem in our own military than we seem to be stirring up in other countries. We need to try to get them out."

The President had been listening and looking over his reading glasses at each of the speakers almost with amusement. However, there was nothing amusing about the situation. The phone in front of David McGee rang. In a meeting like this one only emergency phone calls would be directed into the room, and then only to the White House Chief of Staff. He picked it up and listened. "All right. Put him on." He directed to the operator at the other end. "Madam Secretary, it is Ambassador Brexler from Seoul. Evidently he has some news that we need."

Secretary Anderson picked up her phone. "Yes John, this is Melissa Anderson." She listened for a minute, then broke in. "Just a minute John. Let me put you on speaker phone. You have the President and most of the security advisory team here." She covered the mouthpiece and addressed the President. "Sir, this is John Brexler. Evidently there is some major activity and demands from Seoul." The President nodded.

"Go ahead Mr. Ambassador, this is Robert Madigan." The President addressed the inanimate phone in front of him.

"Mr. President, we have a major situation here. The Parliament just issued me an ultimatum. They have locked up all of their Nationalist Party leaders. Those are the ones I can normally consider as sympathetic to our cause. President Kim was a Nationalist, as you know. Before he was defeated in this latest election he had appointed some pretty powerful folks to key positions in the Cabinet and elsewhere. From what I can gather, they are all under lock and key. Kim himself is under house arrest at his home." The Ambassador sounded tense and afraid.

"Sir, President Lee has summoned me to his office, but has sent word from the Parliament that there are to be no flights in or out of any of our air bases in Korea, that all Americans are hereby confined to base or quarters if outside the bases, and that we are to make immediate plans to transport all of our citizens off the Peninsula. There is a large crowd outside the gates to the Embassy, and the Marine Guards have taken at least three stray bullets. No one hurt yet, but we are basically under siege. I'm not sure how I'm supposed to get to President Lee." The Ambassador paused.

"Don't you go anywhere Mr. Ambassador. Dave, get me Lee on the phone." The President directed his Chief of Staff to raise the Korean President and then returned his attention to the

Ambassador. "Ambassador Brexler, do you have contact with the military leaders?"

"Sir, we do." It was General Marquez. "Major General Steve Woodward is hooked up on a separate line. He's the Director of Operations at PACOM and was placed in charge of the operation from Osan Air Base. We can also get General Jim Schad, the senior officer on the Peninsula."

"Mr. President, I also have a hotline to General Schad, and I had an update from General Woodward just a few minutes ago about the status at Osan." The Ambassador chimed in.

"OK. Ambassador Brexler, you sit tight in the embassy. Take care of your people. Tell the Marines to defend themselves with whatever means necessary, but to try not and provoke anything. We'll work with the military and I'll talk to President Lee shortly. Stay by the phone." The President then pushed a button on the phone that was flashing. "President Madigan."

"Sir, we have President Lee of the Republic of Korea on the line." The operator in another room of the White House explained.

"Thank you. I'll take it." The President waited as the call was put through.

"Good day Mr. President, this is President Choi Lee of the Republic of Korea. I assume you are aware of the situation?" The only lightly accented voice reminded President Madigan that Choi Lee was Harvard educated, and the son of a Korean American family who only recently returned to Seoul when their son came to power. Lee had grown up much of his life in San Francisco.

"What I am aware of Mr. President, is that your government has made demands on us and our people in Korea which we cannot accept. We will not be held hostage in our own embassy and military bases. Surely you understand the seriousness of your actions." Madigan was polite, but firm.

"With all respect President Madigan, I would hope you understand that you do not own the military bases in my country. You are merely tenants. I will admit that officially the embassy is U.S. property, but the requirement for your people to remain there and on the bases is for their own safety. We cannot guarantee their well being. Your actions over the past 36 hours have been most disturbing to us and our people. The fact that you used our territory to launch an attack on our neighbor, and in many cases our extended family to the north, is unconscionable." The Korean was being condescending at best.

"Your extended family? You must be kidding!" The President was livid. "A few months ago they were your hated enemy. Over the last decade you have had at least a dozen incidents when one or the other of you was shooting at the other. Is that what families do over there? President Lee, did you really expect we would let our citizens and one Canadian sit up there in a North Korean jail and rot? Did you really not expect us to retaliate?" The Secretary of State was trying to get the President's attention by motioning for him to calm down. She got a stern look that would freeze a hot bowl of chili.

"Please Mr. President. Let us not be emotional." President Lee was pushing the wrong buttons. "The past relationships we had with our brothers to the north were under a different regime. No doubt you have heard we have Mr. Kim, the previous leader of that regime, under house arrest. He will be tried for treason, as will many of those who followed him. As for your actions to save your countrymen, look what it has done for you. If you had conferred with us and let us in on your scheme we may have been able to work out a different, more successful solution. Our demands are simple. We want an agreement that you will remove all forces from Korea over the next year. We want a detailed schedule for the deployment of forces with\in a week. In the meantime, no America forces will be allowed to come and go without the written permission of the Korean Base Commander. Where there is no commander we are sending an officer to act as one." There were several army posts in the Korean mountains where even the Koreans wouldn't go. They had been "loaned" to the Americans to use.

"Who the Hell do you think you are? You ungrateful…" The President caught himself, much to the relief of his Chief of Staff and the Secretary of State. After a pregnant moment of silence, "President Lee, we will get back to you shortly. In the meantime I would suggest you do everything you can to ensure the safety of our citizens in your country. If one American is killed or injured by your gangs of thugs or your 'toy' military forces, I will hold you personally responsible. Good Day, Sir."

"President Madigan, the fate of your people is in their hands, your hands. I will not…" President Madigan pressed the button and hung up on his Korean counterpart. "That smug Son of a Bitch!" The President slammed his fist on the table. The Secretary of State decided not to say whatever it was she had been contemplating. She valued her job too much and figured it might be in jeopardy at the moment.

"Get me this General Schad. Woodward too." The Chairman went to work on the phones to satisfy his Commander in Chief's demands. "Anybody got any ideas?" The President asked his advisors.

"Sir, once again I can only suggest that having Melanie Han on the ground there is a big benefit." Director Durkee offered. "She's been there before. I think the three of them have a good chance of survival as long as they can keep moving."

"That's crap Charlie." The SecDef was next. "We can't leave the fate of these three patriots to some woman who happens to speak the language. With all due respect Mr. President, the security of the bases we have in Korea works both ways. We can very easily kick the Koreans that are on the bases out the front gates and lock folks out probably easier than they can lock us in. Then we can do whatever we damn well please on those bases, including preparing for and launching an all out attack on downtown Seoul if need be."

"My God Russell. Surely you're not serious." The SecState was aghast. "Sir, the Lee regime is a time bomb at best. This is just the excuse they needed, and if they really have all the Nationalists locked up somewhere there is no voice of sanity in South Korea. At least not one that we would call sane. Anything we do to provoke the situation any further could very well mean permanent expulsion from the peninsula."

"Yeah, well I'm not so sure that's such a bad idea." The President quipped. The Chairman signaled that Generals Woodward and Schad were on the line. The President punched them onto the speaker phone.

"General Woodward, this is President Madigan. What's your status over there?"

"Mr. President, here at Osan we have several hundred dependents and civilians on the base. We are finding them all quarters. There are just as many out there though who have not made it on base, either from their homes or wherever they might have been when all this came down." General Steve Woodward seemed calm and collected. "We have dozens of frantic spouses, fathers, mothers, what have you trying to get out to find their loved ones. Otherwise, we are intact. The ROKAF colonel on base is being very gracious and apologetic about the whole thing, explaining that he is only doing his job. Down at Kunsan they have things in much better hand. There are not many civilians or dependents in the area and they have been able to get all but two on base. Evidently those two are a couple of visiting wives who are up here somewhere in Seoul shopping. I have no idea what's going on at the various army bases."

"I can help there, Mr. President." General Schad broke in. As Commander in Chief US Forces Korea, he was more a figurehead than anything else. The protocol between the U.S. and South Korea called for a four star general in charge. In fact, he had no forces under his direct command, but he certainly had input to their status. "All of our posts are buttoned up. We probably have

15-20 folks unaccounted for – on leave or scheduled day off. Most of them are in the Seoul area somewhere. Yongsan Army Post here in Seoul is basically under siege. There are demonstrators at all our gates. I have given orders for the guards to stay firm but to not get into any confrontations. So far there has been one shot fired and we have one MP with a shoulder wound. We did not return fire, but we used tear gas to break up the crowd."

"Shit!" The President exclaimed. "OK, same thing as I told the Ambassador and his Marines. Have your folks stand fast and firm. You're right – no confrontations, but defend yourselves at all costs. General Woodward, there is a thought here to clear Osan and Kunsan of your Korean 'hosts' and prepare for another attack north. You see any problem with that?"

"Uh, no sir. I guess not. Obviously the ROKAF and the Korean army have significant air defenses that could be used on us as we get airborne. I guess you folks would know better than me as to the likelihood of that. But, no sir. We can do whatever is necessary. By the way sir, the AWACS got airborne just before the crap hit the fan out here. They have made contact with the three on the ground. Ms. Han recommends a later, more western pickup because they are practically overrun with North Korean regulars. AWACS contacts them again within the hour. Do you have any guidance for them?" Woodward was not so calm and collected now.

"Back at you, General." The President replied. "As the closest thing to the war fighter on the ground, and knowing what you know about the military situation, what would you tell them?"

There was a long pause. General Joiner jumped in to "rescue" his two star subordinate. "Mr. President, I do not recommend we try anything without a full blown package of support. We need electronic warfare support – jammers – refueling, AWACS, and full blown close air support package around the pick up. Just getting through the coastal defenses will be dicey again unless we take them out first. Otherwise we run the risk of losing even another pilot and aircraft."

"Sir, I have to agree. We have three squadrons of F-16s here in South Korea and one of A-10s. Certainly they can do a lot of damage, but a mission like this needs more support than we have available. Personally I think we were lucky last night to only lose one, especially after it was obvious the whole mission was compromised." General Woodward added his "war fighter's" opinion.

"So what? You would just leave them there?" The President asked incredulously.

"Sir, perhaps I can help." It was the Chief of Naval Operations, Admiral Mike McGarrity.

"I'm listening."

The CNO went to the map of the Korean Peninsula and its surrounding waters. "We currently have the attack submarine 'Marlin' right about here in the Yellow Sea. She can be close off the coast of North Korea here within 30 hours." He pointed to an area due west of Yongbyon and the three evaders' location. In the meantime, we have another Seal Team on alert on Okinawa, and I believe the Air Force has a couple of C-130s at Kadena." He looked at General Joiner who nodded agreement.

"Those Seals could be dropped in on the 'Marlin' before she gets in too close. She could surface to bring them on board and then surface again off the coast at night to let them loose. If our three nomads can make it to the coast, the Seals ought to be able to bring them in." The CNO sat down.

"That's a big 'if.' How are they supposed to hook up at the right place?" The President asked.

"Mr. President, the Tiger Team has a GPS receiver with them. They should be able to navigate pretty close." General Woodward offered.

"What does everyone think?" The Commander in Chief looked around the room. Everyone nodded, even the Secretary of State. She figured this was the least disruptive action we could do and therefore wouldn't ruffle so many feathers.

"General Woodward? General Schad?" The President asked his war fighters.

Woodward gave his senior officer counterpart a chance to speak first, but when it was obvious the CINC had nothing to say he chimed in. "Sir, as much as I would like to go up there and make the place a parking lot, this alternative makes a lot of sense. I agree with General Joiner, we need more help to do it our way."

The President sat silent for what seemed like an eternity. Everyone knew better than to speak though. Finally, "All right.

General Woodsward, you and the CNO work out a location on the coast and pass the words on to our three patriots. Relay to them my best wishes and whatever words you can that suggest we are not leaving them to the wolves."

"Yes sir." Woodward and Admiral McGarrity sang out in chorus. The President disconnected the phone contact.

"The only thing that pisses me off about this is the obvious cave in to the South Korean demands, and those of our pussy foot allies. I don't like that." The President was working up a head of steam again.

"Mr. President, I do believe we can patch things up with South Korea. We've done significant damage in North Korea and they are sufficiently embarrassed right now. Perhaps we should try a little diplomacy ...." Secretary Anderson went about one word too far.

"Diplomacy my ass!" Madigan was livid. "I'll show them diplomacy! Madam Secretary, you get back to Foggy Bottom and you work your magic diplomacy. Do whatever you have to, but make sure the South knows that there had better not be any American injuries or deaths in their country. Go ahead and prepare the withdrawal plan that Lee wants, and make it one that works. Right now I'm prone to withdraw and let them drown. Russ, General – give her all the help she needs there." The President addressed that last direction to the SecDef and the Chairman, referring to the withdrawal of the military forces.

"David, I want a press release describing last night's action that states we believe there are no survivors. Any help we can give these three the better. If the North believes we think they're dead, maybe they'll quit looking so hard. Hopefully they'll relax their coastal defenses." The White House Chief of Staff nodded and left the room.

"One last thing." The President directed as he stood up to leave. "Mr. Chairman, prepare a major attack on North Korea using all forces available, including those in the South – ESPECIALLY those in the south – to be ready to go if anything goes wrong with this rescue mission. We might just give General Woodward his wish for a parking lot." The President left everyone standing.

CHAPTER EIGHTEEN

ENCOUNTER

At 10 AM Melanie came back up on the radio. "Sentry 61, this is Tiger Team, over." Sentry came right up, they authenticated again and the team heard the words they couldn't believe, much less accept.

"Tiger, this is Sentry." It was a man's voice this time. Probably the controller's supervisor. "I'm sorry to have to tell you this, but the mission has been scrubbed for now. Big Eye passes that there is a plan for a rescue mission by a Seal team off the Submarine Marlin. You are to make your way to a point on the coast."

"You gotta be shittin' me!" Brad exclaimed, half under his breath. Franks just shook his head.

"Roger Sentry. Tiger understands that since we have no hostages to bring out with us, we are expendable, is that right?" Melanie was blunt and to the point. There was a long pause. The AWACS supervisor obviously did not know what to say and was probably wishing he hadn't taken the microphone from his young Captain.

"Tiger, Sentry has no info on the decision. Do you want us to inquire further?" He was hoping she'd say no. "We do have words from the President wishing you the best of luck."

"Negative Sentry. We get it." She released the mic button and said to Brad and Tommy, "Anything you guys want to pass on?" Franks shook his head in disgust. Brad thought a second or two, then grabbed the mic.

"Sentry, this is Conan. Be sure this information is passed to my squadron. Conan and Tiger out."

"Will do, Conan. Standby for coordinates and timing instructions." The controller read them coordinates of a spot on the coast where the rendezvous was to take place in four days, then, "Good luck to you guys. Sentry out." The supervisor handed the microphone back to his controller. He saw that she was wiping back tears. He had a few welling up in his eyes too. They had probably just sentenced three good Americans to death.

Melanie thought a while. It had been many years, but she had been here before – evading the North Korean army and traveling to the west coast. She had no clue what route she and Lee Chun had taken back then. She also remembered that Master Chief Woolsey and his two partners made a similar trek just 18 months ago, but she realized they were in a different part of the country and closer to the coast than they are now. It wouldn't matter now anyway. The three of them would have to be a lot more careful than a teenage Korean boy and a young Korean girl would, or three oriental looking GIs dressed in North Korean uniforms for that matter. The three of them would stand out like black sheep in a flock of albinos. She pulled out the map and they huddled a while to try and pick out a route. They decided that the best thing was to rest during the day, as long as it didn't get too crowded in the neighborhood, and to travel at night. The rain had lightened up a bit and they were able to find some thick bushes to crawl under and keep relatively dry. Sleep however, was hard to come by. Each of them had their own private thoughts and premonitions about their future.

The USS Marlin was one of the Navy's newest submarines. She was small for a nuclear sub and fast. She was armed with several different types of torpedoes and Tomahawk surface to surface missiles. When she was underwater she was virtually invisible, both visually and electronically. But right now she was very vulnerable. No submarine skipper like to be on or near the surface. Commander Josh Moran was no exception, but orders were orders. They had stayed at periscope depth until the C-130 made its first low pass. Then the Marlin surface and fired off a flare to positively ID its position. The C-130 was making its final approach. The big Hercules was at 1800 feet, about as low as a parachutist wants to jump from. Any lower than that and there is no time to deploy an emergency chute if the main one malfunctions.

One by one the four chutes popped open, the bodies at the end of the risers swung twice and then splashed down as close as they dared to the Marlin. Moran dispatched a rescue launch and the four Seals were on board in a matter of ten minutes. The crew quickly battened the hatches and the Marlin headed for safer waters – below.

"Welcome aboard, gentlemen." Moran addressed the team as they put away their gear and dried off.

"Thank you sir. Good to be here." Master Chief Rob McGee answered with a sharp salute. "I assume you've been read in on our mission sir?" McGee introduced himself as the team chief and the rest of Seal Team Foxtrot.

"All we know is that we're supposed to get you as close to a point off the North Korean coast as we can and put you off three nights from now." The Skipper answered. "Then I assume we're supposed to standby for a later pickup."

"That's correct, sir. If everything goes right and our sheep are where they are supposed to be, we should be back on board the next night. I understand there are three of them – one member of Tiger Team, a female CIA agent, and an Air Force flyboy who's lost his wings." McGee bristled at the thought.

"Did you know those guys Master Chief?" Moran referred to the lost Seal members.

"Yes sir. We're one big family. Wilcox here has a twin brother on Tiger." He nodded toward one of his team members. "We don't even know which one is alive."

"Well, make yourselves as comfortable as possible. There's some chow in the galley if you're hungry. 'Cookie' probably has some of his killer pot roast left." With that the Seal team left the bridge and headed to their quarters.

Brad Mitchell was slowing the progress down. His back was stiffening up more and more and he could only travel for about a half hour at a time. Franks was impatient, but Melanie was the soothing factor – in more ways than one. She not only reined Tommy back, she gave a great back rub that helped Brad's pain and disposition a lot. The first night they traveled cautiously but were successful in evading capture, and then dug in to rest.

They were at last in an area where they thought they could at least whisper to one another. Franks had no trouble sleeping, but neither Melanie nor Brad could. It was cold and Brad was aching. Melanie snuggled in behind him and used her body heat to help her hands loosen up his back. They lay like that for several hours and told each other their life stories – at least Melanie told the public version of hers. It was interesting enough and Brad had no reason to think there was more to her than the saga she told. All he knew was that the feel of her body next to him and her hands working on his back was a feeling he wanted to go on forever.

Apparently Melanie was feeling something too. Eventually her hands gave out to the rigors of a strong muscle massage. When she stopped Brad reached back and took one hand in his and pulled it over and up next to his chest, cradled in his own hand. Melanie didn't resist. She rested her cheek on the back of Brad's neck and soon they were both asleep, close and warm.

Melanie awoke with a start. The feel of cold steel on the back of her neck got her attention. She rolled off of Brad and toward her AK-47 but the man standing over her quickly put his bare foot down hard on her chest. The tip of his machete rested on her throat. He just shook his head side to side very slowly. Melanie could see behind him that Tommy Franks was sitting on the ground and leaning up against a tree. His head was slumped over and there was blood on his chest. She couldn't tell if he was dead or alive, but she decided that the man hovering over her meant business.

Brad jumped when Melanie did. He just didn't move as quickly. It was probably a good thing too. Staring him in the face was the muzzle of a rifle. It was Franks' rifle, but the man behind it wasn't Franks. Brad sat up very slowly. The man with the gun motioned to Brad's pistol. Brad gingerly unholstered the gun and laid it on the ground. Quickly the Korean swooped down and picked it up. He smiled and displayed several missing teeth, the rest covered in beetle juice or tobacco stains.

Melanie was allowed to sit up as well and she quickly spoke up, indicating to their captors that she knew their language. She asked them what they wanted and what had happened to Tommy Franks. The toothless one laughed and raked his finger across his neck indicating Franks' throat had been slashed. The older Korean was more reserved and yelled at his younger counterpart to be quiet. Apparently there were only two of them. How they managed to sneak up on Tommy Franks would never be known.

Melanie decided they needed to come clean and see if they could recruit these two who were obviously not soldiers, but just as obviously were of soldier age. They were either deserters or against the government in some way. Melanie knew there were a few bands of rebellious types in North Korea, but they were very loosely organized and mostly made their living robbing and abusing their own kind. She guessed these two were of that persuasion. She explained their situation and that they needed to get to the coast. She offered a reward if the men would help.

"How much of a reward?" The older man asked in Korean. He obviously had an interest in money. Melanie quickly had to decide had to handle this. Obviously the Seal team they were to rendezvous with wouldn't have any money, and she sure didn't.

"That gun, and one just like it, and two other guns." Melanie indicated Franks' sniper rifle.

"Hah! We already have the gun, and yours, and this pistol." The younger one piped in, not impressed with the offer.

"The army is offering gold for you and even for this dead man." The senior Korean said. Melanie's heart sank. The army had put out the word there were some evaders in the countryside. They were likely portrayed as killers and no telling what the reward might be. Anything at all would be more than these two thugs had seen in their entire lives.

Melanie translated for Brad. Meanwhile the young one started going through Franks' pockets, took his watch and most importantly, he took the hand held GPS receiver. The older one stood guard with Melanie's AK-47 leveled at his two captives.

"Do you think he's dead?" Brad nodded toward Franks. About then the young thug grabbed Tommy by the hair and pulled his head up. There was a gash where his throat used to be big enough to stuff a football in. "Never mind." Brad said and looked away. Meanwhile the young gun ripped the chain with Franks' dog tags off his neck.

Melanie tried to persuade the older one that they should let her and Brad go, and that they would get plenty from the army for Franks' body, but that they would also get thrown in jail for desertion or for not entering the army.

"That's why you are going with us." The crafty older man replied. "We will tell the army where to find you, but only after we have escaped them. Now – move together. We will leave in the morning." He motioned for the two of them to sit together. The younger Korean tied them up back to back, lashing their arms together, and then tied up each of their feet. Finally, he put a noose around each of their necks and threw the other end of the ropes over a branch above them. They basically were unable to move. They couldn't even lie down or roll off to one side. They ropes around their necks were tight. Brad thought about how nice it was having Melanie up against him just a few minutes ago. Not quite the same now.

The Koreans finished stripping everything of value from Franks' body and then kicked him over under a bush. They built a small fire and helped themselves to the food they found on the three, although they had trouble deciding how to eat the Meals Ready to Eat (MREs). They didn't know you had to add water and Melanie wasn't about to make life easier for them. The older one spit out the contents of one package, but the younger slob would eat anything. He consumed the contents of two complete MREs dry and then went to the chocolate. When he took out the pill he had found in Franks' pocket and looked at it like he was going to eat it, Brad felt Melanie tense up. They both had the same thought, *Swallow it, you bastard. It's like candy.* No such luck. He threw it into the bushes and settled on some jerky.

After they had eaten, Brad noticed the younger Korean kept eying Melanie, and started arguing with the senior thug. "Are they saying what I think they are?" Brad whispered.

"He wants me. Seems he hasn't had a woman in a few nights since the last time they raped one in a nearby village." Melanie said matter-of-factly. Brad felt her slide her hands down toward her shin. "Knife." She whispered. Brad suddenly then remembered his own knife. It was still strapped to his left calf. He was surprised the Koreans hadn't searched them. Obviously Melanie must be similarly armed. Trouble was, she was moving her left arm too, and that was the opposite arm for him. He decided that she might need hers sooner than he would. The argument was getting louder and it looked like the young stud was winning.

"Stand up!" The young one ordered in Korean. Brad understood though, because he had no choice. The man had cut the ropes binding their feet and was pulling hard on the ropes around their necks. They had no choice but to stand up – or choke. They stumbled to their feet, still bound back to back at the arms. Their assailant yelled back to the old man, who obviously said he was not going to help. The young one tied off the ropes so that both Melanie and Brad were practically on their toes to breathe. He cut the ropes holding their arms and quickly hoisted Melanie even farther. She was practically dangling in the air and gasping for breath. Meanwhile the Korean tied Brad's hands behind his back and then kicked him hard in the groin – just for good measure, Brad guessed. He certainly was not a threat. It was all he could do to stand up, and if he didn't he would choke. He looked over at Melanie. She had a wild look in her eyes, even though she was fighting just to stay conscious.

The Korean cut the rope holding Melanie up and she tumbled to the ground. Brad noticed that as she did she rolled to one side and he saw her hand flash down to her left ankle. The Korean was on her like a wildcat. He pushed her onto her back and began ripping at her clothes. Brad felt a strong sense of emotion. He was enraged, afraid, jealous and disgusted – all at once. This woman had become special to him and he couldn't stand for this to happen to her. He started yelling – yelling at the top of his lungs.

The young one stopped his pillaging of Melanie long enough to yell something to the old man – probably telling him to shut Brad up. One thing they did not want was for the army to find them until they were ready. He went back to Melanie and clamped down hard on her mouth. "Tell him to shut up, or this will be a lot worse." He yelled at her.

"Brad, don't get yourself killed for me. I can handle this." Melanie pleaded to Brad. She knew that she could say anything she wanted in English and these two wouldn't have a clue.

"Bullshit! You don't deserve this." Brad went back to yelling, but the old man couldn't let that go. He yelled something in Korean and then clubbed Brad with the butt of Melanie's rifle. Brad slumped into the noose and the man cut him down to let him fall on the ground. Fortunately, the blow was not as hard as the Korean would have liked, but Brad was dazed and almost blacked out. When he hit the ground he rolled down a slight bank and froze.

The young rapist continued on Melanie. He had her shirt and halter bra completely ripped off and was working on her pants. Melanie decided she didn't have much time. She could see the older man tending to Brad and they were about as far away as they were going to get. Melanie had slipped the knife up her sleeve. It was a large knife and he was bound to discover it soon. She decided why not show it to him now? She reached up and pulled the man down on top of her and said something he wanted to hear in Korean, kissed him wildly on the lips and sank the big knife up to its hilt just above his groin, pulling it violently up. It was a quick, quiet and very bloody death.

Brad was not quite able to slide his arms down enough to his left calf to get to the Bowie knife. But he was at least back conscious again, so he kept yelling. That kept the old man's attention. He poked Brad with the business end of the AK-47 and yelled something in Korean. Brad could see that Melanie's attacker was still and slumped over her. He wasn't sure how far he should push this old man, but he thought that he had to keep his attention. So, he tried a new tactic.

Brad suddenly doubled up and made noises like he was throwing up, groaned, moaned, even managed to puke up a little saliva. The old man looked at him and walked around to the other side, turning his back to Melanie. She moved quickly and quietly, depositing the bloody hulk that was sprawled on top of her off to one side, and rising to her feet. She covered the 20-30 feet between them in a flash and was on the old man's back like a cat, plunging her knife deep into his kidneys, her arm wrapped around his throat from the back. Death came instantly and Brad could hardly believe what he had just seen.

Melanie slowly let the old man drop to the ground in a heap and stood for a moment looking at him. She was topless and her pants were half on, half off. She was covered in blood and the look in her eyes was that of a wild animal. Brad trembled when he saw her.

"You ok?" He asked meekly.

"Melanie looked at Brad and her eyes softened. "Yeah. I will be. Roll over." She ordered and as he did she reached down and cut the rope tying his hands. Then she went over to what was left of her clothes and tried to salvage something.

Brad got up and checked both Koreans, as if there might be a doubt they were dead. The young one's wound was huge. Melanie had basically gutted him like a deer and his innards were all over the ground. Brad retrieved their guns and knives and placed them in a pile near the fire. As he did he heard a muffled sob from Melanie. He looked at her, but she quickly hid her face and turned her naked back to him. Brad went to her and put his arms around her.

"It'll be all right. Here, let me give you my T-shirt." He started to zip down his flightsuit to take it off.

"No." Melanie said with a slight sob. "Just hold me a minute."

They stood in an embrace for several minutes. Brad stroked her hair and kissed her forehead. The feel of her skin was soft and even though the circumstances were slightly less than romantic, he became aroused. Melanie must have felt it. She looked up and peered deep into his eyes, almost pleading. They kissed.

It was a long, warm kiss. The kind both of them had dreams about over the past few years, but neither had experienced. They were slow and tender with each other, and the message was passed between them. Finally it was Brad who cut it off.

"We've got to get you in some clothes." He said, still holding her tight.

She pushed him away slowly and said, "I'll use Tommy's." She went over to the big man's body and rolled him over. His fatigue shirt was basically intact, though it would be huge on her. Together they took off Franks' T-shirt and fatigue shirt. Melanie slipped on the bloody T-shirt and they tailored his fatigues by cutting the sleeves short and she tucked the tails into her own pants. She looked a sight, but at least she was covered. Using what un-bloodied clothing there was from their two assailants she was able to wipe most of the blood off herself. "We'd better get out of here." She finally whispered.

They managed to dig a shallow grave for Tommy Franks using their knives and the young Korean's machete. They dug another hole and poured the bodies of the Koreans in, taking back the valuables that were Tommy's, and especially the GPS receiver. They paused for a moment of silence over Tommy, neither of them knowing what to say. Finally, they scooped up the guns and knives and kicked out the fire.

"You know how to use this thing?" Brad asked Melanie, holding out the GPS.

"I think so. Don't you flyboys use that new technology?" She answered, and for the first time since he could remember meeting her, Brad saw Melanie smile.

"Ours is built into the jet, and all I do is enter coordinates and punch a button." He smiled back. They looked at each other longingly for a few seconds. This time it was Melanie who snapped out of it first.

"It's basically the same. Tommy already put in the coordinates of our rendezvous point. I think we just push the 'Go To' button and follow the pointer." Brad tried it and sure enough, the arrow pointed west and the distance read 62 miles.

"What do we have now, three days?" He asked.

"Yeah, let's go." Melanie pushed off into the dark. Brad shot one more glance toward Tommy Franks' grave and then followed.

CHAPTER NINETEEN

REACTION

"Sir, this is Bullshit! We can't just leave him up there." Ed Howe was furious and he was venting his anger on Nels Rushing, as if the Colonel didn't feel the same way. Howe had convinced General Woodward to convince the South Koreans that he and his wingmen should be allowed to fly from Osan to Kunsan to prepare for their departure from the ROK, as directed. That was a BS excuse, but it worked and Howe wasted no time rolling in on the Wing Commander. Bones Harbinger was in the room too, as was John Lorner, the Wing DO.

"Easy Coach." Lorner advised the junior officer. Dumping on your Wing Commander was not normally a healthy thing for a Lt. Colonel's career. "This decision was made at the highest level. Chances are probably better for Conan and the others this way than if we tried another abortion like last night."

"Believe me Ed, I don't feel right about this either." Rushing spoke up, not that he thought he needed to defend himself, but because he knew they had a job to do. "But this country is about to explode, and there are a lot of Americans who would be in major jeopardy if we did anything foolish. We've got a mission to prepare, and who knows? If we're lucky, maybe we'll get to fly it. Now get your squadron together, along with the Pantons and I want a meeting in 1 hour." Lobo dismissed his two antagonists.

In Seoul things were deteriorating rapidly. The Ambassador and his staff were basically prisoners in their own embassy. Most of the dependents had been able to get into the complex safely, and they were being cared for in the Ambassador's residence. But several were still outside the gates somewhere, and the demonstrators had become very loud and boisterous. Korean TV had much of it on the air, and the police were nowhere to be seen. The whole world watched in horror as a young American mother and her two children were beaten and forced to watch as a black American teenager was wrapped in an American flag and then set on fire within blocks of the Embassy. No one even knew what was happening until it was on television sets all over the world. The phone rang within minutes in President Choi Lee's office. It was the U.S. President.

"President Madigan, I assure you, we do not condone this action and I am sorry for the loss. But you must understand our people's resolve." Lee tried to get the first word.

"President Lee, I will only say this once." Madigan was calm and remarkably subdued. "If you do not deploy your police and military and protect our people you will soon find yourself at war with the United States of America. Do I make myself clear?"

The Korean President could hardly believe his ears. He paused for what seemed like minutes, and President Madigan gave him all the time he needed to absorb the threat. "Mr. President, surely you understand the gravity of a threat like that. You would risk a war because of the death of one black man? I think not." The Korean gambled. Bad move.

"One AMERICAN boy, Mr. Lee. Not a black man, an American teenage boy." The temperature of the rhetoric went up a few degrees. "I will not stand by and watch one more of our countrymen injured, beaten or killed while you do nothing to protect them. I have ordered the 7th Fleet to the Yellow Sea. We are deploying thousands of troops to Japan as we speak, and the Air Force is reinforcing the squadrons in Japan." The President was bluffing, or at least he hadn't really ordered any of those movements yet. "The troops and squadrons in your country now are arming themselves for whatever they need to do to ensure their own safety and that of the Americans still trapped in your streets. Now, are you going to help stop this madness or not?"

Again there was a long pause. Finally, "I will try Mr. President, but I do not have control over the students."

"Then I suggest you get some control, President Lee. You are wasting time." And with that the American President hung up on his counterpart for the second time in less than 24 hours. The Vice President, the Secretary of Defense and the White House Chief of Staff were in the room.

"Russ, follow up on that threat about the 7th Fleet and deploy whatever we need to evacuate our folks from South Korea. Any trouble and we will retaliate." Madigan ordered his SecDef.

"Yes Sir." The Secretary picked up the phone and started making calls.

"David, get me on TV tonight." The President wanted to speak to the American people.

"Be seated." Colonel Nels Rushing walked to the front of the Base Theater and as many as could sat down. Half the entire wing had been assembled. It was decided that this was not just a matter for the fighter squadrons, but that everyone needed to be involved. All of the pilots were in attendance, and as many representatives from every organization on base that could comfortably sit and stand in the theater were allowed in. Security policemen guarded the doors.

"Folks, by now most of you know what went down last night." Rushing began. "Suffice it to say that we participated in a mission up north to attempt a rescue of some Americans being held hostage. The mission was mostly successful in that we hit our targets. However, the hostages were killed, along with their rescuers on the ground. We lost one of our pilots as well." Rushing passed on the same story the President had made that everyone was dead. He didn't want a repeat of leaking intel like two nights earlier. "In the meantime, we seem to have incurred the wrath of the Seoul government and students, and most of the rest of the world. As you know, we have been restricted to base. We have most of our known dependents on base with us and no one is to attempt to leave. If you have been watching TV you have seen what is going on in Seoul."

"The Koreans want us out of their country, and right now at least, the President is in the mood to oblige. Immediately upon leaving here you are to set about preparing to deploy off the ROK. Use your mobility plans in place. However, do not plan on returning. Configure the jets with live munitions as directed by the frag team. We will not go quietly." There was a huge cheer from the audience. "Let's get to work. Carry On." Rushing walked out, followed by his staff of senior colonels. The crowd dispersed with much conversation and a hum of anticipation.

The Eighth Tac Fighter Wing, along with its counterpart at Osan and the various U.S. Army installations in South Korea, prepared for war and deployment at the same time. Everyone who could be was armed. Mobility plans were put into place that basically packed up all essential gear and set it in specific locations, either on the flight lines in the case of the two air bases, or on trucks. Every aircraft that could fly was loaded with cluster bombs or five hundred pounders, live missiles and a hot gun. The ones that were not flyable received increased attention to fix whatever the problem was. Plans were reviewed for moving the nuclear weapons in storage to appropriate pick up points for transport off the Peninsula. The pilots readied themselves for two missions – one directly to Kadena Air Base in Okinawa or Misawa Air Base on Northern Hokaido, Japan, and one that took them back up north again first. The difference in the planning for the second mission this time was a review of the South Korean defenses that could be used against them during their departure.

The South Korean armed forces were relatively modern and well equipped. Their Air Force had just taken delivery of the first 8 of 28 F-16s that were to replace some ancient F-86 fighters and some of their F-5s. The remainder of the F-5s had been upgraded to the latest technology. Their Air Force was purely an air defense force, because the plans in place had the Americans doing the offensive damage up north if there was ever a conflict north of the DMZ. Their defense forces had Patriot and Stinger missiles, as well as the latest in guided AAA. They were much more of a threat to the Americans than the North Koreans were, if it came down to it. Most importantly however, the South Korean Army was large, and although not as big as their neighbors to the north, they were well equipped and could roll in and take over the American bases against only token resistance – at least from the U.S. Air Force. The Army installations in the mountains would be tougher to take, but were really of no threat themselves.

President Lee of South Korea couldn't stand the heat. He acquiesced to the American demands and deployed the police and army to control the riots. It was not much more than a token effort, however. There were a few skirmishes, but in most cases the police would back down when really forced. At least their presence on the streets seemed to calm things a bit, but there wasn't an American in hiding that felt safe enough to come out. Fortunately the embassy still had phone communications and they were able to locate almost all of the U.S. citizens outside the walls by phone. General Schad put together a squad of Army rangers from Yongsan

Army Post in downtown Seoul and the Ambassador put in a call to President Lee.

"Mr. President, we are deploying a team of our army with armored personnel carriers and we are moving them out to rescue and bring in our people who are still outside. We are merely abiding by your orders to restrict all Americans to base. This will help to get them there. We expect assistance from your police and army. Do we have your assurance?" The Ambassador was more informing than asking.

"I cannot guarantee anyone's safety, Mr. Ambassador, but I will give the order to help where we can." The Korean President knew he really had no choice. "Do not provoke any attack yourselves, Mr. Ambassador. Our people are furious with your actions."

"We will do our best." The Ambassador hung up and then called Washington to inform the home front of the plan.

"I'm not sure that's a good idea, John." Secretary of State Anderson did not like the plan. "You will only provoke them."

"Begging your pardon, Madam Secretary, but this is out of my hands." Brexler eased out of it - almost. "This is the Army's idea, but I must say I agree with it. It is the only way to get our people to safety. Will you brief the President?"

"Yes, I suppose so. But John, tell the army to be gentle."

Brexler chuckled, though with his hand over the phone. "Yes Ma'am."

The Rangers made a half a dozen runs, picking up American families and businessmen at locations where there weren't any students or demonstrators. It was basically uneventful. Every once in a while a brave and stupid student would plant himself in front of the oncoming APC, but he didn't stay there long, and the small convoy rolled by, receiving only a stoning or two. Finally, the effort to rescue the mother and her two children that had made the evening news all over the world was mounted. The demonstrators were holding them in a building nearby the embassy and the streets were jam packed with rowdy students and rioters. A few Korean police were assembled nearby, but they were mainly just standing around and watching.

The convoy rounded a corner two blocks away and stopped in the middle of the thoroughfare. At first the demonstrators did not see them, or if they did they assumed they were Korean army. Then someone saw an American flag attached to the lead APC. The throng moved forward. General Schad had a few tricks up his sleeve that even the Ambassador didn't know about. Two Cobra helicopters suddenly swooped down the boulevard very low. They were so low their rotor blades were just 10 feet off the street. Demonstrators dove for cover and there was general chaos. The convoy moved on slowly. The choppers made pass after pass, threatening, but not shooting their 50 caliber machine guns. They were also armed with two pods of rockets each.

As the APCs rolled up to the front of the building where the hostages were kept, the students immediately around the hostages got brave, or at least they got organized. They paraded the young mother and her two children out in front of the building with a gun to each of their heads. All of this was on every television in the world, and it was a horrifying sight. The little girl couldn't have been more than six years old and she was screaming. Her older brother was probably 10 or 11 and he had been slapped around a little. His lip was bleeding and he was holding his right arm. Their mother could barely stand and her head was slumped over as if she was drugged. For a moment the students seemed to have the upper hand. The captain in charge of the convoy had stepped out of the lead APC, but as soon as he saw the situation he barked orders to his men to stand fast. The students started jeering and chanting and making threatening gestures.

The Cobras returned. This time, instead of swooping down the street, the lead Cobra went into a hover directly over the APC and the guns were pointed at the students and their hostages. The noise was deafening, but the Cobra pilot was good. He didn't waiver a bit and it became obvious to the students in charge that many of them were in the line of fire. It was a standoff.

This time it was the American Ambassador who acted. All of the demonstrators in front of the embassy had congregated around all the excitement down the street. The area directly in front of the embassy gates was clear. Quickly and quietly three U.S. Marines slipped out and disappeared into the building next door, directly across the street from the building where all the activity was taking place. The Ambassador climbed into his bullet proof limousine with three big Marines and ordered the gates opened. The driver stomped on it and the big black Chrysler sped up to the scene, coming very close to running over two students. The Marines got out and leveled their weapons at the crowd. A corridor opened up between the Marines and the students holding the hostages. There were now two avenues of threat facing the students. The Cobra kept hovering and had a bead on them from in front, and these three big Marines were moving on them from the side. Suddenly the American Ambassador stepped out of the limo and with a bullhorn spoke directly to the students in Korean. As if on cue, the Cobra backed up a few hundred feet so that the Ambassador could be heard, but still maintained its aim.

"You will give the children and the woman to these Marines." Ambassador Brexler ordered. Back in Washington, Secretary Anderson gasped at the scene on TV. The President smiled. "If you do not, there are three snipers in that building across the street that have a direct aim on you, you and you." Brexler pointed to the three demonstrators holding onto the Americans. "You have no choice. If you harm them you will all die. If you do not release them in five seconds, three of you will die. One! Two!"

The student holding the little girl immediately released her and she ran to her mother. The student holding Mom was confused. Just then the brave American boy turned and thrust his elbow into the groin of the man who had a hold of his arm, wrenched himself loose and ran directly to the lead Marine. The Cobra helicopter moved forward and fired a volley directly over the head of everyone. The crowd screamed and dove for cover and the student holding the mother ducked. When he did the seemingly stoic and quiet mother reached up and dug her fingernails into his eyes, grabbed her daughter by the arm and ran to the Marines. It was over in a matter of seconds. The Marines covered the crowd while the family piled into the limo, the APCs moved forward and escorted the limo to the embassy gate, and the three snipers appeared out of nowhere and reentered their embassy. The Cobras continued to swoop the streets in front of the APCs as they returned to Yongsan. The world cheered and relaxed.

"Good evening." The President spoke from his desk in the Oval Office. "I've asked to speak to you tonight because I want to make sure you are informed as to what is happening on the Korean Peninsula. No doubt you have seen news stories, television coverage and reports that may or may not tell the whole story. Suffice it to say, we have a situation which we are prepared to deal with, but which has and may put American citizens in harm's way. Three days ago the North Korean government took three U.N. weapons inspectors hostage and killed four more. These inspectors were on a sanctioned mission to inspect the suspected weapons grade plutonium factory in Yongbyon, North Korea. The three held hostage were two American citizens and a Canadian. Those murdered were from Australia, Germany, India and Belgium. The North Koreans are blaming this atrocity on the fact that our Navy stopped one of their ships in the Persian Gulf, and their ship's captain and first mate were killed. This ship was carrying illegal weapons grade plutonium and missile parts to the regime in Iraq. Their captain and first mate committed suicide after trying in vain to set the ship on fire. Basically, the Koreans were caught doing exactly what the U.N. has outlawed and what we in this country cannot stand for – they were caught trying to provide arms to terrorists bent on harming the United States or our allies."

"Last night we launched a mission to rescue the hostages in North Korea and to destroy the weapons factory at Yongbyon. Although most of our allies did not agree, I was not about to let American citizens stay in harm's way. We had pre-positioned a team of special forces in country and launched a rescue and strike mission from two of our Air Force bases in South Korea. Unfortunately the mission was compromised and the Koreans knew we were coming. The hostages, their rescuers and one of our fighter pilots were all lost." The President was lying to the American people, but more importantly in his mind, he was promoting a cover story that he hoped would work to rescue the three wayward souls on the ground. As of now, most of the world has condemned our actions. But I will make no apologies, except to the families of the Americans lost. I am sorry we were not successful in our rescue attempt, but I assure the families, the losses of their loved ones will not be for naught. We will protect ourselves and our people. As you probably saw on television earlier today, we were successful in rescuing one very brave American mother and her two young children from the thugs running the streets of Seoul, South Korea. The South Korean government has lost control of their people and as of now they want us out of their country. I am inclined to give them what they want, but the well being of South Korea is vital to our national security. America will not deal with rioters, terrorists, or rogue nations. We will protect our interests and our assets, and most importantly, our people. Our extended future on the Korean peninsula is up for debate right now. However, I assure you, the immediate future of the thousands of troops and civilians in South Korea right now is not. We will fight our way out if necessary, and leave the rest to history – if necessary. Thank you, and rest assured we will keep you informed. May God bless the families of our lost citizens, and may God Bless America."

CHAPTER TWENTY

PYONGYANG

As the supreme leader of North Korea, Kim Jong Un had complete control of everything – everything that is, except his faculties. Kim was described by many western observers as "certifiable." He was certainly demonstrating it today. With word of the attack on Yongbyon, his first order was a declaration of war against America and South Korea. Fortunately, calmer heads prevailed and his advisors were able to calm him down a bit. Nevertheless, his ranting and ravings got the people in a frenzy and exaggerated claims of the deaths of thousands of women and children in Yongbyon helped stir up the rest of the world.

Since there are very few televisions in North Korea, and those that existed were not allowed to be tuned to anything but the state run station, none of the activity in Seoul got out to the people. It did get to Kim, and his advisors wanted to use the fact that the South was uprising against the Americans to convince their leader that he should take advantage and move closer toward reunification. The fact was however, that Kim Jong Un had no intention of reunifying the Korean peninsula. He knew that if he did, the influence of the free society in the south would loosen his grip on the north. He had amassed an enormous personal wealth at the expense of the North Korean people and he had no intention of giving any of it up. He enjoyed the power he held over virtually every aspect of life in his "kingdom." He even had contemplated enacting a law that actually crowned him king, but he settled for "Supreme Leader" instead. Even when the American President alluded in his speech to his nation that the South Korean government was against the U.S., Kim suspected a trick.

"Is it true that all of the Americans are dead? I thought we were chasing them?" Kim asked his commanding army general in a meeting in his palace.

"We are Your Excellency. We believe there are only two left alive. One is a woman, and we think she is a former citizen of the area – a traitor." The general replied nervously. "We just found one dead American soldier and two mountain men from the area about 50 kilometers west of Yongbyon. They were all murdered."

"Tell me more about this woman. What are we doing to capture them? I want them alive if possible." Kim was not displaying a softness, but rather a devious plan to exploit the escapees if he could.

"We think she is this woman." The general handed his leader grainy photos taken of Melanie on the streets of Tokyo. "She goes by the name of 'Lee Han.' Her father was an American pilot our forces shot down during the Great War. He hid in our country rather than go back to his own and lived with a Korean woman in a village not far from Yongbyon. Our security forces got wind of the child and her brother and raided their village. They killed the American pilot and captured the young boy. He is still in our prison here in Pyongyang. You have seen pictures of him, Excellency. He is the blond man who looks very American, though he has always claimed he is one of us. The girl escaped to China with the help of a neighbor boy, Lee Chun. As it is now, Lee Chun is one of our best special warfare leaders. He was forced to help this girl at the time. But since then he has seen the ways of your father and your Excellency's leadership. He is a Colonel in our special forces, trained in the Soviet Union and he awaits in the outer chambers."

"But how do we know this is the same woman?" Kim was skeptical.

"The Russians have been tracking her actions, Excellency." The general felt he was losing his audience. "She has been working for the CIA for several years and they tracked her back to a childhood in China. We are almost certain she is the same girl. Her features are very similar to the man we have in prison. We believe the other American is an F-16 pilot we shot down the other night. Colonel Chun thinks they are heading for the coast to be picked up by another team of Americans. He has a plan to capture them all. It would be a huge coup for us, Your Excellency."

"Bring in Colonel Chun." Kim ordered.

Lee Chun was almost 50 years old. He had returned to his father's home after the trip to the coast with Melanie and kept his mission a secret for many years. He was sufficiently indoctrinated in the school system, and was "recruited" to join the army at the ripe age of 15. He was very bright and showed great promise – so much so that he was noticed by a Soviet major who was training the Koreans in guerrilla warfare. Lee was sent to Vladivostok and then to an interior Soviet training base for four years of intensive special warfare training. He returned to Pyongyang as a Captain in Kim Il Sun's Special Brigade. Lee went on several raids into South Korea and even managed to infiltrate a Japanese naval base for intelligence gathering purposes. In later years he took command of the North Korean training school for special warfare agents.

"Your Excellency." Chun bowed in front of his great leader. Kim nodded.

"So – you helped this woman to escape our country. Is that so?" Kim demanded. The generals were stunned. They did not want their top war fighter punished for something that happened 35 years ago.

"Excellency, that was.."

"Quiet! I know when it was. I also know it was treason. What do you have to say for yourself, Colonel?"

Chun was churning on the inside, but he remained very calm and collected. "Excellency, I did exactly what I was told. My father ordered me to take her to the coast. I did so. As I have learned from you through the years, sire – following orders is paramount for a good soldier. I was not a soldier then, but was destined to be one. Although I regret the fact that this traitor has turned into an American spy, I cannot say I would not do the same thing again if ordered to do so." He shot a glance at the nearest general who was shaking his lowered head in disbelief.

Kim thought for almost a full minute before responding. "So – how do you propose to get these two infidels?" He completely changed the subject. There was an inaudible sigh of relief from the generals.

"Sire, I believe they must be heading to the coast for a pick up by an American Seal team." Chun produced a map and rolled it out on a table. "The Russians have lost track of one of the American submarines that was last detected here heading in a northerly direction. In addition, an American C-130 flew towards our airspace from their base on Okinawa two nights ago. It went under our radar coverage, but it is conceivable that it delivered a Seal team to a submarine somewhere off our shores, about here." Chun pointed out the suspected route of the Marlin and the C-130. "Based on estimating an escape route from Yongbyon, the best area for a pick up would be here." Chun pointed to a relatively uninhabited area on the coast.

"I plan on taking two assault helicopters and 20 men, along with the prisoner we have in our jails to intercept the rendezvous. If we are fortunate, we will capture all of the Americans." Lee Chun had thought out his plan very thoroughly. Kim was impressed.

"Why do you need the prisoner?"

"Merely as a bargaining chip, Your Excellency. I suspect the woman will give up easily if she knows her brother is about to die. Although she would be a great prize for us, her brother is expendable. I do not expect to bring him back to clutter up our prisons any longer." Chun had thought of everything.

"When do you leave?" Kim asked.

"Within the hour, Excellency.... With your blessing of course. I expect it will take the woman and the American pilot another full day to travel to the coast. I also expect the Americans would build in a day or so of flexibility. Therefore, I think the Seals will try to come ashore tomorrow night or the night after. I plan to be waiting."

"Go. But bring this woman and the pilot to me alive." Kim ordered. Then, when Lee had left the room, to his commanding general Kim ordered, "Mobilize our army to attack the south. Be visible on the border. I want to test the resolve of the enemy. If this mission fails we will attack. Even if it is successful, we will avenge our people at Yongbyon. Tell our contacts in Seoul to find out exactly which way the South's government is leaning." The generals left the room to begrudgingly carry out their orders.

In Seoul things had calmed down a little. There were still huge throngs of demonstrators in front of the American Embassy and the gates of military bases of Yongsan and Osan. There was even a small contingent of students posted outside the front gate of Kunsan. The ROK military was on edge. They kept a wary eye on the Americans while looking more to the north for any reaction to the Yongbyon attacks. They stepped up patrols along the DMZ and increased their level of alert. All time off was canceled and the ROK forces were on full combat alert.

So were the American forces. Everyone who was capable was armed and had biological/chemical warfare equipment within arm's reach. In the meantime, they worked hard to prepare for deployment. The jets at Osan and Kunsan were once again loaded for bear – bombs, missiles and hot guns. Equipment was packed up and readied for loading onto cargo planes when they arrived. Each soldier and airman was allowed one "A-3 bag," a large canvas bag for personal clothing and equipment. Civilians were allowed the equivalent. Bags were collected and palletized, and all personnel were listed, categorized (critical, non-critical, combatants, etc.) and given a deployment number. At the fighter squadrons, missions were planned and briefed and everyone was preparing for war.

Elsewhere the U.S. armada was moving to support. The Seventh Fleet was steaming at full speed toward the South China Sea. Estimated Time of Arrival – 12 hours. Military Airlift Command C-17, C-141 and C-5 cargo jets were accumulating at Yokota and Kadena Air Bases in Japan, ready to launch into Korea to evacuate the troops. Air Force fighter bombers at Misawa and Kadena Air Bases in Japan were arming themselves to protect the American assets. Marines were doing the same at their bases, as were the Navy forces on board the carriers. The game plan had come directly from the top. A time frame for deployment/attack was given based on the expected pick up time of Melanie Han and Brad Mitchell. That aspect of when was kept Top Secret. All the forces knew was a time to be ready, not what was supposed to happen first.

Colonel Lee Chun and a crack squad of 20 North Korean special warfare agents launched from a base just south of Pyongyang in two huge Soviet built troop choppers. With them was Chin Ho Han, Melanie Han's brother. He was still in prison garb, filthy dirty and emaciated from years of malnutrition and mistreatment. He could walk, but with a severe limp and he had a hard time holding his head up. He had been beaten and his leg was actually broken when he was first brought to the prison as a young boy. As he grew in the prison cell, he was never moved to a larger room, and in fact he could not even stretch out in the small cubicle he was kept in. His skin was pale and dry and his hair was almost completely white, though filthy dirty now.

The choppers set down on the beach on a small inlet due west of Yongbyon. Chun deployed the men over a five mile stretch of coastline that he had selected as the most logical for a Seal team to attempt to infiltrate. Each man settled in with a radio, binoculars and the latest Soviet night vision goggles. In addition, listening devices were strung up and down the beach even farther. Chun set up in the middle with two other men and his prisoner, chained to a tree. They waited.

CHAPTER TWENTY ONE

INTERLUDE

Brad and Melanie moved as quickly as they could. They encountered no resistance and only came up on two villages with any evidence of civilization. But Brad's back was sore. He could only go for about an hour without some rest. Melanie was becoming impatient, but at the same time she had a strong feeling for this man. She wanted to help him and be with him, and she was confused at her own emotions. Brad also had a strong desire to please Melanie. Ever since that kiss back in the jungle he thought about little else. He watched her move, and he was amazed at the strength and stamina, yet grace and beauty that she personified.

Finally, nearing dusk on the third day they crested a hill that looked down on a small bay. The South China Sea was calm and serene. They decided to stay where they were until the next night when they were to rendezvous with the Seals. Melanie searched the coastline with her binoculars and they made a campsite of sorts – gathering straw and large leaves to make an area to sleep on. A fire was out of the question. They had crossed a stream in the last valley, and Melanie decided to go back and try to clean herself up as much as possible. She was still covered in the blood of the two Koreans she had butchered. They decided it would be best to stay together, and Brad figured he could use a bath or a shower anyway. They retreated down the hill and found an area of clean water flowing over the rocks and into a small pool.

Brad went in first. He did not hesitate to strip down, even though he felt Melanie's eyes watching him. He draped his clothes over a bush and submerged himself in the cold water. Melanie was a bit more bashful. She stripped down behind a tree and told Brad to turn away while she stepped into the water. They both splashed around like little kids, though trying to be as quiet as they could. It was a small pool and invariably they touched each other. At first Brad drew back when his hand accidentally touched Melanie's hip. Then, without warning she reached out and grabbed his hand and pulled him to her.

Melanie drew Brad in behind her and pulled his hands around her waist. Brad moved up against her and felt himself immediately respond. Melanie sighed when she felt his warmth and pressure and leaned her head back onto his shoulder. Her shining black hair draped over Brad and he gently kissed her cheek and neck. Melanie moved one of Brad's hands up to her breast. She moaned a long, slow sigh of contentment and Brad gently turned her around. Melanie wrapped her legs around Brad and he gently, softly and slowly penetrated her warm and ready body. They clung to each other in a gentle slow rhythm and in a long, romantic and passionate kiss. It was over in a short minute, but they were both satisfied and hung on to each other for a beautiful five minutes afterward.

Finally, Melanie shivered. The cold water overcame the heat of passion and they both were freezing. Without a word they kissed and got dressed. Both washed out as much of their bloody clothing as possible and they climbed up to their hideaway on the ridge. They hung out their clothes to dry and settled in together for a long rest while they could. At least, that was the plan.

Through the night they made love at least a half a dozen times. Sometimes slow and gentle. Sometimes wild and passionate. They talked and told each other everything there was to know about themselves. This time Melanie came clean. She told Brad the true version of her life. She managed to leave out the sordid details of her life as a prostitute and the other encounters she had as part of her job, but she even told him about her affair with a co-worker. By the end of the night they had slept very little, but professed their love for one another. What they didn't talk about was "What now?" What do they do when/if they get out of the predicament they were in?

The Marlin surfaced just after midnight and the Seal team was put off in two dark grey Zodiac boats. They each had a very small and quiet electric motor and they headed into shore. The Marlin then re-submerged to wait for its next rendezvous. She leveled off at 30 feet and extended an antenna that just broke the surface for a call back home to Fleet Headquarters. They also got a radio check with the Seal radioman. Loud and clear.

Chief McGee's GPS receiver pointed dead ahead and as they approached the beach he ordered the helmsmen to kill the engine. They paddled and rode the gentle surf in the rest of the way. As soon as they beached they pulled the boats up into the jungle and covered them as much as they could. Two men went back with branches and swept clear the foot prints and other evidence they had been there. Then the Seals dug in for a long day and spread out in a 40 yard wide semicircular pattern, each covering a quadrant of forest. McGee radioed back to the Marlin that they were in position, and the message was in turn passed to military headquarters in Hawaii, Japan, Korea and Washington.

One of Colonel Chun's men was the first to spot the Seals. He almost missed them, but at the last minute he saw the two boats hit the shore and then "disappear" into the jungle. He passed the word to Chun who acknowledged and then called in the rest of his team to a point about a half mile up the beach. He kept half of his force with him and sent the rest inland and then to the other side of the perpetrators, skirting their position and setting up to surround the enemy. The instructions were to move very slowly and to go at least a mile inland before turning parallel the coast. Once in position, the squad was to report in by radio. The plan was to form a corridor for the escapees to funnel into the Seals and then to close in around them. Instructions were given to avoid contact at all costs.

At Osan General Steve Woodward hatched a plan. He had been in contact with Nels Rushing, the Commander of the Wolfpack at Kunsan, and the two of them were concerned for the safety of Mitchell, Melanie and the Seal team. He ran the plan through Pacific Command and from there back to Washington. The fewer people that had to know about it the better. In Washington that came down to the Secdef, the Chairman of the JCS, the President and Johnny Joiner, Air Force Chief of Staff. The State Department was kept out of the loop, although it was decided to let the Ambassador in on the plan just minutes before it actually took place. That way she would not be so embarrassed when she received phone calls from pissed off and inquisitive Koreans.

Both the Marlin and the Seal team on shore had communications. Based on line of sight and power output, the Seals' radio would only reach the Marlin, but the sub's antenna and power boost allowed it to bounce off satellites to anywhere in the world. It was decided that the central command post would be Woodward's position at Osan. It was also decided to launch a round the clock AWACs platform with a dedicated refueling tanker and to put more tankers on standby at Kadena. At pick up time minus six hours the tankers would launch. At two hours prior a flight of four A-10 Warthogs would launch from Osan. Simultaneously eight F-16 Falcons would launch from Kunsan. They would all rendezvous with the tankers and wait until needed.

Melanie and Brad lolled around most of the day, keeping out of sight and enjoying their new found relationship. They finished all the food they had with them and Melanie managed to bag a large rat or mole, or some kind of slow, unsuspecting creature. They had to eat it raw, and it was not very good, but they knew they would need the energy. Periodically they would take turns surveying the shoreline and forest beneath them through the binoculars. At about noon Brad spotted some movement. It was 3-4 soldiers in Soviet style special forces uniforms quietly and slowly moving parallel the coast line about a mile inland. Melanie studied them intently.

"They are Special Warfare agents of the President's own guards. They must be onto something. They never leave Kim Jong Un's tight little circle. What could they be doing here?" Melanie thought out loud.

"Are they looking for us?" Brad asked.

"More likely they are looking for the Seals. They wouldn't know where to look for us." Melanie studied the area closer to the coast. She could see a small wisp of smoke from a campfire about a half mile north of their planned rendezvous point. "I'm thinking this could be a trap." She said. She searched the area where she thought the Seals should be, but could spot nothing. "Let's see if we can raise anyone on the radio.

Sentry 31 had launched from Kadena Air Base in Okinawa with a long mission planned. The idea was to head up and orbit just south of North Korean airspace and out to sea from South Korea as well. Air refueling support was due to join them in a few hours and they had two full crews onboard so they could stretch their mission even longer. Captain Stephanie Michaels was at the first communications console, mainly because no one expected any activity for a while and her supervisors figured she could cover the console while they got some sleep. "Steve" was a good controller, but sometimes a little over-zealous. She was in a relationship with an F-15 pilot at Kadena and sometimes she seemed to want to be his mother as well as his lover. She took every mission very seriously, even the basic training missions, acting like it was her duty to protect the force.

"Sentry or anybody, this is Conan over." The call was weak and broken, but since the AWACs was still over a hundred miles south, it was surprising to Stephanie that she could even hear anything.

"Conan, this is Sentry 31. You're about three by sir." The controller was telling her contact that she could hear him, but with only about 60% strength.

"Roger Sentry, we're near our rendezvous point. Let's go Channel Alpha." Brad did not want to broadcast on the world wide emergency net where everyone was. They switched over to one of the alternate frequencies and Stephanie authenticated Brad to be sure he was who he said he was.

"Roger Conan. Good authentication. What can I do for you sir? How are you holding up?" Stephanie was playing "mom" again.

"We're ok. We're overlooking the rendezvous point, but it looks like we have company down there. Looks like North Korean special forces, over."

"Ok, copy that Conan. Standby. Let me see if I can raise the Navy and pass this on to Osan." Stephanie switched to her high frequency (HF) radio and put in a call each to the Marlin and to General Woodward"s headquarters at Osan. It was only then that she was apprised of the plan in place, and she decided she'd better wake her supervisor.

Commander Moran was informed of the call from AWACs and decided to pass the information on to the Seals. Chief McGee was surprised. His men had seen or heard nothing from their vantage points near the rendezvous. McGee pulled everyone in and briefed them to be more vigilant and to be ready for action.

General Woodward too was alerted that contact had been made between AWACs and Brad. It was decided to pass on details of the recovery plan. Brad got excited at the thought of seeing some friendly Air Force types flying overhead. But Melanie was less than enamored with the whole thing. She kept studying the forest with the binoculars, and worrying that there was a trap in place and that they were the bait.

Back at Kunsan, Ed Howe had put together an eight ship package of his best pilots. They had done their homework and mission planning and were just standing by, waiting for it to get dark. Their plan was to launch off and use the superb thrust to weight ratio of the F-16 to climb in full afterburner almost straight up immediately. That way they would avoid any air defenses that the South Koreans might want to turn into air offenses to keep the Americans from launching another attack from Korean soil. The A-10s from Osan would not have the luxury of a climb like that. The "Warthog" was slow and underpowered. However, it had an excellent turning radius. The plan from Osan was to take off and spiral up over the base, making tight turns and keeping the jet directly overhead until out of range of most surface to air weapons. Neither of these tactics is foolproof. If the South Koreans wanted to, they could shoot at the jets from just off base and create quite a spectacle. The gamble was that the South Korean government would not be quite so stupid as to shoot down an American jet that was obviously no threat -- other than diplomatically.

The stage was set. A small inlet on the west coast of North Korea was about to become the scene of a major conflict if things went wrong – or even if they went right, depending on whose point of view one used. If the Americans were successful and extracted Melanie and Brad, the North Koreans lost even more face and Kim Jong Un might just start something nobody wanted to see. If Melanie and Brad were captured, President Robert Madigan had promised his people and his cabinet he would retaliate. No matter what happened, the situation between the U.S. and Seoul governments had deteriorated to beyond repair in the opinion of many of the pundits. The rest of the world was taking a wait and see attitude, secretly hoping the Americans would get rid of the "pest" in Pyongyang, but publicly condemning American pompousness and arrogance. Time would tell.

CHAPTER TWENTY TWO

RENDEZVOUS

Melanie had decided it would take them about 2-3 hours to negotiate the mile or so of forest between their hilltop vantage point and the rendezvous. They would have to move very slowly and quietly in the dark and once they left the nice view they had now, the forest would engulf them. All they would be able to do was follow the GPS pointer and hope they got close. They dirtied themselves up as much as they could with makeshift camouflage. They had made sure their weapons were fully loaded, although they hoped not to get into a fire fight with North Korean special warfare agents trained by Russians. At about 9 P.M. they crawled off their hill and into the woods.

At 10 P.M. the Warthogs launched from Osan, followed shortly thereafter by the Juvats from Kunsan. They made a lot of noise and it was a pretty sight, watching the F-16 afterburner basically disappear into the night sky. There was no reaction from the South Korean air defenses, but phones started ringing off the hook. Ambassador Brexler, General Shad and General Woodward were inundated with phone calls from Korean government, military and even media leaders. They all pleaded ignorance, which was easy for General Shad. He was never read in on the plan, a fact he was none too pleased about, but one call to the SecDef in Washington and he knew enough to keep his mouth shut.

The launches went off smoothly. The F-16s had taxied 10 to get eight airborne and the A-10s had a spare at the end of the runway as well. None of the spares were needed and they returned to the chocks. The flights joined up with the tankers from Kadena and set up an orbit just south of the AWACs.

President Madigan had convened an inner circle of advisors in the White House War Room. The SecDef, Chairman of the Joint Chiefs, CNO, Air Force Chief of Staff, CIA Director, SecState and the White House Chief of Staff were all there. Those that hadn't been in on the planning were briefed on the operation taking place. Secretary Anderson tried to raise an objection, but she soon saw that the mood in the room was not one conducive to any "dove-ish" ideas. It was also obvious that she was only invited to handle what damage control she could when the world started objecting to this American "aggression." The phone rang.

It was President Lee from Seoul. Madigan put him on speaker phone. "Good evening President Lee. How are things in your fair city tonight?" Madigan was making light of a potentially dark situation.

"Mr. President, I demand to know what you are up to. Why have American fighter jets flown from Osan and Kunsan Air Bases?" Lee was nervously furious.

"Why Mr. President, I am surprised. Did you not order our forces to leave your country? This is just the first of many who are complying with your wishes." The President lied very well. "By the way, my intelligence tells me the North Koreans are massing their forces just north of your border. Are you sure you don't want our help?"

There was a very long pause at the other end of the phone. Lee was obviously conferring with advisors. "We do not believe their movements to be anything more than a reaction to your previous aggression. Our communications with the North have not indicated an intent of hostility." Lee finally replied. "However, we do not believe that you would be deploying your forces back to America in the middle of the night and with such a dramatic exit. Our radar shows them grouped to the west in an orbit with other aircraft. What are you planning on doing Mr. President? Do not under-estimate our resolve."

Madigan lost a little bit of his cool. "I have learned over the last few days not to estimate anyone's resolve amongst our so called allies, Mr. Lee." Secretary Anderson winced. "By the way, I want to offer my congratulations for your lack of resolve in neither helping nor hindering the Ambassador's forces as they rescued our American citizens off the streets of Seoul yesterday. They are safe and sound now, although we still have a few people we cannot account for. I assume you are doing your best to protect them from the hooligans who apparently control your cities now. Now, as far as our aircraft off shore, I will have to contact them and ask them to move out of your radar coverage so that their presence does not give you any more concern. Good night, Mr. President."

Once again the American President hung up on his Korean counterpart. He turned to the Secretary of State. "Ok Madam Secretary, as soon as this little operation is over, assuming we are successful, go to work mending your fences if you can. However, I want a clear and coordinated consensus between you and our intelligence agencies as to whether these fences are even worth our time. I have had it with these people and with kissing their asses every time we turn around. Give me a good reason why we need to stick around on the Korean peninsula. I want that assessment within 48 hours. Any questions?" He looked at his CIA Director and the SecState who both nodded they understood the directive.

"What if we are not successful tonight, Sir?" It was the President's own Chief of Staff who dared ask.

"That's why we're all here now." Madigan looked around the room. "What's the worst case?"

Secretary Matson spoke up first. "I suppose it's the possibility that the Seals and the nomads are captured or killed."

"If I may sir, I believe our biggest threat is a reaction from Kim Jong Un, regardless of the outcome of tonight's operation." Director Durkee sounded ominous. "If he loses face, I sincerely believe he will attack the South. Even if he is successful in capturing our citizens and parading them around the streets of Pyongyang, he could easily take the opportunity to move south." There was general agreement in the room that this would be the worst scenario. As long as the U.S. still had forces on the peninsula, and realistically, even if the forces had already deployed, America would have to come to the aid of the South Koreans. Japan also would likely join in, because they could not afford to have a historical enemy so close to their own soil. There would be pressure on the Russians and the Chinese to aid the North, though no one expected they would do so – at least not overtly. The big problem would be how the rest of the world viewed the whole thing. The Brits, Aussies and maybe a few others of our close allies would line up with the U.S., but witnessing the latest position taken by much of the world, most would blame the U.S. no matter what happened.

Madigan resisted the temptation to say "Screw the rest of the world," although he certainly wanted to. Instead he thought for a minute and then addressed the group. "Ok. Where are we on the planning and timing of an all out strike on the North? I want a quick and severe hit. I want Kim Jong Il's head on a platter. We need minimum collateral damage, but give the generals and admirals the leeway to do their job."

"Sir, obviously the more forces we can have in position the better, but the fleet and our deploying Air Force units can be in position in two days." It was Chairman of the Joint Chiefs Marquez. "Targets are being scoped out now. Our first hits will be on air defenses, then the palace and government buildings. Finally, we take out as many nuclear facilities and military installations as we can. The big problem is that we do not have the intelligence on the ground in Pyongyang that we need. We really can only guess at where Kim will be. To be honest – if we get him, it will be the 'golden BB.'" The President shot a glare at Director Durkee.

"I'm afraid the General is correct sir." Durkee tried to defend his agency. "Although we have a handful of agents in North Korea, the communications in and out are archaic at best. In addition, we have not been able to penetrate Kim's inner circle. He trusts no one and he is a master of disguise. He comes and goes as he pleases, but he has doubles and stand-ins at every street corner. I'm sure you remember our unsuccessful attempt to get him a year or so ago. I think the only way to even be close to thinking we got him is a massive strike that basically takes out half the City of Pyongyang."

"Surely sir, you don't ….." Secretary Anderson tried to protest, but cut herself off when she felt the wrath of her President's glare.

"You know, I can sympathize with Kim when you say he can trust no one." Madigan fired a shot at everyone. No one knew whether to take it personally or not, except Secretary Anderson. She did. The president offered her a carrot. "Melissa, what about the Chinese and the Russians? Can we work on them to rein in this turkey? Like you all, I don't suspect they will come down against us militarily, but can we get them to help us?"

"They both have people in North Korea, sir – both as advisors and especially as entrepreneurs. The Russians especially are after significant mineral rights in the country. However, for that reason as well, they would not want us to level the place. The Chinese see the North Koreans as inferior and Kim as more a fly in the ointment than anything else. It's possible we might be able to get them to threaten sanctions – both of them." The Secretary was beginning to feel useful again.

"All right people, keep pressing. Prepare for the worst. If we lose our folks tonight, or worse, if they are captured, consider them casualties of war and start that war as soon as we can. Use the forces we have identified so far. If you can cram more into the fray, so be it, but don't delay. In the meantime, Melissa, bring me that assessment of our extended status in South Korea. As many who wish to are welcome to stay here through the operation tonight. But, if you have stuff to get done, get to it." The President was being Commander in Chief. They waited for word from the front.

The men in Colonel Chun's outer ring of forces were very still and quiet. At about 11:30 one of them heard some rustling in the bushes. It sounded like an animal moving slowly toward the coast. He could not see anything, but he alerted his comrades by radio. Melanie and Brad had been detected. They kept moving, stopping every few yards to listen ….. nothing. The Koreans closed in behind them and slowly, quietly followed. They were experts at this, while Brad Mitchell was big, clumsy, injured and tired. Melanie was slightly better off, but she too was very tired and concerned that they were walking into a trap. A justifiable concern.

Soon Melanie could hear the lapping of the waves on the shore not too far ahead of them. That was good news. The bad news was that the sound served to muffle out the noise made by the force massing behind them.

"Hold it!" A voice said quietly, but sternly. Brad just about jumped out of his skin. The voice came from no more than 10 feet in front of him and he could see nothing but the dark silhouette of a bush. He froze. Melanie reached out and touched his arm. He heard her chamber and cock her AK-47. The bush moved.

"No. No! Put the weapon on the ground." The bush said softly. "We are American Navy. Identify yourselves." Brad breathed a sigh of relief. They quickly confirmed who they were and the man disguised as a bush led them out to the edge of the forest and down to the south a few hundred yards. There they met up with Master Chief McGee.

There were quick introductions and a few questions about the first Seal team, especially from Wicox's brother. McGee kept it professional and cut off the interrogation. "We've got work to do people. Let's contact the Marlin."

The radioman signaled the Marlin and was in the middle of passing the fact they had completed the rendezvous when there was gunfire from the perimeter. In a matter of seconds they were surrounded by North Korean soldiers and severely outnumbered. McGee quickly realized he had no choice but to surrender. One of his men was killed in the quick skirmish. One other was pushed into the center of their group, his weapon confiscated. Colonel Chun walked out into the open.

"Lay down your weapons American infidels." Chun said in broken English. Melanie felt a twinge of sensation. There was something familiar about that voice. She started to speak in Korean.

"Silence traitor!" Chun snapped. "Or you will join your brother as a casualty of war." Melanie was startled and confused. Her brother? Who was this guy?

"What is it you want?" McGee spoke up. "We are here to retrieve our citizens and then leave your country. We mean no harm to anyone."

"Tell that to our countrymen who these two butchered back in the hills and to the hundreds of women and children this coward murdered with his bombs." Chun thrust his gun barrel in Brad's stomach, doubling him over with a gasp. "You will all come with us. Our President awaits you."

"We aren't going anywhere with you. We are leaving in our boats or we will die right here." McGee was holding the line and none of his remaining men had relinquished their weapons.

"Lee Chun? Is that you?" Melanie thought she recognized the face of the Colonel as the teenage boy who had helped her escape many years ago.

"Quiet woman!" Chun spoke firmly, but not shouting – keeping his eye on McGee and McGee's gun. "You do not know me, and I do not know you. You deserted your country many years ago. I have atoned for my sins and have served the Great Leader."

Melanie was more and more convinced with every word that this man was the same boy she credited with saving her life, but she decided now was not the time to discuss it.

During all of this, Radioman Wilcox had kept the microphone of his radio keyed. Commander Josh Moran heard everything from the Marlin. He quickly got on the horn to AWACs and General Woodward at Osan. Within minutes the Juvats led by Ed Howe and the A-10s pushed off from their orbit and headed directly toward the Seal team's position. Stephanie Michaels was busy at her console on AWACs, making sure everyone could relay whatever direction they needed through her. She finally felt needed.

Howe pushed the nose of his jet over and lit the afterburner. They had recently topped off their tanks in the refueling track and within seconds they were all doing about 1.4 Mach (1.4 times the speed of sound). The inertial navigation system and GPS said the "target area" was on the nose and 11 minutes away at this speed. From AWACs they got the Marlin's frequency and a quick call to the sub told them what frequency to find the Seal's on. Howe sent his flight over to the Seals VHF frequency with instructions to listen only – no transmissions. Any in flight transmission by the Juvats were to be made on the FM or UHF radios.

Colonel Chun was confused and angry. He shouted at his men and they moved forward to disarm the Americans. "You will drop your weapons now or I will start with this coward and kill each of you one at a time." Chun motioned and one of his men clubbed Brad, took his gun and held him up for Chun to further threaten.

Melanie stepped forward. "Stop!" She yelled in Korean. "Take me and leave the rest. It is I who you want anyway. I am the one who betrayed my country. I am the one who killed the mountain men. I am the one who ordered the air strike." She piled it on thick – some true, some a bit over inflated.

Chun was not impressed. He responded in his native tongue. "That's an interesting concept, Miss Han. Perhaps then you could be persuaded to convince your friends to comply with my requests." He shouted out to someone hiding in the forest. Soon, a blond man in Korean clothes and with his hands shackled was pushed out into the clearing. Melanie gasped. It was her brother. She tried to move to him, but she was restrained by an AK-47 and a very ugly soldier.

"I believe you will recognize this man, Miss Han. He is your brother, another traitor of the State, spawned from the same disgusting relationship as you were after the Great War. He has been a prisoner, taking up space in our jails for decades, and he is expendable to us. I suggest you convince these stupid Americans to turn over their weapons now or this infidel will die along with the American pilot." Chun had Melanie in a real predicament.

Her flesh and blood and the man she had come to love – both in danger of losing their lives.

Melanie's brother was weak and emaciated. His eyes were bloodshot and he looked to be drugged. But he obviously understood what was being said and he looked at Melanie with both awe and disdain. He saw no good way out of this for himself. "Ptooey! I spit on this woman. I am not of her lot. I am loyal to our Great Leader. Spare me, sire." He threw himself at Chun's feet. Chun looked down disgusted and kicked the coward off to one side. A soldier grabbed him and yanked him to his feet.

"It seems you are surrounded by cowards, Miss Han. Should we just kill them for you?"

"What's going on, Mel?" It was Brad. He could see that Melanie knew the blond man and she was definitely affected by what the Colonel was saying.

"This man is my brother whom I have not seen for almost 30 years. They want me to convince you all to give up or they will kill him and you, Brad." She looked at Brad with warm, loving eyes. The glance did not go unnoticed.

"I hate to break up the party folks, but I'm the one in charge here." McGee was feeling his oats. He turned to Chun. "Colonel, it seems you have a problem. With the possible exception of that coward you brought with you, none of these people are going to come with you … alive. It seems to me you have only one choice here and that is to let us go quietly. You can work out how you can save face with your leadership."

Chun became enraged. "Corporal!" he yelled at one of his men and motioned by pointing to the middle of the circle that had formed in front of them. The soldier nearest Brad pushed and kicked him severely, tumbling him into a heap at the colonel's feet. "I will take pleasure in killing you first, infidel." Chun screamed as he pointed his revolver at Mitchell's head.

Just then all hell broke loose. Coach Howe had heard it all and dove for the coastline directly at the box on his Heads Up Display that designated where his GPS thought the action was. He had directed the rest of the flight to follow but at about a 1000 feet higher. It was dark and the terrain was severe – no place for a wingman to be trying to fly formation at extremely low altitude. Howe came across the group on the ground at significantly faster than the speed of sound. The "boom" of his breaking the Mach was ear shattering. The noise of the jet engine itself was deafening and the jungle shook and blew with the vibration of the mach stem screaming by. Everyone on the ground either jumped out of their skin or dove for cover. It was complete chaos – just what Howe had hoped for.

Chief McGee took advantage and his men followed suit. They were the first to recover and a short firefight ensued. Six of Chun's men were dropped in their tracks. Eight more were still scrambling around for cover. Melanie was able to free herself and rolled into a bush toward McGee. The closest Seal to Brad dragged him off into the dark. Chun was left standing alone in a clearing with only himself and Melanie's cowering shackled brother.

"Seal Team Alpha, the Juvats are at your service. Anything we can do for you?" Howe was smug and hoped his arrival had been successful. The radioman acknowledged his presence.

"Roger Juvats. We certainly heard you. Standby for further action." He crawled over to McGee and let him know he had radio contact with the fighters. McGee was otherwise occupied.

"Colonel Chun, drop your weapon. You are surrounded and I will not hesitate to shoot." McGee stepped out in front of the Korean. It was a face off. There was sporadic gunfire from the woods – more likely Chun's men shooting at shadows in their effort to escape.

"Comrades, show yourselves! Shoot this man!" Chun screamed in Korean as he froze, not taking his eyes off McGee. They both aimed their weapon at the other's chest. There was no reaction from the dark reaches of the clearing – at least not from the Koreans. One by one, the Seals made themselves barely visible, still keeping one eye each out for movement from the perimeter. Melanie ran to Brad and they too stood on the edge of the area. There was a long, quiet pause. It was obvious that the remaining Koreans had either fled the scene, or they knew they were in no position to help their colonel.

"Drop it now, Colonel. Don't make this any more difficult." McGee spoke softly but firmly. "That was an F-16 – one of several loaded with bombs and rockets. There is another flight of A-10 fighter bombers right behind them. If they have to they will annihilate this entire jungle, with all of us in it. You cannot escape unless you cooperate with us."

Colonel Chun looked around him. He paused when he saw Melanie and Brad, almost rekindling the fire in his eyes. Then he softened. He lowered his gun, but did not drop it. "You must allow me to save face. I will not return a failure."

"Come with us, Colonel" Melanie said in Korean, stepping forward and toward her brother. "The Americans will treat you right. You would be a valuable asset." Melanie quickly translated what she had said to McGee and the rest.

"Ma'am, I'm not sure we can…" McGee tried to protest. He stopped when he got the hardest stare he had ever experienced from a woman.

"There are too many of my men out there alive." Chun replied softly in Korean, indicating he was not completely averse to the idea, just worried if it didn't work. Melanie translated.

It was Brad who came up with a solution. "The Juvats and Warthogs can take care of that. Unless those guys are miles away already, we could turn this beach into a parking lot of death and destruction."

"We could never be sure we got them all." Melanie replied. Then she had an idea. "Radioman, contact your submarine. How many extra bodies can they take." McGee tried to protest again. This time he got the cold palm of Melanie's hand in a "hold it, Chief" signal. He nodded for the corpsman to make the call.

"Colonel, how far out do you expect your men are, and how many are there?" Melanie asked Chun.

Colonel Chun looked around at the bodies he could see. "I suspect there are 14 to 15 left and all within listening range. What are you thinking?"

"If you tell them to, will they return and surrender to us?" Melanie translated as she went.

"Absolutely! They will do exactly what they are told, but I will not sacrifice my men. I do not believe you when you say we will be cared for. I wish to end my life honorably, but not the lives of all my men as well. I will not make that decision for them, nor will I put them in that situation." Chun was not cooperating.

Melanie walked over to the radioman. "Give me the fighters." She commanded.

"Yes Ma'am. And the Marlin says they can take only 5-10 more than our team and you and the Major, Ma'am." He switched the radio frequency to the Juvats and handed her the microphone.

"Juvat Lead, this is Dingaling, do you copy." She still hated that callsign, but now was not the time to change it.

Coach Howe was a bit surprised to hear a female voice, but he realized who it was. "Roger Dingaling, got you five by."

"Juvat, when you flew overhead you were slightly offset to our north – maybe 50 yards. I'm going to launch a flare and we need you to light up the forest all around us. Get close, but try to spare us from the carnage." Melanie looked at McGee who pulled out a flare. Then she looked intently at Colonel Chun.

"One last chance Colonel." The Korean did not flinch.

McGee launched the flare into a small clearing in the trees. Howe immediately acknowledged "Flare in site, Juvats are in." The Seal Team hunkered down while Colonel Chun stood straight and tall.

The night sky lit up like the Fourth of July and the noise was deafening. The bombs went off within 50 yards of the group, but fortunately the thickness of the forest kept the fragmentation from hitting anyone in the immediate vicinity. Not so for the bulk of Chun's men spread out in the woods. Although there was no way to tell how many had been hit, there were moans and screams of pain and death after the explosions subsided.

"Nice shootin' Juvats. Now stand by for further direction." Melanie had taken charge.

"Roger Ma'am. We've got three bombs each left. Can give them to you in a string or one at a time." Howe came back.

"Colonel Chun, once again – call your people in. If you do not, the next set of bombs will be targeted on you. We will march you out onto the beach and make you visible to the bombers." Melanie wasn't kidding around. McGee took it all in with amusement. Brad's feeling was more of amazement. He was in love with this woman, but more than a little afraid of what she could do.

Chun still held his pistol in his right hand. He slowly looked around him as if surveying the situation. One by one the Seals had stepped back out into the clearing. McGee was still pointing his rifle at the Korean's chest. What happened next was quick and violent.

"Comrades, attack! Attack! Do not give up. Do not let these infidels escape!" Chun screamed as loud as he could in Korean. At the same time he jumped and rolled over to where Melanie's brother was cowering in a lump. Chun screamed at Melanie. "I will kill him or we will walk out of here together – you, your brother and me."

McGee was startled. He wanted to shoot the bastard, but wasn't sure about this American looking shield that Chun crouched behind. Melanie too was torn between blood and country, but only for a moment. She lifted her weapon – the AK-47 she had lifted from the last Korean she had killed – and unleashed a burst of fire, killing her brother immediately and hitting Colonel Chun in the shoulder and hip. He rolled off to one side, sat up straight, almost like in a yoga position, lifted his pistol putting the barrel in his mouth, and pulled the trigger. The forest was quiet.

Melanie ran to her brother, knelt down beside him, checked his pulse, softly closed his eyes with her fingertips, and breathed a long audible side. Brad came to her and Melanie melted into his arms sobbing uncontrollably.

"We gotta go, folks." McGee took back over command. He waved his men to the beach. Brad pulled Melanie away from her brother and they followed. They pulled the Zodiacs out of the cover they had made from branches and leaves and dragged them down to the water, all the time with two men keeping watch on the forest for any sign of Korean soldiers responding to Colonel Chun's last command.

"Chief, what about the fighters?" The radioman asked. McGee looked to Melanie for advice. Brad stepped in.

"Seems to me the fewer witnesses we leave the better, Chief. What do you think? The F-16s and the A-10s behind them can do some hefty damage on this place." Brad wished he was flying one of those jets right now.

"Not sure that's our decision, sir …. But I'll ask." McGee replied then took the microphone.

"Juvats, this is Foxtrot. We're egressing to sea now. Can you give us covering fire on and around the original target? The Korean leader is dead, but some of his men are out there with orders to capture us." McGee made his case.

"Roger that, Foxtrot. The Warthogs are on station as well. Can you give us a flare when you push off? We'll make crispy critters out of them." Howe did not even hesitate although the 'crispy critter' comment is one he would regret later.

"Roger that Juvat. Flare's away." McGee popped a flare and it launched up into the sky as they pushed the boats out into the surf. The good news was that the fighters could see the "friendlies." The bad news was that so could the Koreans. There was sporadic fire at them from the shore line. One Seal was hit and one of the boats took a round as well.

"Juvats, fire from just north of our position – probably 100 yards up the beach." Brad had grabbed the radioman's microphone.

"Tallyho, Conan. Juvats are in." Howe recognized his squadron commander's voice. He rolled his Viper into a tight turn and dove straight at the muzzle flashes on the shore. He dropped his last three bombs in a string, and all the F-16s followed. That part of the beach and forest was soon ablaze in an inferno that looked like a California wildfire. Nothing within a half mile of the drop zone could have survived.

The A-10s did the rest. They sprayed bombs and cluster munitions all over the area. Then they rolled in with their big cannons and hosed the whole area down with gunfire. If there was anyone or anything alive in the general vicinity, they were gravely injured. The A-10s "escorted" the boats back to the rendezvous point with the Marlin, just in case there was any attempt to intercept from shore. They set up a figure eight pattern above the boats at about 3000 feet while the F-16s climbed out toward the tanker to take on fuel and be available for any air to air action. They also had a loaded and armed gun if necessary for follow on strafe requirements.

The wounded Zodiac was designed to be able to take a round or two of gunfire. They had several chambers of air and self-repairing capability. The trip out to sea was uneventful and the Marlin surfaced right on time and target. Within an hour the only evidence of activity on the North Korean coast was a smoldering fire in an area the size of a small city.

The Marlin submerged after taking on her passengers and made a beeline for Naha Naval Base on Okinawa. The Juvats and Warthogs also recovered on Okinawa, at Kadena Air Base. It seems their departure had roused suspicion and the wrath of the government in Seoul. President Madigan had followed the entire proceedings as the mission unfolded. Since President Lee had been hostile and threatening, the brass decided not to take the chance recovering back on the Korean peninsula, especially since Madigan had described their departure a few hours before as permanent.

Now it was a waiting game and a matter of mending political fences.

CHAPTER TWENTY THREE

AFTERSHOCK - TREMBLE

It took several days for Pyongyang to figure out what had happened. Only two of Colonel Chun's commandos survived the bombings. One was so critically wounded he couldn't be moved from a local village and he could not even speak. The other was unscathed, but mainly because he had run so far and fast at the first pass by Coach Howe's jet that he was far enough away when the bombs came raining down. He had no idea what had taken place, and in fact, had not returned to the scene to try and hook up with his unit. He had basically deserted. When he was discovered by army officials he made up whatever story he could to stay out of trouble. No one was sure what to believe.

Several local villages were affected by the bombing and there were villagers willing to describe at least the attacks from the air and the sporadic gunfire on the ground that preceded them. Remains of Colonel Chun and a few others were recovered, though

251

badly burned and maimed. The army leadership could only guess at what to tell their Great Leader. It was obvious however, that there were no Americans and no direct evidence of a foreign "invasion." Kim Jong Un was furious, but fortunately for the rest of the world, he was not stupid. He also knew that things were in an unraveled state in Seoul, and that patience might be the best trait he could exhibit right now. Patience however, was not one of Kim's best assets. He ordered his Army to increase its presence even more on the DMZ and made lots of noise through diplomatic channels about how the South and the Americans were in cahoots and had "savagely attacked his country, killing hundreds of innocent civilians."

In Seoul matters were still in a state of disarray. The government basically had minimum control, but as long as Americans kept a low profile, the students and radicals seemed satisfied to just get together periodically and yell and scream and find an excuse to party. The military was very nervous however. They saw the forces massing to the north, and they knew that if the North Korean horde came over the line, there would be no way to stop them before they got to Seoul. More than one ROK general had often wished his capitol city was not so close to the action. Even though South Korea was a democracy, there still was very strong military influence on the government. Generals were powerful. All of the strong politicians had been military generals in a distinguished first career. Most importantly to international relations however, there were very few leaders in the ROK government and military who actually believed they could ever defend themselves from attack from the north without American help. It wasn't so much a matter of numbers – even a mass of all the American troops on Korean soil would be nothing more than a speed bump to the North Korean juggernaut. The technology the U.S. possessed in its arsenal, and especially the nuclear weapons threat were quite possibly all that had kept Kim Jong Un, and his father before him, from marching south sooner. Even President Lee was soon convinced that he had to retract his demand that the Americans withdraw. That, he thought, would be the easy part. The hard part would be convincing his own people and keeping peace in the streets. He felt he must have some concession from the Americans as a "peace offering" to keep the rabble from rebelling.

In Washington the mood was jubilant. The Seals and Mitchell were all in route back to American soil with only minor scratches, and the aircraft recovered at Kadena unscathed. The plan had gone well, and since the rest of the world knew little or nothing about what they would describe as the U.S. playing the "cowboy" role, generally there was a sigh of relief. The only problems now were the situation in South Korea and the massive army to their north. One more time the President's phone rang.

"Mr. President, I assume your forces have returned safely to wherever you are hiding them." President Lee tried to put his American counterpart on the defensive. Not a great idea.

"President Lee, as I told you, our forces were merely following your orders – or at least the orders of whoever leads your country now." Madigan shot back. "We were leaving for friendlier ally bases. By the way, my intelligence sources tell me that the North Korean army just north of your border is armed with Scud missiles – probably targeted at you right now. I assume you have a safe place to hide should they attack?"

"We still do not believe the North will attack us, but that is what I called you about." The Korean President sounded nervous. Madigan shot a glance at his Secretary of State, who also seemed very nervous.

"You have a proposition for us?" Madigan questioned. "I assume you bring with it a guarantee that all Americans on your soil will be safe and safe guarded?"

"I am doing my best to do just that, Mr. President. In fact, my proposal should help to insure their safety. Both the leadership in the north and the students and activists in my own party will be appeased, and hopefully we can get our relationship back to normal." Lee was almost pleading. Secretary Anderson sat forward in her seat, eager to hear the proposal.

"A normal relationship?" Madigan warmed up. "A few hours ago it seemed we had no relationship and you ordered all of our citizens and forces out of your country. Now you want to get back to normal? What do you have in mind?"

"A token removal of some of your forces." Lee put forth. "I'm not sure what would be appropriate. Perhaps you and your Cabinet could tell me. I am looking for a removal of American forces enough that would cause Kim Jong Un to back down on his side of the border, and our more radical politicians and people to calm down. Perhaps your nuclear forces at Kunsan Air Base?"

Secretary Anderson frowned and SecDef Matson shook his head vigorously. Madigan noticed their response and motioned for them to maintain silence.

"President Lee, I will be very honest with you. Since your edict to us a few hours ago, and because of the obvious dislike for Americans right now in the streets of your cities, I have asked my people to tell me why we should remain in your country at all." The President looked at his SecState and CIA Chief. "Unless they come up with a better reason than to protect you from the hordes to the North that most of your people would rather be in bed with anyway, you can expect our forces to continue to leave, and we will be out of your country completely by the deadline you gave us. However, now that you have apparently changed your tune, I will need a little time to respond. In the meantime however, you need to determine what you are willing to do for us. The United States will not be at the mercy of a bunch of thugs in the streets of Seoul and in your Parliament, anymore than we will bow to some mad man who lives to your north. If we decide to pull only a token force out of Korea, what will you do to enhance the safety of those left behind and to bring stability back to your government?"

"You are correct, sir. This will take some time." Lee responded after a minute. "But we may not have much time. If you are correct about the Scud missiles, I need to do something now."

"Tell you what, President Lee…..you get on the phone or whatever communications you have with Pyongyang and tell them that if they do not pull back their forces immediately, the entire combined forces of South Korea and America will attack." Madigan was shooting in the dark. "Tell them they have 24 hours to begin to redeploy. In the meantime, if you haven't already, put your forces on alert, and tell them to direct their attention to the north as opposed to our direction. Our forces are already on alert and ready to launch a strike within hours." The President shot a glance toward Chairman Marquez, who nodded in agreement. "Then I would suggest you tell your people that you are negotiating a deal with the U.S. and that they should return to their college classes or tea houses – wherever it is they hang out. Quietly however, I want you to release all the Nationalist Party political prisoners you have locked up, especially President Kim. He is a good friend of the United States. If he wants asylum in our country we will grant it." This time it was Secretary Anderson who was able to nod in agreement when her Boss glanced her way. "You will restore the powers and positions the opposition party held and get back to what we call a democratic government. We here will discuss what, if any forces we will withdraw, or if we will withdraw them all. Any questions?"

Again there was a long pause. Finally President Lee meekly replied. "You give me more credit for power and control than I believe I have, Mr. President. There are many in my government and in our streets who believe the Nationalists are traitors and puppets of the United States. I…"

"How about you, President Lee? Is that your belief too?" Madigan interrupted.

"Of course not." Lee waffled. "I believe we are strong allies and should remain so." President Madigan and most of his Cabinet just shook their heads, remembering the demands that came from this "strong ally" just hours ago. Lee went on.. "I am not a dictator and I do not have the same kind of veto powers you have sir. I also believe that the activities of the past few days have severely strained our relationship, and…"

"Bull shit!" Madigan cut off his counterpart again. "President Lee, we're finished here. You have my response to your request. I would suggest you take steps to comply. My people will contact you with our decision on which and how many forces to withdraw. Good day sir." Conversation over!

"So, what do you think folks?" Madigan asked his assembled advisors.

"Sir, one thing for sure is that we do not want to remove the nukes from Korea." SecDef Matson spoke first. "By many analyses, those nukes are the only deterrent from North Korea using theirs. At the very least we should continue to use their presence as a bargaining chip to get the North to quit developing and dealing in nukes."

"I beg to differ sir." SecState Anderson chimed in. "Obviously the presence of nukes in the South have done nothing to deter Kim Jong Un's programs, and in fact this whole issue started over his development of nuclear weapons. The only thing we have done is stir up a hornet's nest of resentment in the south. Removing the nukes would go a long way to mending those fences."

"Mr. President, it seems to me that no matter what we give in to, it will be seen just that way – the U.S. caving into the demands of a bunch of thugs." The CIA Director offered his opinion. "I would suggest we move in the opposite direction – do what we can to topple the current regime in Seoul and reinstall the Nationalist Party. If we have to give them a token carrot to offer the students, then we do just that – offer a token – nothing formidable like nuclear weapons."

"How do you propose we do that, Chuck?" The President was interested. He'd had enough of the whining and waffling President Lee.

"Sir, there are several high ranking military officers in South Korea who are fed up with the current government, and in fact see themselves out of a job soon if the regime has its way. It would not take much for them to pull off a coup, maybe even placing President Kim back in office." Durkee explained.

"Mr. President, I MUST advise against this." Melissa Anderson was squirming again. "We CANNOT be involved with a coup of a legally elected democratic government." The President shot her one of his "get off your high horse" looks and then returned his glance to his CIA Director.

"We don't have to be involved, sir." Durkee went on. "I believe that all we have to do is let them know we will not oppose them and it's a done deal. They are strong and powerful and have a huge backing amongst the troops. Especially if Lee releases the Nationalist Party members, they too can help. It could all be over in a few hours, with minimum (if any) bloodshed. Since all of our citizens are under lock and key anyway, there should be no threat to American citizens."

"Sir, we have no way of guaranteeing that. The students could get very violent at any time." Anderson tried one last time. She saw her opportunities to sway the President oozing away.

"What do the rest of you think?" The President looked around the room.

"It could work, sir, and General Joiner and I have been talking." The Chairman spoke up. "If we need a token withdrawal, let it be the A-10s at Osan. They can't do much from there anyway. The defenses up north are so formidable that except for action like the past few nights, slow moving Warthogs are sitting ducks. They could be withdrawn to Eielson in Alaska and the F-16s could take up the slack. In fact, if you wanted to, we could give up the whole base at Osan. There is enough room at Kunsan for the Osan F-16 squadron, and the command and control functions of 7th Air Force could be moved too. The only real hit would be the loss of the runway for logistics support. Kunsan's a lot farther away from Seoul."

"That's not all bad either. Having our forces displaced from Seoul gives them a little more survivability should the horde come south." Director Durkee added.

"Anyone else?" Madigan asked around. "OK. Chuck, go to work. Make it quiet and keep us out of it."

"Mr. President, I MUST disagree, I...." Anderson was beside herself.

"Noted, Madam Secretary. Now sit back and be quiet." Madigan had listened all he was going to.

"Get in touch with President Kim. See if he wants the helm again, and if not, who does he suggest? Offer the A-10 squadron as a bargaining chip. Keep Osan in our hip pocket for now. General, contact Generals Schad and Woodward and anyone else appropriate, and tell them to sit tight and keep their heads down." This last order was directed at Chariman Marquez. "Be vague. They don't need to hear what is going to happen, just that something is cooking. That goes for anyone outside this room, people. We must keep a low profile. Melissa, contact your Ambassador and pass on the same guidance." The President finally gave his Secretary of State a reason for living. "Anything else?"

There were no questions or comments. The advisors went out to do their business. The President sat for a while, then looked at his Chief of Staff and said after everyone else had left. "God, I love this job!"

CHAPTER TWENTY FOUR

HERO

It was over quickly, just as CIA Director Durkee had predicted, but not without bloodshed. There were fights in the Parliament House in Seoul, and two of the most radical ministers shot themselves, one with world television coverage. The ROK army also had several "skirmishes" with the students, in one case leveling the library at Seoul University and killing at least 100. Their use of force was denounced around the world. Even the United States expressed "dismay at the unfortunate circumstances," but otherwise stayed quiet. President Choi Kim was installed as an "interim" president at his request. Elections would be held within one year. President Lee and many of his followers were thrown in the same jail cells their predecessors had occupied. The beds were already made.

The United States did eventually move the squadron of A-10s from Osan, and generally scaled down the presence on the peninsula by about 30% over the next two years. Forces were redeployed to combat a growing terrorist threat in the Mideast.

Although North Korea was still seen as a major contributor to that threat, it was not as an exporter of terrorism, but as an exporter of the means. The general feeling in Washington, and with the new Seoul regime, was that the status quo of keeping a lid on Kim Jong Un was still the best policy. Token talks of reunification continued, with both sides denouncing the other and the North denouncing the presence of American troops. Progress was made very slowly. There were increasing numbers of family visits across the DMZ and more and more cultural exchanges. Plans were made for a unified Korean Olympic team for the next games.

There was still the looming threat of a North Korean nuclear arsenal. More pressure was levied by the U.N., and China finally chimed in to help restrict Pyongyang's involvement in the production of plutonium. The U.S. Navy stepped up its interception of Korean vessels. The market for weapons was still out there, but the price of doing business was expensive. This didn't please Kim Jong Un very much, but he realized he was between a rock and a hard place. Especially with China and Russia breathing down his neck, he could not afford to rock the boat too much for fear of losing the vast personal wealth he had accumulated at the expense of his people. He seemed satisfied to sit in Pyongyang counting his money, and taking periodic pot shots at the South and its American ally.

The U.S. Air Force in Korea quietly got back to normal. After the coup, the F-16s and A-10s returned to their home bases from Okinawa and the bases came down off their increased readiness status. Within 6 months the A-10s deployed out, joining a sister squadron in Eielson AFB, Fairbanks, Alaska. The 7th Fleet and deployed air forces maintained their positions of readiness for a few days, and then quietly withdrew to a "normal" distance, always keeping an eye on the mad man up north. AWACs went about their normal over-extended routine, supporting activities all over the world. Stephanie Michaels only got to see her fighter pilot boy friend once or twice a month.

Melanie Han and Brad Mitchell spent several days in the hospital at Kadena AB, on Okinawa – Brad a few more than Melanie. She was debriefed by CIA personnel, allowed to gather her gear in Tokyo and reassigned to headquarters at Langley. The feeling was that Japan was too close and that she could be an easy target for retaliation. As it turned out, it was for the best anyway. She and Brad only had a few moments together here and there, but they vowed they would be together soon. It seems the powers that be agreed.

Brad was treated for his injuries and it turned out he had a compressed vertebra. It basically meant he would often have a sore back, but unless it got any worse, he would eventually be returned to flying status. However, the Air Force and the Defense Department had other ideas for him. He was transported back to Kunsan and had just long enough to pack up his gear and enjoy a rip-snortin' Juvat farewell party. Then it was off to the Pentagon, where Brad was assigned to the Fighter Shop of the Air Force's Deputy for Operations. His job was as staff officer in charge of fighter training for the F-16, but in fact he was hardly around to do the work. Brad Mitchell was touted as a hero and paraded around the country to various Air Force functions, open houses, conventions, reunions, even political conventions, where he told his story and was the "Poster Boy" for patriotism – badly needed in a country that had become constantly under attack by terrorism. Brad was awarded the Silver Star, Distinguished Flying Cross, and Purple Heart. The hoopla was not his cup of tea, but he really had no choice. The Chief of Staff himself, General Johnny Joiner, personally "asked" him to participate, and even if they weren't graduates of the same college (VMI), Joiner was the boss – Mitchell was just the Lt. Colonel. He endured the excitement, and after a few months things settled down. He was able to get to work at his job, all along working on when he could get back to the cockpit and another operational unit.

At least with Melanie stationed in McLean and Brad at the Pentagon, they were in the same city whenever he wasn't on the road. She too was traveling a bit, having been switched back to the Middle East desk. She started to have some physical problems a couple of months after returning from Kadena, and finally had to go to a doctor.

Brad and Melanie had decided to share a condo in Arlington. They both knew that what had happened to them in the forests of North Korea was something special, but they also knew they wanted to slow down a little – especially Melanie. She still had memories of a bad relationship. However, the doctor's news threw another iron on the fire. Melanie was pregnant. Their interlude in the woods had produced more than just feelings for one another.

Brad was ecstatic. Along with a good moral upbringing, which told him to do the right thing and marry this girl, he truly knew he loved Melanie. He could think of nothing better than to spend the rest of his life with her. Melanie had initial reservations because she was such a dedicated professional. She worried about how she could continue to work. But she too was deeply in love, and after they talked it out, she decided that she could maintain a double life - one as a spy and one has a mother and wife. They were married two months later, just before Melanie really started to show. It was a gala affair with guests from all walks of their lives. The Chief of Staff of the Air Force, even Chief McGee from the Navy Seals was there. As many ex-Juvats that were in country flew in and Melanie had lots of co-workers there as well. CIA Director Chuck Durkee gave the bride away, and the President sent his best wishes.

Four months later Melanie and Brad Mitchell had a beautiful baby girl. She looked a lot like her mother, except with blond hair. She had the same blue eyes, and even a hint of an oriental complexion. They named her Kristi Han Mitchell.

Melanie continued working, though her traveling was curtailed. She stayed at Langley most of the time. Brad too did not travel as much as when he first arrived in the D.C. area, and finally after another two years of agony driving the beltway and pushing papers instead of flying, Brad got an assignment back to the cockpit. He was also promoted a year early to Colonel. After a couple years of being a poster boy Brad read the handwriting on the wall. He was not going to get a wing command and be put on the short list for general. His propensity to call a spade a spade, especially with his superiors earned him a reputation of being more of a rebel.

EPILOGUE

Brad Mitchell retired from the regular Air Force and accepted a job as the wing commander of the 113th Air National Guard Wing at Andrews Air Force base just outside of Washington. The wing was home to the 121st Fighter Squadron of F-16s that were instrumental in protecting D.C. after 9/11. In addition, Brad and Melanie were the hosts when the President and First Lady came and went through Andrews on Air Force One.

Melanie Mitchell worked "part time" as a Middle East operative, periodically taking trips to Libya, Egypt, Israel, and elsewhere in the region coordinating with "assets" needed by the U.S. intelligence corps. She and Brad, because of their availability in the Washington area, and because of their experience in the field, were part of a top secret special operations unit formed with Seal, Army Ranger, CIA, FBI and other agency special forces personnel. The team was tasked with all sorts of clandestine activities, working directly out of the White House.

Ed Howe was assigned to the Australian War College after his tour at Kunsan. Six months later he was assistant director of the "fighter shop" in the Pentagon, working for Brad and charged with the responsibility of Air Force fighter operations world wide.

Within a year however, he was resigned to Spangdahlem Air Base in Germany as the squadron commander of the 10th TFS. It was unusual for a Lt. Colonel to get two squadron commands, but the job in Germany was a special case and he really only had the Juvat squadron for a few months after Brad left. The Air Force had closed several bases after the fall of the Soviet Union, but then, with the ramped up activities of Russia in Crimea and the Ukraine, the 10th squadron was quietly brought back in country for a show of force. It was expected that Howe would make colonel within a few months and move up to the Spangdahlem wing hierarchy.

Nels Rushing was promoted to Brigadier General and assigned to Pacific AF headquarters as the command Inspector General. As such, he once again was in a flying job, though as a general officer he was forced to fly with an instructor pilot in most aircraft. He held that position for two years when he too read the handwriting on the wall. It seems the Air Force wanted its high ranking generals to be married. Lobo decided not to take a "token" wife, but to retire to Montana and the family ranch he grew up on.

Korea remains a hot spot of nervous leaders and population. President Kim prevailed in their election a year after being put back in office. He maintained a stronger presence and succeeded in keeping the students in check. He was also able to get talks going once in a while toward some sort of reunification with the north. However, just when there seemed to be a break through, Kim Jong Un would pull one of his stunts by testing a nuke or launching a "practice" missile. The U.S. vehemently insisted that Kim Jong Un give up his nuclear program and stop supplying weapons to terrorist groups, especially in the Mideast. It was a standoff that made everyone **tremble**.

The End

ABOUT THE AUTHOR

Colonel Dana Duthie's career as an Air Force fighter pilot is the basis for many of the experiences in "Tremble." His Air Force career spanned 24 years, from pilot training in Georgia and instructor in Texas to the skies over Southeast Asia, and from the F-4 phantom in Germany to the F-16 Falcon in South Carolina, Korea and Germany. The theme of "Tremble" spawned from his tour as the 80th Fighter Squadron Commender in 1985-86. He also "paid his dues" with three headquarters assignments and professional schooling. Colonel Duthie retired in 1992. He lives in Broomfield and Steamboat Springs, Colorado with his wife, and two children and four grandchildren nearby. One grandson is currently assigned to the USS Carl Vinson, nuclear carrier in the Pacific.

FROM THE SAME AUTHOR

Don't miss the next chapter in the career of Brad Mitchell. DARK RAIN is author Dana Duthie's first book, but actually the last in the sequence of the career of Air Force fighter pilot, Brad Mitchell. Iranian terrorists strike the U.S. military in four simultaneous attacks. An Iranian mole steals an American F-16 armed with a nuclear bomb and flies it to Libya to meet up with his Iranian master. The intention is to bomb Israel. Colonel Brad Mitchell and a select group of special Operators, under the direct supervision of the White House, put together a massive raid and covert operation to return the jet and its weapon. DARK RAIN is full of intrigue, air battles and adventure. Available in hardback, paperback and E-book.